I0831600

The Great World and the Small

Other Books by Darrell Schweitzer

Novels
The White Isle
The Shattered Goddess
The Mask of the Sorcerer

Collections and Story-Cycles
We Are All Legends
Tom O'Bedlam's Night Out
Transients
Refugees from an Imaginary Country
Necromancies and Netherworlds (with Jason Van Hollander)
Nightscapes
Echoes of the Goddess (forthcoming)
Sekenre: The Book of the Sorcerer (forthcoming)

Poetry and Light Verse
Groping Toward the Light
Non Compost Mentis
Poetica Dementia
Stop Me Before I Do It Again!

Non-Fiction
The Dream Quest of H. P. Lovecraft
Pathways to Elfland: The Writings of Lord Dunsany
Lord Dunsany: A Bibliography (with S. T. Joshi)
SF Voices (interviews)
SF Voices 1 (interviews)
SF Voices 5 (interviews)
Speaking of Science Fiction (interviews, forthcoming)
Speaking of Horror (interviews)
Windows of the Imagination
On Writing Science Fiction: The Editors Strike Back
(with George Scithers and John M. Ford)

As Editor
Discovering H. P. Lovecraft
Exploring Fantasy Worlds
The Ghosts of the Heaviside Layer by Lord Dunsany
Discovering Modern Horror Fiction (two volumes)
Discovering Stephen King
Discovering Classic Horror Fiction
Discovering Classic Fantasy
Tales from the Spaceport Bar (with George Scithers)
Another Round at the Spaceport Bar (with George Scithers)

The point is not tilting at windmills,
but making the giants appear.

—Jeffrey Quilt

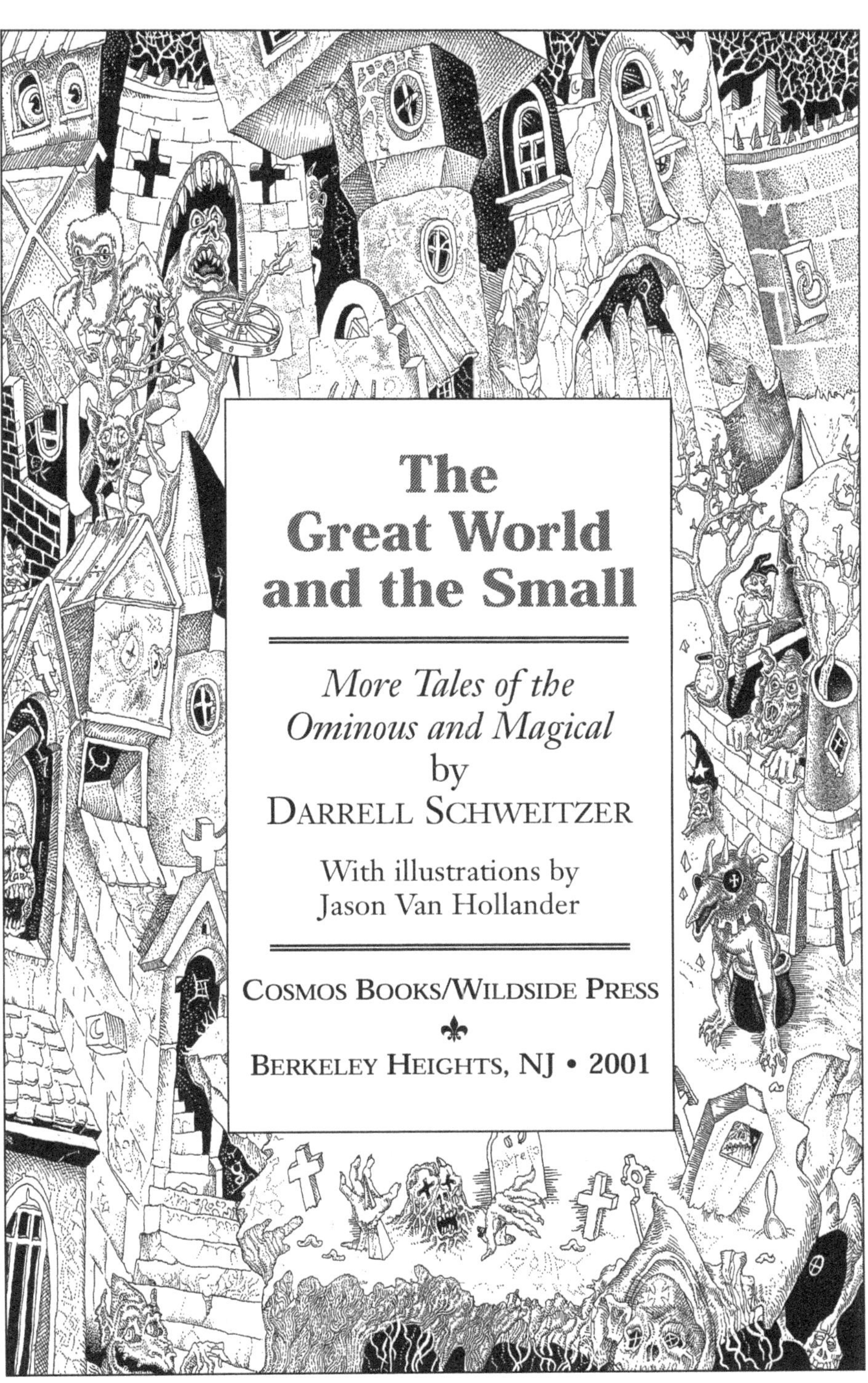

The Great World and the Small

More Tales of the Ominous and Magical

by

DARRELL SCHWEITZER

With illustrations by
Jason Van Hollander

COSMOS BOOKS/WILDSIDE PRESS

BERKELEY HEIGHTS, NJ • 2001

Acknowledgements:

"The Dragon of Camlann" first appeared in THE CHRONICLES OF THE ROUND TABLE edited by Mike Ashley. © 1997 by Darrell Schweitzer.

"Believing in the Twentieth Century" first appeared in *Terra Incognita* #1. © 1996 by Terra Incognita.

"Ghost" first appeared in *Interzone* #139, January 1999. © 1999 by Interzone.

"The Adventure of the Death-Fetch" first appeared in THE GAME IS AFOOT edited by Marvin Kaye. ©1994 by Darrell Schweitzer.

"The Unwanted Grail" first appeared in THE CHRONICLES OF THE HOLY GRAIL edited by Mike Ashley. © 1996 by Darrell Schweitzer.

"I Told You So" first appeared in ZODIAC FANTASTIC edited by Martin H. Greenberg and A.R. Morlan. © 1997 by Darrell Schweitzer.

"The Murder of Etelven Thios" first appeared in *Weirdbook* #14. © 1979 by Darrell Schweitzer.

"The Other Murder of Etelven Thios" first appeared in *Weirdbook* #15. © 1979 by Darrell Schweitzer.

"The Final? Murder? Of Etelven Thios?" first appeared in *Weirdbook* #15. © 1979 by Darrell Schweitzer.

"Wanderers and Travelers We Were" first appeared in ANDROMEDA 3 edited by Peter Weston. © 1978 by Darrell Schweitzer.

"Silkie Son" first appeared in *Weirdbook* #29. © 1995 by Darrell Schweitzer.

"Just Suppose" first appeared in HORRORS! 365 SCARY STORIES edited by Stefan Dziemianowicz, Martin H. Greenberg, and Robert Weinberg. ©1998 by Darrell Schweitzer.

"We Are the Dead" first appeared in *The Horror Show* Winter 1988. ©1988, 1992 by Darrell Schweitzer.

"Tom O'Bedlam and the King of Dreams" first appeared in *Weird Tales* #317, Fall 1999. ©1999 by Terminus Publishing Co.

"The Invisible Knight's Squire" first appeared in *Marion Zimmer Bradley's Fantasy Magazine* #48, Summer 2000. © 2000 by the Marion Zimmer Bradley Living Trust.

"The Great World and the Small" first appeared in *Marion Zimmer Bradley's Fantasy Magazine* #18, Winter 1993. © 1992 by Marion Zimmer Bradley Ltd.

Published in 2001 by Cosmos Books and Wildside Press. Wildside Press, P.O. Box 45, Gillette, NJ 07933-0045. http://www.wildsidepress.com

Paperback edition ISBN 1-58715-345-9
Hardcover edition ISBN 1-58715-210-X

To my beloved Mattie, to whom I have not dedicated anything in several minutes.

Table of Contents

The Dragon of Camlann

"I hope to God everything will be settled this day, once and for all," said my older brother Constantine, that same one who later became king of the Britons.

I rode by his side as the armies arrayed themselves on the field of Camlann.

"Whether by fighting or by truce?"

"Either way. Over. Done. Damn it all."

He spurred his horse and galloped toward his own company, then drew rein, turned, and came halfway back, standing in his stirrups to shout, "Oh Artegall, I almost forgot! There was a message from Mother this morning! For you! She says take care of Valentinus!"

He waved. I think he was laughing as he turned again and went to join his men.

I cursed. I actually smote my mailed hand with mailed fist, making a loud crack.

It figured. Constantine and I were sons of a great lord, of Cador of Cornwall. We were mighty men. Great deeds were expected of us, and already Constantine had won fame. His exploits were celebrated by the singers. But me? What was the message for Artegall? *Take care of your baby brother.* Don't let the little darling come to harm. He's such a sweet boy. Well, maybe so, but I didn't think he would make much of a knight. He was too young, thirteen, short and slender, his voice still soft; and never before out of Cornwall, innocent to the world, horribly incongruous here, *now*, when everything *was* likely to be settled in a single day and a lot of brave men would be in Hell by suppertime.

Such were my own dark thoughts as I assumed my own position, at the far end of Arthur's right flank, facing Mordred's left.

And the dear boy Valentinus came riding up to me.

"Isn't it *exciting*, Artegall? Isn't it? Look at all the knights!"

He wasn't my brother anyway, but a foundling, deposited on our doorstep by some stray knight or holy hermit perhaps, or, as was sometimes whispered, by an agency less holy, one more mystery of our rocky, shadowed land.

But he was my squire, and I was stuck with him.

"Isn't it grand?" he jabbered again, standing up in his stirrups for a better look. "Oh! There's the King's standard. And Sir Mordred's."

I turned to look.

"So they are."

At that moment, the last hope of Britain hung in the balance. Already there had been fighting, at Dover and elsewhere, when Arthur returned from France in all his wrath, the unfinished campaign against Lancelot left behind him. Heroes were already dead, including Sir Gawain. I wept for him, and for the others. This was no childish game. It wasn't exciting. It wasn't grand. Men who had fought and feasted as brothers, knights of the Round Table, were at one another's throats. God, yes, I wanted it to be over too, but I was so very afraid of how it would have to be resolved.

But as those standards stood together, as the final parley was held, there was still a chance for peace.

I couldn't explain any of this to Valentinus, who would probably be sorry to miss the fun of a good battle.

"You're a bloodthirsty little barbarian," I said to him suddenly.

"Huh?" He sat down in his saddle.

"You don't have the slightest idea of what any of this means, do you?"

He looked at me as if I'd suddenly grown an extra head, like a giant in a story. "Of course I do! A battle is a time for a knight to win *glory!*"

Then suddenly there was no time to explain anything. You've heard how in the midst of the parley, a serpent made to strike one of the knights. (On whose side? Does it matter?) The knight drew his sword to defend himself, and at the sight of flashing steel *everybody* rushed forward with a great roar—

I don't know. I was in another part of the field. It might even be true. Certainly there was a roar, as the fighting rippled toward us, as the two armies came together like waves closing over a spot where a stone has been hurled into the sea.

Nobody had time to give any orders. Arrows whizzed like bees. One struck Valentinus's shield and he let out a surprised yelp. I twisted in my saddle to see that he wasn't hurt and yelled, "Stay close, boy! Stay close!"

It was all a rage, a rush, a muddle, thundering chaos. Nobody made a proper charge. There wasn't room for that. Long lances were useless, the ground too rough for horses to get up speed. I remember the great mass of mounted men, pressed close together, coming at us. We closed together against them. I struck here, there, as I thrust and parried, as my sword hacked through shields and mail, clove breastplates, shattered skulls. Men shouted; horses screamed; men died as their mounts stumbled and the riders plunged beneath the mass.

Once again I heard a shrill, wordless cry, and turned again, afraid that I had lost Valentinus after just a few minutes. *A child! A child! What a damned stupid place for a child!* And I fought my way toward him, like a swimmer against a tide, and just as I reached him the whole mass of our army went tumbling backward into a deep, wooded ravine.

Trumpets blasted. Shouting rebels rushed upon us, like a tide, yes, a tide of death, closing over us one last time; a wave of flailing steel that bore me out of my saddle and landed me among sharp stones with a crash.

But I was not badly hurt. I caught hold of a man, pulled him out of his saddle, raised myself, lost hold of the horse again, but at least I was standing, and the wave had passed over me, the armies losing all definition, the Battle of the Ditch degenerating into an incoherent mass of struggling men and horses.

I caught a glimpse of Valentinus again, his helmet gone, his yellow hair flying wild, his pale face smeared with blood, his eyes filled with a panic that bordered on lunacy. He was swinging his mace with both hands, like a bat, because it was too heavy for him. I'd told him over and over not to do that. It leaves your guts open, to be skewered on the next available spear.

He went down and I fought my way to him, my mind quite far from any thoughts of glory. I grabbed somebody by the collar and yanked him up, and beheld a dark, snarling face. Was this a knight I had once feasted with? I struck the head off. Blood exploded over me.

Then I had hold of Valentinus, who wriggled like a hooked fish while three skin-clad Saxon mercenaries came at us all at once. The only thing I could do was swing the boy like a club, his feet flailing into their faces; then I rolled one of them off my shoulder and caught him under the chin with a vicious jab of my spiked elbow.

That was when the marvels truly began, I think, the delirium, the miracles; the *silence*, where time itself ceased to flow and arrows hung motionless in the air. It seemed that the sky darkened, that it was already night, but instead of stars the sky was filled with fiercely burning torches, which flickered down through the treetops.

And the forest spoke with a vast sigh, as shadows rushed out from the trees and washed over me; and I was very cold, my body gone numb, drifting on a great wave of blood and darkness, like a twig in a whirlpool. Valentinus was still with me. I felt him struggle, then cling to me. I too was struggling, drowning, and it seemed that the earth opened up.

A mouth appeared in the side of the hill, and it spoke to me, saying, "Artegall, you who would serve King Arthur, enter freely and of your own will."

But I'm not sure how freely I did anything. I can't remember. Maybe I replied something. There was absolute darkness. Then a lantern floated before me, flickering and sputtering, its fire burning blue. Strange knights rode beside me, in slow, pantomime motion. Perhaps I was borne on a bier of some sort. I saw the knights, clad all in glimmering green, their horses like things of dust and shadow given shape by some magic; and at times there were no knights at all, but animals and birds, ravens circling and shrieking, foxes and bears and stags running before me, led by an exquisitely white hind, which was not a hind at all, but a lady mounted on a white mare, clad in the blue of the morning sky, with the sunlight in her hair.

I cried out in amazement that she must be the Queen of Heaven, but she only laughed, and her laughter was like a winter wind rattling icy branches.

Valentinus was nearby somewhere, shrieking and gibbering.

And the mouth of the hillside closed over us and swallowed us up, and there was only darkness and silence and the smell of damp earth.

* * *

Some while later I awoke in twilight, on a hillside, looking out over a landscape that was all shadows, shot through with blues and greens, the colors and shapes shifting like the deep sea when faintly struck by sunlight.

Lights danced around me like fireflies; and grew larger, resolving into shrouded human figures, into animals and birds, then fading into a faintly luminous smoke. The air filled with exquisite music no earthly instrument or hand could have produced.

Glowing faces floated in the air like wind-borne leaves, human faces or nearly so, their mouths forming words I couldn't make out.

Valentinus stirred beside me. He sat up and stared in amazement, while groping about, for his mace I suppose, though to what purpose I neither knew nor cared.

Now the lights assumed shapes again; and I beheld the supernally beautiful queen and all her train, her knights mounted on horses of wind and dust, her courtiers hollow behind, like incomplete shapes of gossamer filled with a faint breeze and given a semblance of life. When they turned just so, their open backs revealed, they were almost invisible.

"Where *are* we?" Valentinus whispered.

As his knight, I was responsible for his education. Like a schoolmaster, I demanded, "Where do you think?"

As the phantom train drew around us and the queen came forward, the boy said, "I think only that our souls are in gravest peril."

That was a wise and careful answer. Were I his schoolmaster, I would have commended him. But I wasn't. I lost all control. I leapt to my feet and harangued the boy, the queen, anyone and everyone, the very sky itself with its alien stars.

"We don't have *time* for any of this! Not *now!*"

Valentinus let out a yelp as if I'd struck him. He grabbed my hand, to restrain me from who knew what.

He probably thought I'd gone mad when I turned my back on the beautiful lady and her knights as if Valentinus and I were alone, and continued my discourse.

"Don't you *see?* Don't you *understand?* Isn't it all so terribly *customary?* Where are we? On the border marches of death, if not in the grave itself. What's going on? We're having an *adventure.* There will probably be a *quest.* All very grand, the sort of thing to tell to the Christmas court when everybody's at the table swilling themselves silly and it comes time to review the year's chivalrous accomplishments. But we haven't time for any of that, Valentinus. Truly. Arthur may be *dying.* He needs us *now.* Sure, we may illuminate our souls and gain wisdom in the course of a fine adventure, but what's the use if there's no Camelot left and Arthur's head is on a pike and Mordred sells the country directly to Hell? Well? Well? Answer me that."

The boy could only gape. It was the queen who spoke, and the sound of her voice made my whole body go chill and numb.

"Artegall, son of Cador, I find you deficient in courtesy."

I turned and bowed to her.

"I crave your pardon, then, Lady. The passion of the moment got the better of me."

She laughed, and her courtiers laughed also. The sound was like a wind rattling icy branches.

"Artegall, you are a knight of the Round Table and therefore bound by certain oaths, one of which is never to refuse a lady a favor. Isn't that so?"

"You know that it is."

"Very well then. There is a dragon to be slain, a most terrible beast, which impedes the execution of all my designs."

"Lady," I said, bowing once more, trembling as I did so, not so much for any concern about my soul or my reputation or any chivalrous obligation I might be trying to evade, but simply for fear of what might be happening to Arthur. "Gladly will I undertake this task for you, as any knight would, be he of the Round Table or otherwise, for what man can possibly refuse such a beautiful lady? But I ask a favor of *you.* Can't it *wait?* My king is fighting for his life. The last I saw of the battle, it didn't look good. Please. Wait. If this makes me less than a perfect knight, so be it. Let me come back and serve you afterward."

Her manner grew more firm, and she did not laugh.

"No, I cannot wait. I charge you now. But remember that time in this land is not the same as it is in yours, so perhaps none at all will pass on the battlefield."

I bowed my head. "Very well, then. I shall undertake this quest."

Valentinus stood up beside me and declared, "I too will undertake it, for I am this knight's squire and—"

His voice broke into a shrill squeak. I never thought him more ridiculous than at that moment. I wanted to swat him for his presumption, for speaking out of turn in front of a queen, if nothing else.

But the queen smiled on us both, and the anger left me.

Then the wind bore us up into the darkness, and for some time the fairy knights rode beside us on their horses of air and dust. Then they were gone and we found ourselves alone in a rocky tunnel. We climbed toward the night sky and the familiar stars and finally emerged onto a battlefield, where black birds circled by starlight and wounded men cried for succor. Here and there, robbers came to rob the dead and dispatch the dying.

I threw my sword down, cursing, and I probably would have blasphemed had not Valentinus caught me by the hand and said, "Hold! Remember that quests come from God for his own purposes! It's not for us to understand!"

"That's something you read in a damned, pretty book, in some damned, pretty story. Who the Hell cares? We've been betrayed. It's all over. Arthur's dead and we weren't even there to die with him!"

I fell to my knees and the tears streamed down my face like blood.

Valentinus knelt beside me and pressed my sword back into my hands. "You don't know that. Our side might have won."

"I rather doubt it," I said sourly.

"Still you must hope—"

My reply was incredibly foul.

"Take up your sword," said Valentinus, "remember your courtesy, and let us fight the dragon together."

I didn't even swat him for his ridiculous presumption. Here he was instructing *me.* The problem was, he was right. A knight accepts death gladly, but he does not despair.

The boy stood up. He'd acquired a spear and shield from somewhere. He looked all the proud warrior. I sat back and gazed up at him and sighed.

"You think this is a game, don't you?"

"No! Look! There's the dragon!"

I leapt to my feet and looked to where he pointed, and I too beheld the dragon, as huge as a cloud rising up over the horizon, blotting out the stars.

"Come on then," I said, and like a couple of lunatics chasing after the Moon, we pursued the dragon throughout the night, shouting war-cries to draw its attention, waving our weapons, banging on our shields. But ever it remained vast and remote, like a shadow that had fallen on the whole world as we straggled across the battlefield and along roads strewn with corpses, past burnt castles and towns.

We did not catch it, nor ever drew near, though we heard always the thunder of its voice, like the sound of water rushing into a great cataract.

At last the dawn came. We both fell down exhausted, in tears, knowing that we had failed. The sun began to rise. It dazzled our eyes, but then we found ourselves once more in twilight, on the purple hillside in Faerie—for I did not doubt the place—and the queen and her court gathered around us once more.

"You have not fulfilled your quest, Sir Artegall," she said.

"I'm not done trying."

"Even so, I grant you a respite. Come and feast and make merry with us."

"I cannot make merry because my king is in peril, but I will come with you, because I cannot refuse a lady, as you are well aware."

"I am indeed," she said, and she laughed again, that exquisite and infuriating laughter. I wanted nothing more than to draw my sword and strike off her head, chivalry be damned; but somehow I controlled myself.

Besides, I was supposed to be educating this stupid boy, and that would hardly set a good example.

Knighthood, as I had told him a hundred times, is not glory, not gratification, but sacrifice. It is doing what you *don't* want to do because it has to be done.

So we entered into a wondrous hall, filled with many marvels, where the floor was of black glass and the stars of the Earth's night sky swam like glowing fish beneath it. Wizards in brilliant robes, all blue and golden and scarlet, with wands in their hands, leaned over to study the stars and learn what was to come upon the Earth. Every so often one of them would dip his wand through the glass, as if into the water of a still pond; and the glass would ripple faintly; and the wizard would draw his wand out again, all aglow with unearthly fire; and holding the burning wand aloft, the wizard would rise into the air, to vanish into the darkness above. I looked up to see the specks of firelight wink out, one by one, like stars eclipsed by a slow-moving cloud.

In that hall I saw a fountain that spewed gold, a bronze head that prophesied; there were books that turned their own pages and spoke. An island of glass swam in a lake of blood, somehow encompassed within that place, where distance and time were not as human senses knew them, and I seemed to be walking forever without crossing any distance, and sometimes distances shifted in ways I cannot describe, and I seemed to walk a hundred miles in a single step.

Pipers played on silver stairs. The lords and ladies danced to the music, whirling like leaves and dust in a great storm.

The lady bade Valentinus and myself to sit beside her at a high table atop a dais, and a repast was served: the most succulent meats and fruits the eye has ever beheld.

The boy reached for an apple. I caught hold of his wrist.

"Do *not.* I charge you upon your life. If you take even one bite, you become of this place, and you won't be able to leave."

Wide-eyed and afraid, Valentinus drew his hand away.

The queen looked on, whether amused or angered that we did not eat, I could not say. Her face was an unreadable mystery.

It was a greater agony to just sit there, watching the dancers, watching the wizards work great illusions, watching the centaurs or the fairy-folk dance, *wasting time*—a far greater agony that any wound I'd ever suffered in battle, far worse than anything a torturer could devise. Here was the iron resolve of knighthood tested.

It was time for sacrifice.

"Lady! Great Queen! Let me go *now* and fight the dragon and get this over with! Please!"

She looked at me once more with her inscrutable gaze.

"Do you really think you can?"

"Yes, if I can get close. Or die trying!"

"Then go at once."

She clapped her hands. The hall vanished. There was an instant of darkness, a sound of thunder; and I found myself in a pit of fire, where the very stones burned and ran molten and the sky was filled with smoke and red flame.

Valentinus huddled beside me. We both covered our dazzled eyes with our shields, but then a gentle voice spoke and someone pulled my shield away.

"Brave Artegall. Brave Valentinus. Fear not. The fire cannot burn you, not yet."

I lowered my shield and in time I could see again. I let out a cry, first of joy, then of terror, for I was face-to-face with an old friend, with Sir Gawain, but I knew that Sir Gawain had died for Arthur at Dover when the war against Mordred began. Indeed, I could see on his face the terrible wound that had killed him.

"I'm looking for a dragon—" I amazed myself as I blurted that out.

"I know where it is to be found."

So we followed him through the land of fire, across a battlefield where dying men lay all aflame, screaming in their agony, while robbers robbed them, for all that they likewise burned and screamed; where cities and castles burned; where fiery champions crashed into one another on the roads, their spears and shields shattering, their steeds crumbling into ash.

"Artegall!" my squire shouted above the universal roar of burning, tugging on my belt for attention. "Are we in Hell?"

"On its border, I think. But this is where we have to go."

He clung to my belt as we both bent against fiery wind, as cinders and hot stones bounced off my shield, as we climbed a mountain that streamed with liquid fire; as we followed Sir Gawain into a castle made of half-molten gold where there were precious stones set into the walls and men screamed and burst into flame and died even as they tried to pry the stones out of the walls. Others fought among themselves over what they had stolen, oblivious to their own pain.

Truly this was like Hell, but there were no demons here, only men, tormenting themselves.

In the great hall of that castle, we discovered even more treasure, heaps inestimable and undreamed of, deadly to the touch.

There, too, stood a great mirror.

"Here is your dragon," said Sir Gawain. "Go on. Slay it."

I raised my sword to strike the mirror, but as I did so the knight reflected therein raised his visor and I saw my own face. I paused only an instant, and in that instant the face was transformed into that of a dragon more terrible than may ever be described. Its voice was a human one, like thousands of men shouting all at once, in lust and anger and agony.

Yet I fought it, there, in the place of fire, as the monster burst out of the mirror, huge and covered with golden scales too bright to look upon, a mountain of fire and living metal and molten earth, its black, smoking wings spread to cover the whole world. I fought against its great claws and gnashing teeth. I knelt behind my shield against the fury of its breath. Valentinus hurled his spear down the dragon's throat, but that was of no consequence, any more than was my sword. I struck once more every blow I had ever struck in every battle I had ever known. Madness and hurt and furious memory swirled together like lurid paints stirred in a pot.

I fought for King Arthur, raging that I should be here and not at his side when he needed me most. I fought to get this damned quest over with and get back to Camlann, even if all I'd ever do there was get hit by the first stray arrow or be run down by a riderless horse.

No, I told myself. No. I cannot die *here.*

Thus I fought the dragon in an endless, timeless moment, throughout eternity; but to no use, for my weapons could not pierce its armor, even those few times when I could get through the flames close enough to strike.

Valentinus fought bravely beside me. I will give him credit for that.

He fought, just as uselessly as I.

In the end I could only stand up and weep as the dragon snatched the sword out of my hand; it swatted me about for a time, as a cat does tormenting a mouse; then I was in its crushing jaws, looking up in despairing amazement at the enormous, golden tooth which protruded from my chest like a spear; for the dragon had impaled me, and I hung there dangling, pierced to the heart, impossibly still alive.

"Arthur!" I cried out. "I'm sorry!"

I dreamed then a terrible dream that went on forever, that Sir Gawain led me through a forest of pikes standing in the earth. On each was the head of a knight I knew, all of them alive, their eyes filled with fire as if their faces were furnace doors with little eye-holes cut in them. They mocked me, saying, "You didn't do very well, did you Artegall? You deserted your king when he needed you the most."

I tried to argue with them, pushing through the pikes, searching for Arthur. I didn't find him. I should have taken hope from that. But the search was as endless as the number of the slain at Camlann, and I took only despair.

* * *

When I awoke again, hurt full sore from many wounds and burnt with fire, but somehow not dead, I opened my eyes on the pale blue sky of an earthly dawn. There was mist all about, slowly thinning.

The world swayed, rose, fell.

It took me a while to realize that I was on a boat.

The queen I had seen before leaned over me where I lay. She touched my burnt face with her soft hand, and the pain went away. But now a glamour had fallen from her, and I could never have mistaken her for the Queen of Heaven. This was a beautiful woman, truly, but a woman I knew, whom I had seen before. She was Morgan le Fay.

"You are my master's enemy." I tried to rise, but she gently pushed me back.

"I hated Arthur because I loved him, and loved him because I hated him. It's all a muddle, a mystery, but it's too late for that, Sir Artegall. Alas, the battle of Camlann is over. Most of the knights are dead. Mordred, too, is dead, and Arthur lies near death, from a blow Mordred dealt him."

Then I could only weep from the uttermost depths of my despair, knowing I had failed in all things. I was like Job, but without his faith; and I would have cursed God, had not Valentinus intervened.

"Artegall," he said, his voice more steady and grave than I had ever heard it before, "did you riddle the meaning of our adventure?"

"I don't have time for riddles . . ."

I rolled over and beheld him where he sat at a table. A feast had been set before him. As I watched, he ate of an apple. But I saw too that this was not the first bite he had taken. And I saw that he was dressed in a gown of purest white, and there was not a wound or a burn or a streak of dirt on him.

I had lost him too. Everything.

He put down the apple.

"I have discovered the meaning," he said.

"And what makes you so smart?"

"While you were resting, I ate of the Apple of Knowledge and of the flesh of the Salmon of Wisdom. This latter is a most marvelous fish, which lives in a pool in the Forest of Broceliande. No matter how many times men partake of it, it remains whole, and swimming in Broceliande."

"That's funny. I thought it was Scotland."

I was losing my reason. I was babbling. I wept all the more.

"Why do you weep, Artegall?"

"If you're so knowing and so wise, it should be clear enough."

"I know that Queen Morgan seeks, at the very last, to aid King Arthur, to carry him in this boat to Avalon, where he may be healed. But first the dragon must be slain, which blocks her way, the dragon of pride, of avarice, of the wrath of men. Only then may she come to Arthur. That is the meaning of the riddle."

"But the dragon is still in the full vigor of its health. So we haven't accomplished very much, have we? I haven't even managed to keep you out of trouble . . ."

Once more I wept.

"Artegall," said Valentinus slowly, "you always told me that knighthood means sacrifice, not glory. You would gladly have sacrificed yourself for Arthur, wouldn't you?"

"You know I would."

"Even so, I sacrificed myself. I ate of the apple, freely, for Arthur's sake."

"But the dragon still lives—"

"I know how to kill it, at least for a time. I am sure it will return, for the world is filled with wrath and pride, and no one in it may be free of sin. I have made myself *not* of this world, and now the task is mine."

"This is how my knighthood ends," I said, falling back, sobbing inconsolably, "bested by a boy."

Queen Morgan's attendants raised me up, and I watched as Valentinus walked upon the water of a misty lake. He wore no armor, only the diaphanous white robe, and the sunlight seemed to shine through him at times, making him almost invisible. His bare feet spread ripples from his path. He blew on a tiny silver horn, and the waters parted and the dragon rose up in all its fierceness.

Mindlessly, I fumbled for my sword. Morgan le Fay stayed my hand.

The dragon opened its terrible jaws. Its teeth gleamed, silver, then golden, like swords in the sunrise. Yet Valentinus walked between those teeth, into the great mouth, which closed over him.

Then the dragon sank down, leaving only bubbling foam behind.

And the queen held up a magic glass, in which I could watch the boy's progress. He wriggled in the dark, through the endless labyrinth of the dragon's guts, never faltering from his course, until he reached the very center, where he cut out the dragon's heart with a silver dagger and stilled its thunder.

And he returned, walking across the lake out of the mist, holding up the steaming heart. Then the boy was beside me once more, not bloody, but transfigured, like an angel, his face so bright that I could not look on him.

Yet I had the presence of mind to tell him to kneel. With my eyes closed, I got out my sword, and groping gently with the blade, I touched him on one shoulder.

"I'm sorry. I'm the only one here to do this and I'm afraid I don't really have the authority." I touched him on the other shoulder and said, "Nevertheless, arise Sir Valentinus, knight of the Round Table."

* * *

"And that's it," I said to Morgan le Fay, somewhat later. "My knighthood is at an end. What use am I now? "

"Of much use," said she, "for you are a knight of great worship, if flawed like all men; for in your travails you sought only to serve Arthur and protect Valentinus, never desiring glory or fame for yourself. That is why the fires burnt you only a little and did not consume you. That is why even the dragon's tooth did not kill you."

"But what use?"

* * *

The rest may well have been a dream. So might have been the whole adventure, dreamed in delirium as I lay stunned in the ditch at Camlann. Men say that Arthur died there, that he impaled Mordred on his spear even as Mordred struck him a terrible blow with his sword, piercing him unto the brainpan. Maybe. I didn't see. I was in another part of the field.

But I can tell you that a smaller boat came alongside Morgan le Fay's vessel, and in it was King Arthur, his face and armor all covered with blood, for he was wounded unto death, yet a little alive. The women there, even Queen Morgan, wept as they saw his terrible wound. I touched it. I tried to raise Arthur's head up when he was too weak to raise it himself.

His blood burned me. It made that white scar on my hand, *there.*

He opened his eyes. I think he recognized me. He tried to speak, but blood poured from his mouth.

Some men say that Arthur was carried to Avalon and is not dead. That may be so, but I cannot bear witness, for I was too much of the earth, never having partaken of the Apple of Knowledge or the Salmon of Wisdom; and when the queen's boat passed into the mist again, I was not on it, but found myself knee-deep in water.

I waded ashore, and there met Sir Bedivere, one of the very few knights left alive. He told me how he had hurled Excalibur into the lake.

That was his story. I told him mine.

Who is to say which stories are true? These things are riddles, to be told again and again until the meaning comes clear.

In this way, humbly, patiently, we serve Arthur.

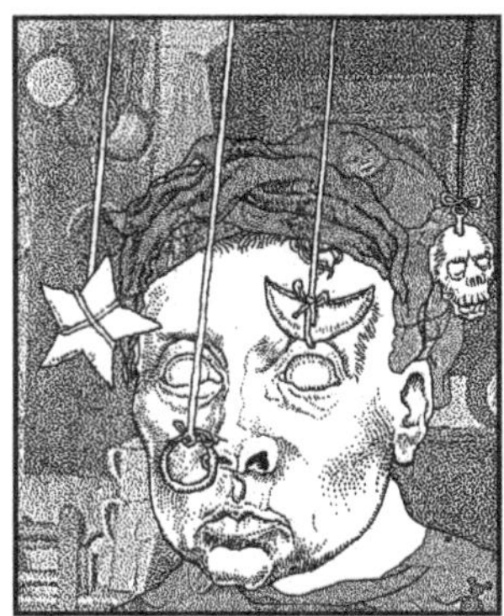

Believing in the Twentieth Century

About the time they reached the twentieth century, Egon wondered what had ever caused him to marry Draxilla. Maybe she had her redeeming features. Maybe he'd even loved her once. But now there were only her crazy obsessions, which ran her life, and his: twentieth-century clubs, twentieth-century fashions, tableaus, re-enactments, rituals, research, facsimilies, holo-resurrections. And when that wasn't enough—

He felt increasingly queasy as the last few decades slipped by.

She kept on arguing.

"It's all true," she said. "*Now* you're going to find out—"

He sighed. "You're endlessly credulous. Such things were never possible—"

"Close minded skeptic—!"

The time-bubble burst. Pop. Thud. The two of them tumbled into a deserted field. He lurched to his feet, gingerly brushing strange particulate matter from his bare skin.

"We're *here,*" she said. "Welcome to the twentieth century."

"I loathe it already."

He found that he could not cleanse himself. He rubbed his arms and sides hard, and realized he was shivering from . . . what was the word? The auxiliary data-brain embedded in his skull behind his ear kicked in and supplied the answer, silently, inside his head: cold. The atmosphere was uncontrolled. Appalling. The thought of gases drifting randomly made him vaguely nauseous.

"In the twentieth century," Draxilla said, the patronizing tone in her voice terribly unsubtle, "people wore body-coverings called clothes." She touched the subcutaneous implant beneath her chin and ludicrous coverings materialized over most of her body, doubtless the properly researched costume for the period. "It's part of the experience. Learn to enjoy it."

"I don't think I can." Already he longed for the rational, sanitary world they'd left behind–or ahead–thirty thousand years in the future, when things made sense, the laws of nature were understood, and there were no miracles.

They had come here in search of miracles. That was the essence of the twentieth century, she insisted, that miracles still happened. It was a time to *believe* rather than to *know*. The data-brain supplied an endless stream of non-sense words: *psychic healing*, *UFOs*, *telepathy*, *astrology*. All of them had been a part of daily life, if the literature of the era was to be taken seriously.

(His data-brain supplied a bibliography: MacLaine, von Däniken, Dixon, a complete sequence of something called *Weekly World News*.)

"Please," he said. "Let's just go back now—"

She hooked a finger under his chin; and he too was clothed, scraped and clawed from every direction by repulsive vegetable and animal fibers he didn't care to ask the data-brain to catalog.

"Come along," she said, dragging him. "Yes, Dear."

"What a wonderful twentieth century expression! You have been doing your homework!"

"Homework?"

"Never mind. Come."

They rose into the air. By moonlight he could see that the field was filled almost to the horizon with gently swaying objects . . . plant-matter . . . crops, the data-brain told him. Stationary, living organisms the people of this barbaric epoch ate for food. Wheat.

He couldn't bring himself to care that the bursting time-bubble had flattened some of the wheat in a broad, circular pattern. The whole thing was too revolting to contemplate.

He alighted beside Draxilla on a pathway of some kind, made of what must have been molded stone. (*Asphalt*, said the data-brain.)

"No more antigravity from now on," she said. "We can't attract attention—"

"If we can' t use the most rudimentary conveniences, I'm leaving—"

"You are not, until our argument is settled. Remember. You promised."

"Yes," he said. "I did." He'd made that promise in a moment of weakness, in the vain hope that it would put an end to Draxilla's absurdities.

(*Marital psychology*, said the data-brain. *Data inadequate for full explication.)*

"You and me both," Egon whispered under his breath.

"Did you say something?" Draxilla asked.

"No, no. nothing."

The asphalt path entered a gloomy stand of larger plants. (*Highway*, *forest*, the data-brain supplied. *Trees*.) Something ugly and green, uncomfortable to the touch, brushed into Egon's face and broke off in his hand. (*Leaf*.) He threw it after Draxilla, who pressed fearlessly onward. The highway looped and twisted in an erratic manner utterly offensive to civilized aesthetics.

"Can't we just stop?" he gasped, already out of breath. "Let's just pretend we were here. Tell your friends back home anything you want."

She stood still, sucking in the cool, strangely-scented night air. "No. We've only just begun. We're *fated* to be here. It is our *destiny!*"

"Utterly irrational!"

"Gloriously so. Now stop complaining— Oh" She held both hands to her temples. "Oh! I'm having a psychic flash! Something is near, an intelligence, non-human . . . Oh!"

"You're faking."

"I—"

A huge manlike shape, startled, stood from where it had been crouching by the edge of the highway. All he could make out in the darkness was that the creature was easily twice his height and covered with fur. It grunted, bared its fangs, and loped off into the forest on enormous feet.

"I knew it!" she said. "I *told* you so! In the twentieth century there are such things!"

"An animal," he said. "Yes, they had animals running around loose. A bear, I think." (But his data-brain insisted it had not been a bear.) "How could it have been anything else? There are no gorillas in North America." (The data-brain backed him up on that. It offered one more nonsense word: *Sasquatch.*)

"Never mind," she said. "You'll *see.*"

But as they approached a town in the morning twilight, it was far worse than merely *seeing* anything. Massive, uncontrolled vehicles roared past. Irrelevant, disturbing thoughts touched his mind, as lightly and irritatingly as a feather, tickling him. (The data-brain supplied the imagery.)

Something was clearly wrong. He couldn't concentrate. If either his primary, organic brain or the implanted data-brain malfunctioned, he knew, he would be helpless. He wouldn't be able to make himself understood. He'd have to return home at once. He almost hoped it was his brain "on the blink," as the local idiom had it.

"I have a bad feeling about this," he said.

"That's *wonderful!*"

"It is? Why?"

"It s an essential twentieth-century experience. You're having a *premonition!*"

"I feel sick."

Now the feather-tickling had become iron spikes driven into his head. The twentieth century was *bedlam.* (Images, metaphors supplied by the data-brain.) Even among the crowded buildings, vast metal machines hurled perilously through the streets. The noise. The smells. The thousand voices jabbering in his mind, extraneous thoughts, repulsive imagery, as if all the strangely garbed citizenry shouted their innermost thoughts directly at him.

But Draxilla was ecstatic.

"That *proves* I'm right! We're experiencing telepathy!"

Only after concentrated effort was he able to reply. "The human mind has no such capacity! It is biologically impossible."

"Here in the twentieth century, no one cared about that. They believed in telepathy, so they experienced it."

"The next thing you'll be telling me is that they believed the Earth was flat, so it was flat."

"Some of them *did* believe, but not enough. It remained round."

He was in too much discomfort to argue. The sensation of telepathy was wretched. He tried to remember how it had been in the future, floating alone in silent, sanitary light, but he couldn't hold the thought as Draxilla hauled him through the streets for what must have been hours. She touched innumerable minds *deliberately*, sometimes joining hands with passers-by to feel their "energy" (a word she used with decreasing precision). She led him into a shop where, by some medium of exchange he couldn't understand (the data-brain muttered something; he didn't bother to listen), she acquired two fragments of crystalline quartz strung on animal-tissue fibers. She placed one over her own head, so that the crystal hung down her chest, and insisted he do the same with the other.

"It's very powerful," she said. "Don't you feel the vibrations?"

As much as he wanted to deny it, he did indeed feel the vibrations. Whether they had any significance or not, he didn't care to discuss. He tried to reserve what little mental coherence he had left for the formulation of a theory that the chief, and in fact *only*, experience of the twentieth century was, by definition, mass insanity.

"Oh!" she shouted aloud, clapping her hands, leaping into the air, dancing and twirling on the (*sidewalk* said his data-brain), "it's everything I had hoped for, a whole new *world* filled with wonders!"

Twentieth century people turned to stare.

(*Is she on something?* The thought came to him from somewhere. The data-brain researched the metaphor, but could not define it.)

"It's so different from our own," she continued. "Here each individual is *special*. What they *feel*, that is real. Nothing else. How did we ever give it all up?"

He shrugged wearily. His data-brain launched into a history lecture until he told it to stop.

"Never mind," she said. "Now what I want to know is the *future*."

That snapped him out of his stupor. He grabbed her by the arm and yanked her to a halt.

"We have to return home right now. You are obviously dysfunctional. You forget that we're *from* the future!"

She made a face at him, stuck out her tongue (*Twentieth-century mode of communication*, said his data-brain, *meaning uncertain*), and wriggled free of his grasp. "Silly! This is what I mean—"

She snatched a sheaf of (*Newspaper*, said his data-brain) from a sidewalk stand, flipped through it, and read aloud: "Taurus. Today marks the beginning of your ultimate quest." She closed the paper. "There you have it. The stars have spoken."

"The stars, you know perfectly well, are masses of fusing hydrogen. They do not speak."

"Here in the twentieth century, they control our lives. As long as you're here, you're going to have to get used to it."

"We're leaving—right now!"

But the future, their future, from which they had journeyed in the time-bubble, seemed unreachably far away just then. Was this another . . . what was it? (*Premonition.*)

"Not so fast," she said, grabbing hold of him as he had grabbed her. She waved her free hand in the air. "Taxi!"

One of the hurtling metal machines screeched to a stop. They climbed inside. Incomprehensible transactions with the device's operator followed. (The very idea of a machine directed by a living being seemed too fantastically cruel for words. *Slavery*, the data-brain suggested, searching for a more precise analogy.) His stomach seemed to heave one way, his head the other, as the *taxi* sped through the streets, finally slamming to a halt at a location Draxilla and the operator had somehow agreed upon.

When they got back home, he swore, he was going to pop the module out of her data-brain some night while she slept and purge this twentieth century rubbish from memory. All of it. He didn't care about the legal consequences.

Draxilla shoved him out of the taxi.

Outside on the sidewalk, he swayed dizzily for several seconds before blearily noting the sign on the building in front of them. The script said (as his data-brain translated): MADAME ESTELLA, PSYCHIC READER.

Draxilla herded him up the walkway to the door and rang the bell. Footsteps approached from within. "This is very special indeed. Think of it as a shrine to the collective faith of the twentieth century."

(*Church*, his data-brain said.)

"Not a church," Draxilla said. "Something more important." So now she could read his mind too. It only figured.

The door opened. The old, bent woman standing there was eccentrically dressed, even by twentieth century standards. (*Gypsy*, the data-brain supplied, then supplied an ethnological treatise that did not seem immediately relevant.)

"Ah," the Gypsy woman said, "I was expecting you."

(*Yep, another premonition*, Egon's data-brain observed dryly. *Are you surprised, I mean, really?* He felt a moment of helpless terror. He was becoming corrupted. Here in the twentieth century, machines allegedly developed personalities. All he needed now to make the nightmare complete was a wise-cracking data-brain.)

Inside, they sat around a table in semi-darkness, in a curtained room filled with the paraphernalia of the Gypsy's profession: crystal ball; astrological charts; a paperback *Necronomicon*; statues of multi-armed, dancing figures; a shrunken head; numerous crystal pyramids, some with razor blades beneath them; and much more the data-brain could not identify. The old woman served them cups of a hot beverage which had, he admitted, a genuinely pleasant odor. For an instant he almost relaxed, but as he went to stir his drink (*tea*) the instrument provided for the purpose (*spoon*) suddenly bent itself into uselessness for no apparent reason. The Draxilla and old Gypsy woman likewise held damaged spoons.

Childish laughter came from an adjoining room.

"Junior!" shouted the Gypsy. "That's enough! Stop it at once!"

"Sorry, Gramma."

They put their spoons aside and drank their tea. Then the old woman took his hand in hers and traced the lines on his palm with her index finger.

Her eyes widened. "This is very strange. You don't seem to have any fingerprints."

"Of course not," he said in his most patronizing voice ("You ignorant savage," he wanted to add, but restrained himself). "No one has had individual markings since the middle of the twenty-fourth century at least—"

Draxilla kicked him under the table, hard and painfully. (*Twentieth-century method to tell you to shut up*, her voice announced inside his head, telepathically.)

"Nevertheless," Madame Estella continued, "I see quite clearly that you have come on a long journey, and that very soon your existence will undergo an abrupt transition—"

(*You can hardly deny now*, Draxilla continued inside his head, *that I've won the argument. This is what the twentieth century is all about.*)

He yanked his hand away from the startled Madame Estella. "I can't take any more of this! Look! Look! I'm psychic too! I foresee a definite parting of the ways, Dearest." He glared at his wife. "That means I'm *leaving*, right now. You can stay here if you like. I don't care anymore! That's my prediction! I can do it! I can do it! I prophesy a divorce!"

He ran out of the building, down the steps, into the street.

Machine parts squealed. (*Truck*, the data-brain identified the oncoming vehicle as it hit him.)

* * *

Egon's organic mind was filled with murmurings, like a gentle tide. (The data-brain, damaged, supplied the imagery, but failed to define.) Draxilla wept over him (whatever weeping was) and held his hand, begging him to let the healing "energy" flow into him. (By now that term seemed to mean anything she wanted it to, or nothing at all.) They were in a room somewhere, surrounded by others, amid burning plant-matter (*herbal incense*). He watched dully as crystals and assorted brightly-colored stones were placed on the injured parts of his body. Fortunately there was no pain. In his own time, in the future, people learned how to shut off pain in earliest childhood.

Once he thought he'd known what the future was. Now he wasn't sure. How could anyone? The very idea involved several logical fallacies.

The people around him were chanting words he couldn't make out. His data-brain failed to translate. Someone asked what his spirit-animal was.

"Oh," Draxilla whispered to him. "How I envy you! You're so lucky!"

"Lucky?"

"This is the core experience of the twentieth century. Haven't you learned anything?"

"I don't know . . ." he said.

"I wish I could share it with you . . ."

"Didn't you once say that in the twentieth century wishes are everything?"

He couldn't hear her answer. Somehow he managed to slip off into sleep, into a dream in which he struggled to climb a glass slope up out of darkness and into light; but he made no progress at all, slipping ever downward despite his desperate efforts. As he slid, his body changed, becoming coarser, bent, covered with hair. Somehow he knew his brain was getting smaller. (*Australopithicus*, the data-brain said before it shut off once and for all, no longer able to fit into his diminishing skull.) Near the very end he seemed to have scales and fins, as he flopped in the muck at the edge of a dark, cold sea, gasping for breath, unable to care about anything anymore.

And then he was in a different place, strangely serene, completely at peace. His beloved Draxilla stood beside him in the moonlight at the edge of the same field where the time-bubble had deposited them. He felt increasingly light-headed.

"At last," he said. "We're going home."

"You are," she said, "in a sense. But to a new home."

He searched his mind for his data-brain, but it wasn't there.

"I don't understand. Aren't you coming with me?"

"This is where we part," she said. He thought he detected genuine regret in her voice.

"But . . . I'm returning to our own time, aren't I? Why can't you come with me?"

"I could return to our original time," she said, "if I wanted to. But you couldn't exist there."

All his anger had left him. "Please explain," he said softly.

"Look at yourself. Look closely."

He saw that he was naked once more, but somehow his body had become transparent as smoke. It glowed slightly.

She sobbed. "We couldn't save you. There was just too much negative energy. You shut us out by your refusal to believe."

"I—"

Something bright and round moved across the sky. It wasn't the moon, he realized.

"You have to go away now," she said, "the way many people did, in the twentieth century."

The flying saucer settled into the field as gently as a cloud. Its hatchway opened in a burst of blinding light. Hesitantly, he made his way toward it, until at last he could make out faces in the light, smiling at him. Voices beckoned. Even without the data-brain he recognized some of the people there . . . JFK, Marilyn, Elvis . . .

He turned back toward the field only once, and waved briefly.

"I guess you win," he said.

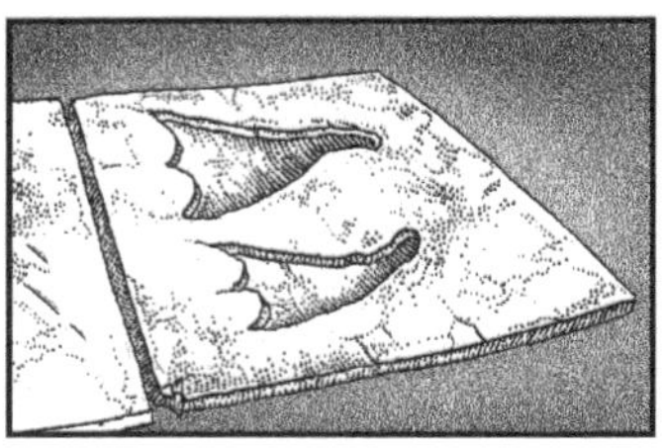

Ghost

"You can never get used to this town, Henry," I said. "Even after five years, the weirdness is still in my face, daily."

"So nu? It's Tinseltown, Hollywood U.S.A., kiddo. You were expecting maybe Little Rock, Arkansas?"

"I don't know what I was expecting—"

"*You're* the one who lives here. I'm from New York, remember?"

That was only one of the infinite number of things which, subtly, didn't make any sense at all. Henry Jessel was from the one city in the country where most people don't have cars, or even feel the need for them, and *he* was driving the rented car he'd insisting on getting at the airport to pick *me* up at my place. Here we were on the Harbor Freeway, amid some of the worst driving conditions in the world, where you can theoretically get from anywhere to anywhere in forty-five minutes but in practice sometime between half an hour and next week. *He* was the one who wanted to be independent, or absorb the L.A. experience or something. He was driving. I think he did it to impress upon me that he was in *control.*

"Yo! Look out!"

He swerved. The lunatic who had never head of turn signals and probably thought solid matter could pass through solid matter if you only wish upon a star cleared our fender by inches.

"Tinseltown, kiddo," Henry said again, remembering to breathe.

Henry Jessel was nine years my junior, but he'd always somehow been the leader in our friendship or partnership or whatever it was. He had all but seized control of my life, which entitled him to take fifteen percent of my income and call me "kiddo." Henry Jessel was my literary agent. He got me my first novelization job, *Captain Cut-Throat*, the book version of a pirate movie which had lasted in the theaters almost a whole day; a book which sold *dozens* of copies. Then he loaded me on a plane for the Coast, where I, Jerry Jack Miller, became one of the least-known, best-paid writers in Hollywood, or anywhere else for that matter.

And I didn't even work in movies. Not exactly. Which was the problem. I was a ghost. My specialty was writing novels for TV stars who pretended to be novelists, which paid extraordinarily well, but my name seldom made it even into the dedication. I felt like I was pouring my talents down a black hole.

"I just can't *do* it anymore," I said. "I stare at the blank screen and I *can't.*"

"You *are* behind on your next book," Henry said, gravely.

As we absorbed the quintessential Los Angeles experience, sitting gridlocked in traffic in the dry-roasting August heat while the car's air-conditioner strained desperately to cope, it all came out, how I'd loved it all at first, and done all the touristy things in the first few weeks out here: Disneyland, Universal, Hollywood Boulevard and the Walk of Fame—and that was where the disillusion began to set in, because Hollywood Boulevard is a wreck, with many of the great Deco theaters just burned-out shells between blocks of shabby storefronts and outlets for we-want-your-bucks religious cults; and there's even a crack in Elvis's star, right there in the sidewalk and nobody really cares except maybe the enormous plastic dinosaur looking down over the rooftops; but for a while still I found the smaller weird things, the fun things, which kept me going for a while, like the Ackermansion and the Museum of Jurassic Technology and Frankenstein's Restaurant (where the tables are haunted); and Venice Beach is really very nice, and I even made the pilgrimage to Bronson Canyon where they filmed any number of matinee westerns, not to mention *Robot Monster*; but I suppose it was when I saw *Donald Fucking Duck's* footprints in the cement in front of Grauman's Chinese, right next to Shirley Temple's and Humphrey Bogart's that it came to me, *Hey, this whole goddamn town is a lie, which makes me the lie behind the lie—and—and—*

Henry reached over and put his hand on my shoulder in a fatherly way and said, "You don't have to live in Hollywood, not at this stage of your career. Later, yes, but for now you could write your books just as well from a trailer park in Nebraska, and if you'd like me to arrange it—"

"That's not the point, Henry."

"No it isn't. You aren't getting to the point. Jerry, when you talk to me, I will listen. But when you just *kvetch*, I will let it wash over me like water over a stone until you get to the point. And, incidentally, Donald Duck doesn't have a middle name, so watch it."

Traffic started moving again. In time we squeezed by the scene of a multiple-car accident, where it didn't look like anyone was hurt but there were cops everywhere and people waving their arms and shouting; only we couldn't hear what they were saying because the windows were up the and the air conditioning was on (which made it all unreal, like a movie with the soundtrack turned off), and that was when I got to the point we'd both been waiting for.

"I'm *nothing*, Henry, nobody. I'm not an *writer.* I'm the guy who does space-operas for Carl Sanderson to put his name on. The man is an absolute *fake*. He's a Schwarzenegger rip-off and even his muscles are fake. He's supposed to be this square-jawed hero, but I happen to know that his jaw's a fake too. It's prosthetic. He got it from the same company that does Jack Palance's cheekbones and Kirk Douglas's chin. Christ, the way that moron gets on the talk shows you'd think he actually thinks he wrote those books, or can even read them."

"The man is an *actor*, Jerry. That's his job. He's been a cowboy, a gladiator, the robot on *Cybercops*, and now he's the mercenary captain on *Galactic Avengers*. He's fully capable of playing the role of a writer if the powers that be back in New York want to shell out hundreds of thousands of bucks for books with his name on them, and if he doesn't actually know how to spell 'the' the same way twice in a row, that is a small and incidental detail which you and I are paid very well to take care of."

"I'm just a hack, Henry. I want to be something more, something real."

Since we were caught motionless in traffic again, Henry was able to turn to me with a look of genuine alarm on his face and say, "Jerry, you're not having an attack of artistic integrity, are you?"

"Well I—"

"Jerry, remember what you were before I made you what you are. You'd published a few pretty sonnets in quarterlies which paid you in copies, and then there were your short stories for which the publishers sometimes threw in a packet of bird-seed; and then I said to you, 'Put yourself in my hands,' and you put yourself there, and now you live in a gorgeous house in Palos Verdes and you got a gorgeous wife and gorgeous kids, and your bank account is not at all below six figures. I'd say you're doing pretty well, Jerry, but remember, it's part of a bargain you and I made five years ago, and I get plans for you in the future too, but for it all to work, you've got to do your part while I do my part. I am sure you understand that, Jerry. I do not phrase that as a question. I made you an offer and you accepted, of your own free will, knowing what it would entail."

"Ah, Mephistopheles—"

Once more he touched me on the shoulder in that father-knows-best sort of way and said, "I will take care of everything, Jerry. I'm your agent. Trust me."

And again the traffic started moving, pretty briskly this time, and all I said now was, "Where are we going anyway?"

"You haven't figured out?"

"Henry, this is Los Angeles, which is like Manhattan only horizontal. It's so big you can see the curvature of the Earth in some of the parking lots. No, I don't know where we're going or what it is exactly we're trying to accomplish."

"Think of it as emergency therapy, Jerry. Something to get the creative juices flowing."

"A sanatorium then, for shock treatment?"

"More of a secret, something which, as they'd say in the military, is available on a need-to-know basis. Now you need to know, so that's where we're going."

"Ah, I see."

"No you don't."

"So you're psychic now, too?"

"No need, Jerry. But as your literary agent, I *do* have certain talents."

"You and Carl Sanderson both."

"Exactly."

There was an ominous resonance to that last line, but I didn't say anything more and just stared out the window as we got off the Freeway a little past Burbank and turned and turned again and again; and if Henry knew where he was going then maybe he really did have special powers. Maybe I even dozed off for a while because as the sun went down I start I looked at my reflection in the windshield and for a long moment of helpless, utter horror, I saw not my own face, but that of Carl Sanderson, heroic space mercenary of large screen and small; then I was clawing away at my face and it came off and underneath was a robot and cowboy and a gladiator and Kermit the Frog and a bug-eyed, drooling Smile Face and then just a skull, which cracked into dust and bits, and there I was sitting in the car next to Henry with no head at all, and he reached over and screwed a giant light bulb into my neck; which he switched on somehow, and put a paper mask on top of it, which started to burn through from the heat of the bulb—

And then the car came gently to a stop and Henry nudged me.

"Hey, kiddo."

I put my hands to my face to make sure I was really me.

"We're here," he said.

Here was somewhere north of the Hollywood Hills, where the desert almost starts, in a non-committal way. We walked across a parking lot just a little bit too small to have its own moon to a completely nondescript bungalow which had a little brass sign by the door that read SIMULACRUM STUDIOS INC., which told me nothing at all, but told Henry enough that he got out an I.D. card of some sort, slid it into a lock, and the door buzzed open.

"I hope we're not late," I said. "The traffic."

"They know about that."

After a minute or two, I didn't doubt that "they" knew about everything, because we'd just walked into what could have been the set for a spy movie. Henry used the I.D. card again, and again. Doors buzzed open. Panels slid back. Guys in uniforms made phone calls in hushed tones. We had to place our hands on scanners. The next thing, I was sure, was that we'd be crowded into a phone booth and there'd be *no question* that Henry knew what the secret number was, and then the floor would drop out . . . but no, it was just endless escalators, like the ones at Universal Studios where by the time you're halfway down you realize you've left your stomach behind in the stratosphere and there's a dinosaur waiting to eat you up at the bottom in the *Jurassic Park* ride . . . but I digress, and down we went, and down, and down, until we came to yet another series of vast, sealed off, secret rooms where scientists in lab coats passed silently this way and that and there wasn't a crackling Jacob's Ladder or cackling hunchbacked assistant in sight.

At last a very polite lady who could well have been the Chief Assistant Sub-Deputy Aide at the C.I.A. ushered us into a little circular theater of some kind and closed the door behind us.

I thought I heard air hiss, as if we'd been sealed into a space capsule.

The lights dimmed.

"Henry, what is this?"

"Be quiet. It's what you've got to see."

A panel slid back in the ceiling. Apparatus lowered.

And for a moment after that I thought we were going to die, or at least be blinded by the searing flash, because the thing coming out of the ceiling looked was a dead ringer for the gigantic laser that almost took Sean Connery's balls off in *Goldfinger*—but the beam was gentle. It just touched the floor in front of us and then other beams shot out from the walls on either side, and in front of us, and right over our heads, and all these beams of light mixed and *whirled* somehow, like paint you drop onto one of those little gizmos that spins the paper; only the result wasn't just sunburst splotches and streaks. Not after a second or two anyway. A shape began to form in the middle of the air. It spread out, and split, until it had what were distinctly two *legs*, which lowered themselves down to the floor. The lights changed color now, and texture, if light can be said to have texture. From the apparatus came a high-pitched whining and the smell of ozone. The light *rippled*, like a reflection on a pool in sunlight, and the thing before us was definitely human-shaped now, a man, yes; I could make out the face, a little, a bit more.

Then the machinery stopped, the lights came back up, and *there he was*, standing in front of us, as real as could be, if such words have any meaning anymore.

My agent got up and went over to the man in the *Galactic Avengers* uniform who stood in the middle of the circular floor. Then he turned back to me.

"Jerry Jack Miller, I'd like you to meet Carl Sanderson."

I didn't know what to say or do. I just gaped.

He, *it*, Sanderson or the thing which looked like Sanderson, square jaw and all, flashed me his famous smile, twinkled his blue eyes, and said, "Don't bother to get up."

He held out his hand, and I reached for it, but he missed and his hand passed *right through* my forearm. Sparks flew. I felt a shock and gave out a yell and drew back.

Sanderson *rippled,* his whole body shifting side to side real fast, and his head seemed to jerk in a way no living human being's head could ever move, and he said, "Pl—please—pleased to—"

"Sometimes it takes them a moment to get the calibrations exactly right," Henry whispered. "Don't worry. Everything's fine."

Henry flashed me *his* famous smile, which is closer to what a rat sees when confronted by a hungry cobra who says to him, *Let's make a deal;* but he was my agent and I remembered that he was on my side.

Then Sanderson shook my hand, and his touch was warm and firm, and he said, "Always pleased to meet one of my fans."

The C.I.A. lady came in and said, "Would you excuse us? Mister Sanderson has to meet the press before tonight's appearance."

The two of them went out and it was *Sanderson* who very solidly opened and closed the door for the lady, being a far more impeccable gentleman in "life" than he was on TV.

I stared at Henry.

"So, what was *that?* Is this the big secret, that Sanderson's even more of a fake, that they've got holograms to take his place for his public appearances—?"

"It's not a hologram, exactly. It's a multiple-task, self-programming, holographic AI."

"AI?"

"Artificial Intelligence. It's generated as you have seen. If they put enough power into it, it can retain its integrity for weeks at a time. A single zap and a Virtual Cast Member can last through an entire film shoot."

"But this is ridiculous. No, it's *obscene.* What does the *real* Carl Sanderson do, just hang around in his palace, get laid, and collect his checks?"

"That *was* the real Carl Sanderson, Jerry. He does everything an actor is expected to do, only better. He never forgets his lines."

"I'll bet."

"That would be a very safe bet, Jerry. He is totally reliable."

"But the original, *human,* flesh-and-blood Sanderson—?"

"You don't get it, Jerry, do you, unless I have to spell it out. There *is no such person* as Carl Sanderson, not anymore. There is *only* the simulacrum. The guy who started out as a TV cowboy in the '60s, well, his career didn't go forward. Only a few of his, you might say, talents, have continued—"

"But that's awful—"

"So as you see, his famous square jaw is not a prosthetic. *He* is a prosthetic."

"Oh, shit. . . . What does it *mean?*"

"What it means, Jerry, is that *you* are the author of all those books you write.

You and nobody else. Even AI programs aren't smart enough to write novels yet. So doesn't that cheer you up? Isn't everything all right now, kiddo?"

I was almost in tears then.

"No," I said. "No, it isn't."

"Jerry," he said sternly. "You knew what you were getting into when you became my client. Grow up, kiddo. If you can't take the heat, get out of the damn swimming pool."

"Metaphors were never your strong point, where they Henry?"

"I got plenty of strong points. But you, kiddo, need a good talking to."

* * *

So I got a good talking to, later, at Frankenstein's Haunted Restaurant (now a chain, under new management) where one of the trick tables nearby tipped over suddenly while the waiter was taking an order, and everybody tittered nervously. I looked up. When I looked down again a hand rose up out of our table top and put an eyeball in my drink, which lit up like a Christmas ornament and winked.

When I looked up from that, Boris Karloff as the *The Bodysnatcher* was sitting across from me, and explaining in that sinister, lisping voice of his, "We're all dust in the end, Jerry, or random electrons. What does it matter? It's what you do in the meantime that counts."

Then something crashed somewhere and when I looked again, it was a completely wasted F. Scott Fitzgerald, with dark bags under his eyes, saying, "They ruined me, but they don't have to ruin you, if only you'll just play the game—"

Then it was Orson Welles leaning over, whispering into my face, telling me what it was all about.

I also had a talk with Hemingway who said, "When they made *For Whom the Cash Register Tolls*, I thought it was crap, but the cash register kept on tolling no matter what."

Humphrey Bogart and Fred Astaire both explained that the TV commercials they're doing these days are just warm-up exercises, and both planned full comebacks.

"I might want to write a book with you one day, kid," Bogart said.

Every time the cast changed, the eyeball blinked. It was a projector of some kind.

I even met Donald Duck, whose flippers still had cement on them. He assured me he had no middle name. He was looking for somebody to collaborate with him on his autobiography. The money involved would have been enough to jumpstart the economy of a Third World nation.

"I couldn't do it without *you*," said the duck.

Henry leaned over the table, into the light of the glowing eyeball in my drink.

"That's the beauty of it, Jerry. Maybe some *actors* have something to worry about these days, but *you're* sitting pretty."

I faked a smile. "Because there are no holo-whosit-AI writers, is that it?"

"Yes. Precisely. That's it. Actors, directors, producers, yes, but *you're* better off than all them. So start counting your blessings, kiddo."

"I feel like slitting my throat. Do you think there'll be any virtual blood?"

That was when he hauled me out of there by the collar and *threw* me back into the car.

"Not on *my* fifteen percent, you don't!"

* * *

So we drove back to Hollywood Boulevard, and on the way it was Henry Jessel who worked his magic on me, not any AI of William Shakespeare or Edward D. Wood or whoever, just my old pal, whom I'd known since he was still in high school and we were both trying to break into paperback science fiction, as if that were the way to make oneself part of the stellar firmament. Just Henry, who did what he does best, and so the ending of my story is a trifle mysterious, a trifle vague, because even I don't know precisely how he did it, but he is my *agent*, and agents have mysterious powers, and I guess he just put the whammy on me.

What he did was come up with a really good metaphor for once. It could have been a Zen riddle.

He said, "If everyone is wearing masks all the time, how do you know it's really them?"

Precisely. There might even be Virtual Publishers in New York, but they weren't on the same wavelength as the folks in Hollywood, and in fact only agents like Henry could connect the two. Only he knew the secrets of both. Only he could have shown me what he had shown me.

"Your *editor* is a big Carl Sanderson fan," he said. "She's dying to meet him. Maybe someday soon we can all get together."

That is, if my editor thinks that Carl Sanderson is a 1960s cowboy star made good, for whom books are being ghosted, and Carl Sanderson is a guy with *clout*, who can call up the aforesaid editor and demand that the whole direction of a storyline be scrapped because *he* has a better idea, and all the editor can do is meekly pass the instructions on to me—well, then, who precisely is in charge here?

"All you have to do," Henry explained, "is put on the mask and your editor will never know the difference. Nor will the reading public. What Carl Sanderson wants, Carl Sanderson gets. If *you* are Carl Sanderson, aren't you on top of the world?"

Ah Mephistopheles, indeed. He took me to the mountaintop. He showed me all the kingdoms of the world, which he would give me, if only I played along.

"Trust me, I'm your agent," he said.

I think I sold my soul all over again that night. If Carl Sanderson wanted to be James Joyce, he could be James Joyce, Henry told me. If he wanted to be Edgar Rice Burroughs, he could be Edgar Rice Burroughs. Or anything in between. Just use the magic name. It has that much clout.

"I won't let the publishers interfere, kiddo. I got connections, remember?"

"Yes, I remember."

And for just one horrifying second he seemed to flicker and jerk from side to side impossibly, but I convinced myself that was just a trick of the light.

We parked a couple blocks away from the Boulevard, and hoofed it along the Walk of Fame, counting the stars (You'll be glad to know they've repaired the crack in Elvis's), and we got to Grauman's Chinese Theater (which may be under new management but is still Grauman's Chinese in the hearts of millions) in time for the midnight ceremony in which Carl Sanderson's footprints and hand prints and the impression of his graviton-blaster were recorded in cement, right next to those of Shatner and Nimoy and all the crowd—and, for that matter, Donald Duck—and afterward I asked him to autograph a copy of *Galactic Avengers in the Nebula of Death* for me; and he shook my hand firmly and said, "I'm always pleased to meet one of my fans."

And after that Carl Sanderson entered a whole new, entirely remarkable phase of literary creativity.

The Adventure of the Death-Fetch

In retrospect, the most amazing thing is that Watson confided the story to me at all. I was nobody, a nineteen-year-old college student from America visiting English relatives during Christmas break. I just happened to be in the house when the old doctor came to call. He had been a friend of my grandfather long before I was born, and was still on the closest terms with my several aunts; and of course he was the Doctor John Watson, who could have commanded the immediate and rapt attention of any audience he chose.

So, why did he tell me and only me? Why not, at least, my aunts? I think it was precisely because I was no one of any consequence or particular credibility and would soon be returning to school far away. He was like the servant of King Midas in the fairy tale, who can no longer bear the secret that the king has ass's ears. He has to "get it off his chest," as we Americans say. The point is not being believed, or recording the truth, but release, from the sheer act of telling. The luckless courtier, fearing for his life, finally has to dig a hole in the swamp, stick his head in it, and whisper the secret. Not that it did him much good, for the wind in the rattling reeds endlessly repeated what he had said.

There being no swamp conveniently at hand for Dr. Watson, I would have to do.

The old gentleman must have been nearly eighty at the time. I remember him as stout, but not quite obese, nearly bald, with a generous white moustache. He often sat smoking by the remains of our fire long after the rest of the household had gone to bed. I imagined that he was reminiscing over a lifetime of wonderful adventures. Well, maybe.

I was up late too, that particular night, on my way into the kitchen for some tea after struggling with a wretched attempt at a novel. I chanced through the parlor. Doctor Watson stirred slightly where he sat.

"Oh, Doctor. I'm sorry. I didn't know you were still there."

He waved me to the empty chair opposite him. I sat without a further word, completely in awe of the great man.

I swallowed hard and stared at the floor for perhaps five minutes, jerking my head up once, startled, when the burnt log in the fireplace settled, throwing off sparks. I could hear occasional automobiles passing by in the street outside.

Dr. Watson's pipe had gone out and he set it aside. He folded his age-spotted hands in his lap, cleared his throat, and leaned forward.

He had my absolute attention. I knew that he was about to *tell a story.* My heart almost stopped.

"I am sure you know there were some cases of Sherlock Holmes which never worked out, and thus went unrecorded."

I lost what little composure I had and blurted, "Yes, yes, Doctor. You mention them from time to time. Like the one about the man and the umbrella—"

He raised a hand to silence me. "Not like that, boy. Some I never found the time to write up, and I inserted those allusions as reminders to myself; but others were *deliberately suppressed,* and never committed to paper at all, because Holmes expressly forbade it. One in particular—"

At least I didn't say anything as stupid as, *"Then why are you telling me?"* No, I had the good sense to sit absolutely motionless and silent, and just listen.

* * *

It was about this same season (*Watson began*) in the year 1900, a few days after Christmas if I recall correctly—I cannot be certain of such facts without my notebooks, and in any case the incident of which I speak was never entered into them—but I am certain it was a bright and brisk winter day, with new-fallen snow on the sidewalks, but no sense of festivity in the air. Instead, the city seemed to have reached a profound calm, a time to rest and tidy up and go on with one's regular business.

Holmes remarked how somehow, in defiance of all logic, it appeared that the calendar revealed patterns of criminality.

"Possibly the superstitions are true," I mused, "and lunatics really *are* driven by the moon."

"There may be scattered facts buried in the morass of superstition, Watson," said he, "if only science has the patience to ferret them out—"

We had now come, conversing as we walked, to the corner of Baker Street and Marylebone Road, having been abroad on some business or other—damn that I don't have my notes with me—when this train of thought was suddenly interrupted by an attractive, well-dressed young woman who rushed up and grasped Holmes by the arm.

"Mr. Sherlock Holmes? You *are* Mr. Sherlock Holmes, are you not?"

Holmes gently eased her hand off him. "I am indeed, Miss—"

"Oh! Thank God! My father said that no one else could possibly save him!"

To my amazement and considerable irritation, Holmes began walking briskly, leaving the poor girl to trail after us like a common beggar. I'd often had words with him in private about these lapses of the expected courtesy, but now I could only follow along, somewhat flustered. Meanwhile the young lady—whose age I would have guessed at a few years short of twenty—breathlessly related a completely disjointed tale about a mysterious curse, approaching danger, and quite a bit else I couldn't make head or tail out of.

At the doorstep of 221B, Holmes turned on her sharply.

"And now Miss—I'm afraid I did not catch your name."

"Thurston. My name is Abigail Thurston."

"Any relation to Sir Humphrey Thurston, the noted explorer of Southeast Asia?"

"He is my father, as I've already told you—"

"I am not sure you've told me much of anything—yet!" Holmes turned to go inside. Miss Thurston's featured revealed a completely understandable admixture of disappointment, grief, and quite possibly—and I couldn't have blamed her—rage.

"Holmes!" I said. "Please!"

"And now Miss Abigail Thurston, as I have no other business this morning, I shall be glad to admit you." As she, then I, followed him up the stairs, he continued, "You must pardon my abrupt manner, but it has its uses."

When I had shown her to a chair and rung Mrs. Hudson for some tea, Holmes explained further, "My primary purpose has been to startle you into *sense*, Miss Thurston. A story told all in a jumble is like a brook plunging over a precipice—very pretty, but, alas, babbling. Now that the initial rush of excitement is past, perhaps now you can tell me, calmly and succinctly, why you have come to see me. I enjoin you to leave out none of the facts, however trivial they may seem to you. Describe the events *exactly*, in the order that they occurred, filling in such background as may be necessary to illuminate the entire tale."

She breathed deeply, then began in measured tones. "I am indeed the daughter of the explorer, Sir Humphrey Thurston. You are perhaps familiar with his discoveries of lost cities in the jungles of Indo-China. His books are intended for a limited, scholarly audience, but there have been numerous articles about him in the popular magazines—"

"Suffice it to say that I am familiar with your father and his admirable contributions to science. Do go on."

"My mother died when I was quite small, Mr. Holmes, and my father spent so much time abroad that he was almost a stranger to me. I was raised by relatives, under the supervision of a series of governesses. All this while Father seemed more a guardian angel than a parent, someone always looking out for my welfare, concerned and benevolent, but invisible. Oh, there were letters and gifts in the post, but he remained *outside* my actual life. Each time he came, we had to become acquainted all over again. Such is the difference in a child's life between six and eight and twelve. *I* had changed profoundly, while he was always the same, brave, mysterious, inevitably sun burnt from long years in the jungles and deserts; home for a short time to rest, write his reports, and perhaps give a few lectures before setting forth again in the quest of knowledge. So things have continued. This past month he has returned again, after an absence of three years, to discover his little girl become a *woman*, and again a stranger. He has promised to remain this time until I am married and secure in a home of my own—"

"Then it should be a happy occasion for you," said Holmes, smiling to reassure her, the corners of his mouth twitching to betray impatience. The smile vanished. "But I perceive it is not. Please get to the point then. *Why* have you come rushing to Baker Street on a winter's day when you would surely be much more comfortable in a warm house in the company of your much-traveled sire?"

She paused, looking alarmed once more, glancing to me first as if for reassurance. I could only smile and nod, wordlessly bidding her to continue.

"The first few days of his visit were indeed happy, Mr. Holmes, but very suddenly, a shadow came over him. For a week and more, he seemed distracted and brooding. Then five days ago he withdrew into his study, refusing to venture out for any reason. He is afraid, deathly afraid!"

"Of what, pray tell?"

"I cannot discern the central fear, exactly, only its broader effects. Certainly he has become morbidly afraid of his own reflection. He will not allow a mirror to be brought anywhere near him. He even shaves with his eyes closed, by touch alone, rather than risk seeing himself."

"This *is* extraordinary," I said. "But surely," said Holmes, "this sort of mania is more in Doctor Watson's line than mine, work for a medical man of a specialized sort, not a detective."

"Oh no, Sir! My father is completely sane. I am certain of that. But I am equally certain that he is not telling me everything, perhaps in an attempt to spare me some horror—for it must be a horror that makes so bold an adventurer cringe behind a locked door with a loaded elephant gun across his knees!"

I leaned forward and spoke to her in my most soothing medical manner. "I am sure, Miss Thurston, that your father has a very good reason for acting as he does, and that, indeed, his chief object is to protect you."

"Yes," said Holmes. "I am certain it is."

"His very words were, 'Summon Sherlock Holmes, girl, or I shall not live out the week!' So here I am. Please come and see him, Mr. Holmes, *at once!*"

Holmes shot to his feet. "Watson! How foolish of us to have even removed our hats and coats. Come!" He took our guest by the hand and helped her up. "As I said, Miss Thurston, I have no other business this morning."

* * *

It was but a short cab ride to the Thurston residence, in the most fashionable part of west London. We rode in silence, crowded together, the girl in the middle, Holmes deep in thought. Unconsciously almost, Miss Thurston took my hand for reassurance. I held her firmly, but gently.

It was admittedly an intriguing problem: what, if not a sudden mania, could cause so brave a man as Sir Humphrey Thurston to be paralyzed with fear at the sight of his own reflection?

As we neared the house, the girl suddenly struggled to stand up in the still moving cab.

"Father!"

She pointed. I had only a glimpse of a tall, muscular man on the further street corner, and noted the tan coat and top hat, white gloves, and silver-tipped stick. He turned at the sound of Miss Thurston's cry, revealing a gray-bearded face, dark eyes, and a broad, high forehead, then moved speedily away in long strides, not quite running. Abruptly, he vanished down a side street.

Holmes pounded on the ceiling of the cab for the driver to stop and we three scrambled out, I attending to Miss Thurston and the driver while Holmes set off at a furious run, only to return moments later, breathing hard, having lost all trace of Sir Humphrey.

"I don't know what explanation I can offer," said Miss Thurston. "Perhaps my father's difficulty, mania or whatever it is, has passed, and I have wasted your time."

Holmes nodded to me.

"Mental disease is not my specialty." I said, "but from what medical papers I've read, and from the talk of my colleagues, I do not think it likely that so powerful a delusion would go away so quickly. It makes no sense."

"Indeed, it does not," said Holmes. "One moment, the man behaves as if he is faced with mortal danger. The next, he is out for a stroll as if nothing had happened, but he flees the approach of his beloved daughter and vanishes with, I must confess, remarkable speed and agility."

"What do we do now, Mr. Holmes?"

"If you would admit us to his chamber. Perhaps he left some clue."

"Yes, yes. I should have thought of that. Pray forgive me—"

"Do not trouble yourself, Miss Thurston. Only lead the way."

She unlocked the door herself. Although it was a fine, large house, there were no servants in evidence. I helped her off with her coat and hung it for her in a closet off to one side. As we ascended the front stairs, she hastily explained that another of her father's inexplicable behaviors was to give leave to the entire staff until—she supposed—the crisis had passed.

"Oh, I do fear that it *is* a mania, Mr. Holmes." I was beginning to fear as much myself, but scarcely a moment to consider the possibility when a voice thundered from above, "Abigail! Is that you?"

Miss Thurston looked to Holmes, then to me with an expression of utmost bewilderment and fright. I think she all but fainted at that moment. I made ready to catch her lest she tumble back down the stairs.

Again came the voice, from somewhere off to the left of the top of the stairs. "Abigail! If that's you, speak up girl! If it's Hawkins, you damned blackguard, I have my gun ready and am fully prepared to shoot!"

Holmes shouted in reply, "Sir Humphrey, it is Sherlock Holmes and his colleague Dr. Watson. We have been admitted by your daughter, who is here with us."

"Abigail?"

"Yes, Father, it is I. I've brought them as you asked."

Heavy footsteps crossed the floor upstairs. A door opened with a click of the lock being undone.

"Thank God, then . . ."

Holmes, Miss Thurston, and I ascended the stairs and were admitted into Sir Humphrey's study. I was astounded to confront the *same man* we had seen on the street. The broad shoulders, bearded face, high forehead, dark eyes, and athletic gait were unmistakable. But now he wasn't dressed for the outdoors. He wore a dressing gown and slippers. An elephant gun lay across the chair where he had obviously been sitting moments before. On the table by his right hand were a bottle and glass of brandy, a notebook, a pen and an uncapped ink jar.

"Thank God you are here, Mr. Holmes," he said. "Doubtless my daughter has told you of my distress and seeming madness. If anyone on Earth may convince me that I am *not* mad, it is you, Mr. Holmes. I can trust no one else to uncover the fiendish devices by which I have been made to see the impossible."

We all sat. Thurston offered Holmes and me glasses of brandy. Holmes waved his aside. I accepted out of politeness, but after a single sip placed it on the table beside me.

Sir Humphrey seemed about ready to speak, when Holmes interrupted.

"First, a question. Have you been, for any reason, outside of the house this morning?"

Thurston looked startled. "Certainly not. I have not been out of this *room* for five days—" He paused, as if uncertain of how to proceed.

It was Holmes's turn to be astonished, but only I, who knew him well, could detect the subtle change in his manner and expression. To the others he must have seemed, as before, calm and attentive, purely analytical.

The silence went on for a minute or two. Now I that had a chance to examine our surroundings, the room proved to be exactly what I expected, a cluttered assembly of mementoes and books, a large bronze Buddha seated on a teakwood stand, strangely demonic Asian masks hanging on the walls amid framed citations and photographs. In a place of honor behind his writing desk hung a portrait of a beautiful woman whose features resembled those of Abigail Thurston but were somewhat older. This I took to be her mother.

"Do go on, Sir Humphrey," said Holmes, "and tell us what has taken place during these five days in which you have never once left this room."

"You'll probably think I am out of my mind, Mr. Holmes. Indeed, I think so myself, whenever I am unable to convince myself that I am beguiled by some devilish trickery. For the life of me, I cannot figure out how it is *done.*"

"How what is done, Sir Humphrey?"

"Mr. Holmes, do you know what I mean when I say I have seen my *death fetch?*"

Abigail Thurston let out a cry, then covered her mouth with her hand.

Holmes seemed unperturbed. "In the superstitions of many races, a man who is about to die may encounter his spirit-likeness. The German term is *doppelgänger,* meaning double-walker. Certainly such an apparition is held to be a portent of the direst sort, and to be *touched* by this figure means instantaneous death. You haven't been touched by it then, have you, Sir Humphrey?"

Thurston's face reddened. "If you mean to mock me, Mr. Holmes, then my faith in you is misplaced."

"I do not mock. Nor do I deal in phantoms. My practice stands firmly flat-footed upon the ground. No ghosts need apply. Therefore I must agree with your conclusion, even before I have examined the evidence, that you are the victim of trickery of some kind. But first, describe to me what you *think* you have seen."

"*Myself,* Mr. Holmes. My daughter has surely mentioned my sudden aversion to mirrors."

"Don't we all see ourselves in mirrors?"

"I saw myself *twice.*"

"Twice?"

"Five mornings ago, I stood before the mirror shaving, when a second image appeared in the glass, as if an *exact duplicate of myself* were looking over my shoulder. I whirled about, razor in hand, and confronted *myself* as surely if I gazed into a second mirror, only the face of this *other* was contorted with the most venomous hatred, Mr. Holmes, the most absolute malevolence I have ever beheld. The lips were about to form an utterance which I somehow *know* would mean my immediate death.

"So I slashed frantically with my razor. I felt the blade pass through only the air, but the figure vanished, like a burst soap bubble."

"And it did not harm you in any way," said Holmes, "any more than a soap bubble—or some projected illusion of light and shadow."

"Oh no, Mr. Holmes, this was no magic-lantern show. It was a fully three-dimensional image. Each time I saw it, it was as real to my eyes as you and Dr. Watson appear now."

"You saw it, then, more than once?"

"Three times, Mr. Holmes, until I had the sense to remove all mirrors and reflective surfaces from the room. That is how it *gets in*. I am certain of that."

"And I am certain, Sir Humphrey, that *you* are certain of far more than you have told me. Unless you give me *all* of the facts, I cannot help you, however much your daughter may entreat me. Who, for instance, is the 'blackguard Hawkins' you took us for on the stairs?"

Thurston refilled his glass and took a long draught of brandy, then settled back. "Yes, you are right, of course, Mr. Holmes. I shall have to tell you and Dr. Watson everything." He turned to his daughter. "But you, my dear, perhaps should not hear what we have to say."

"Father, I think I am old enough."

"It is not a pretty story."

* * *

"My early years were wild," Sir Humphrey began. "I was no paragon of scientific respectability at twenty-one, but little more than a common criminal. I have never before admitted that I was dismissed from the Indian Army under extremely disreputable circumstances and only escaped court martial because a sympathetic officer allowed me time to flee, change my name, and disappear. The offense involved the pillage of a native temple, and the officer's sympathy had been purchased with some of the loot.

"And so, under another name, I wandered the East. I had no means by which to return to England, nor had I any desire to present myself to friends and family as a failure and a disgrace. Once in a very great while I dispatched a letter filled with fanciful, if artfully vague, tales of confidential adventures in government service.

"In the course of my travels I picked up several languages and a profound education in the ways of the world's wickedness. I fell in with the roughest possible company, and was myself more often than not on the wrong side of the law. In the gold fields of Australia there was a certain dispute and a man died of it, and once more I had to vanish. In Shanghai I worked as an agent for a wealthy mandarin, whose true activities, when they became known to the Chinese authorities, caused his head to be pickled in brine.

"But the blackest depths were in Rangoon, for there I met Wendall Hawkins. He was a vile rogue, Mr. Holmes, even among such company as I found him. Murderer, thief, pirate, and more—I am sure. He was a huge, powerful man with an enormous, dark beard, who used to jokingly boast—though I think he half believed it—that he was the reincarnation of Edward Teach, the notorious buccaneer commonly known as Blackbeard.

"Reckless as I was, my normal instinct would have been to avoid such a man as I would a live cobra, but he had something which fascinated me: an idol six inches in height, of a hideous, bat-winged dog, carven of the finest milky green jade, stylized in a manner which resembled the Chinese but wasn't. Its eyes were purest sapphires.

"Mr. Holmes, I was more than just a thieving lout in those days. Already the direction of my life's work was clear to me—though I had yet to learn its manner—for if ever I suffered from a true mania, it was the craving to penetrate the deepest secrets of the mysterious Orient. Oh, I wanted riches, yes, but more than that I hoped to come back to England famous, like some Burton or Livingston or Speke, having brought the light of European science to the darkest and most forbidden corners of the globe.

"I knew what this idol was, even before Wendall Hawkins told me. It was an artifact of the Chan-Tzo people who inhabit the Plateau of Leng in central Asia, in that unmapped and unexplored region northwest of Tibet, where theoretically the Chinese and Russian empires adjoin, but in fact no civilized person has ever set foot—for all the ravings of Madame Blavatsky contain much nonsense about the place. The very name, Chan-Tzo, is often mistranslated as 'Corpse-Eaters,' and so occultists whisper fearfully of the hideous rites of the 'Corpse Eating Cult of Leng.' In truth necrophagy is the least of Leng's horrors. The Chan-Tzo are 'Vomiters of Souls' . . . but I am far ahead of myself.

"Hawkins had the idol and he had a map—which had been acquired, he darkly hinted, at the cost of several lives—written in an obscure Burmese dialect. He needed me to translate. That was why he had come to me. Otherwise he would share his treasure-hunt with as few as possible—for that was what it was to be. We would journey to Leng armed to the teeth, slaughter any natives who stood in our way, and return to civilization rich men. I tried to console my conscience with the belief that I, at least, would be traveling as much for knowledge as for wealth, and that through my efforts this find could be of scientific value.

"Hawkins and ten others had pooled funds to buy a steam launch, which we christened, to suit our leader's fancy, the *Queen Anne's Revenge.* Once we had secured sufficient ammunition and supplies, we slipped up the Irriwaddy by night and journeyed deep into the interior, beyond the reach of any colonial authorities, ultimately anchoring at Putao near the Chinese border and continuing overland.

"I don't have to tell you that the trip was a disaster. Supplies went bad or disappeared. We all had fevers. What native guides we could hire or seize at gunpoint misled us, then got away. I alone could read the damned map, but it was cryptic, even if you could make out the script. Much of the time I merely guessed and tried to find our way by the stars.

"Many times I was certain that none of us would get back alive. The first to die was the crazy American, something-or-other Jones, a lunatic who carried a bullwhip and fancied himself an archaeologist. We found Jones in his tent, bloated to half again normal size, his face eaten away by foot-long jungle leeches.

"One by one the others perished, from accidents, from disease that might have been poisoning. Gutzman, the South African, caught a dart in the neck one night. Van Eysen, the Dutchman, tried to make off with most of our remaining food and clean water. Hawkins shot him in the back, then killed the Malay when he protested, and the Lascar on general principles. Another Englishman, Gunn, got his throat cut merely so that there would be one mouth less to feed.

"Since I alone could read the map—or pretended to—I was certain Hawkins needed me alive. In the end, there were only the two of us, ragged and emaciated wretches staggering on in a timeless delirium of pain and dread. It was nothing less than a living death.

"At last we emerged from the jungle and climbed onto the windswept tableland of central Asia. Still the journey seemed endless. I had no idea of where we were going anymore, for all I made a show of consulting the map over and over so that Hawkins would not kill me. Each night I dreamed of the black and forbidding Plateau of Leng, which was revealed to me in a series of visions, its ruins and artificial caverns of shocking antiquity, perhaps older even than mankind itself, as were the immemorial blasphemies of the Chan-Tzo.

"What Hawkins dreamed, I cannot say. His speech had ceased to be coherent, except on the point of threatening me should I waver from our purpose. I knew he was insane then, and that I would die with him, likewise insane, unless I could somehow escape his company.

"I was past thinking clearly. How fortunate, then, that my plan was simplicity itself—almost the bare truth rather than some contrived stratagem.

"I fell to the ground and refused to rise, no matter how much Hawkins screamed that he would blow my brains out with his pistol. I said I was dying, that his pistol would be a mercy. *He* would offer me no mercy. I was counting on that.

Instead, he forced me to translate the map for him and make notes as best I could. There was nothing to write with by a thorn and my own blood, but I wrote, and when he was satisfied, he laughed, folded the map into his pocket, took *all* our remaining supplies, and left me to my fate on the trackless, endless plain.

"And so we parted. I hoped I had sent him to Hell, deliberately mixing up the directions so he'd end up only the Devil knew where. He, of course, assumed I would be vulture's meat before another day or two.

"But I did not die. Mad with fever and privation, my mind filled with fantastic and horrible hallucinations, I wandered for what might have been days or even weeks, until, by the kindness of Providence alone, I stumbled into the camp of some nomads, who, seeing that I was a white man, bore me on camel-back into the Chinese province of Sinkiang and there turned me over to a trader, who brought me to a missionary.

"This proved to be my salvation, both physical and otherwise. I married the missionary's daughter, Abigail's mother, and largely through the influence of her family I later found a place on a much more respectable Anglo-French expedition to Angkor. That was the true beginning of my scientific career. Still the mysteries of the East haunted me, but my cravings were directed into proper channels until I achieved the renown I have today."

* * *

At this point Sir Humphrey paused. The only sound was the slow ticking of a great clock in some other room. Abigail Thurston's face was white from the shock of what she had heard. She scarcely seemed to breathe. Holmes sat very still, his chin held in his hand, staring into space.

I was the one who broke the silence.

"Surely, Sir Humphrey, there is more to the story than that. I don't see how your luckless expedition or whatever fate the rascal Hawkins must have met has anything to do with the here and now."

Thurston's reaction was explosive.

"Damn it, man! It has *everything* to do with my predicament and what may well be my inevitable fate. But . . . you are right. There is more to tell. After many years of roving the world, giving lectures, publishing books, after I was knighted by the Queen—after my past life seemed a bad dream from which I had finally awakened—I thought I was safe. But it was not to be. *This past fortnight I began to receive communications from the fiend Hawkins!*"

"Communications?" said Holmes. "How so?"

"There. On the desk."

Holmes reached over and opened an ornately carven, lacquered box, removing a sheaf of papers. He glanced at them briefly and gave them to me.

"What do you make of them, Watson?"

"I cannot read the writing. The paper is an Oriental rice-paper. The penmanship shows the author to be under considerable mental strain, perhaps intoxicated. Notice the frequent scratchings and blottings. Beyond that, I can make out nothing."

Sir Humphrey spoke. "The language is an archaic—some would say degenerate—form of Burmese, the script a kind of code used by criminals in the Far East. Between these two elements, I am perhaps the only *living* man who can read what is written here, for Wendall Hawkins *is not alive*, if his words are to be believed."

"Surely if he is dead," said Holmes, "your troubles are at an end."

"No, Mr. Holmes, they are not, for all of these letters were written *after* Hawkins's death—long after it. It seems that he *reached* the Plateau of Leng, which I saw only in visions. There the almost sub-human priests of the Chan-Tzo murdered him after what might have been *years* of indescribable tortures, then brought him back into a kind of half-life as an animate corpse at their command, hideously disfigured, the skin flayed from his face, his heart ripped out, the cavity in his chest filled with inextinguishable fire. He is in implacable now, driven both by the will of his masters and his own rage for revenge against me, whom he blames for his unending agony. He knows all the secrets of the Chan-Tzo priests, and the conjuring of death-fetches is easily within his power."

"He says all *that* in these letters?" I asked.

"That and more, Dr. Watson, and if it is true, I am defenseless. My only hope is that Mr. Holmes and yourself can prove me to be *deluded*, the victim of a *hoax* perpetrated by the vile Hawkins who has no doubt returned, but returned, I still dare to hope, as no more than a mortal villain. If you can do this, I certainly have the means to reward you handsomely for your services."

"My services are charged on a fixed scale," said Holmes, "but let us not concern ourselves with the monetary details now. I shall indeed collar this Hawkins for you and unmask his devices—which I am sure would make the tricks of our English spirit mediums child's play in comparison—but they are devices none the less. For what else can they be?"

"Mr. Holmes, I will be forever in your debt."

"We shall watch and wait until Hawkins is forced to show his hand. But first, I think Dr. Watson should escort Miss Abigail to a safer place, my own rooms, which I shall not be needing until this affair is concluded." When Thurston's daughter made to protest, Holmes turned to her and said, "You have been a heroine, but now that the battle is actually joined, I think it best that you remove yourself from the field. Will you go with Dr. Watson?"

"Whatever you say, Mr. Holmes."

"Splendid. Now I must busy myself examining the house inside and out, to discover any way our enemy might use to gain entrance."

Thurston picked up the elephant gun and lay it across his lap, then began idly polishing the barrel with a cloth.

"I've survived five days like this. I think I shall be safe here behind the locked door for a little while longer yet. Your plan makes excellent sense, Mr. Holmes."

We left Sir Humphrey alone in the room. As Holmes and I escorted Miss Thurston down the stairs, the detective asked me, "Well, Watson, what do you think?"

"A unique case, Holmes. One worthy of your talents."

"About Sir Humphrey. What about him?"

"I judge him to be of fundamentally sound mind, but what superstitious fears he may harbor are being played upon by the murderous Hawkins, who sounds himself to be completely mad."

"Mad or not, he shall have to manifest himself in a decidedly *material* form before long, at which point he will be susceptible to capture by mundane means."

"One thing doesn't fit, Holmes. Who, or what, did we see upon our arrival here? Sir Humphrey hadn't been out of the room."

"An impostor, possibly a trained actor in league with Hawkins. I agree that all the pieces of the puzzle are not yet in place. But have patience. You know my methods."

"I am so glad that you and Dr. Watson will help Father," Miss Thurston said softly as we reached the base of the stairs. "You are sent from Heaven, both of you."

Holmes smiled indulgently. "Not from nearly so far, but we shall do what we can."

Alas, we could do but little. As we stood there at the base of the stairs and I helped Miss Thurston on with her coat, she turned and chanced to look back up the stairs. Suddenly she screamed.

"Good God!" I exclaimed.

Near the top of the stairs was a figure who appeared to be Sir Humphrey, but dressed for the outside, in coat and top hat, as we had seen him before. He *could not* have gotten past us.

"You! Stop!" Holmes was already in pursuit, bounding up the steps three at a time. The figure moved so swiftly the eye could hardly follow, and soft-footedly. I heard only Holmes's boots pounding on the wooden stairs. Then there came a cry from within the study. Sir Humphrey shouted something in a foreign language, his tone that of abject terror, his words broken off in a gurgling scream. The elephant gun went off with a thunderous roar.

I left Miss Thurston and hurried up after Holmes. By the time I reached the study door, which was blown apart from the inside as if a cannonball had gone through it, Holmes was inside.

He rushed out again, his eyes wild, his face bloodless, and he saw Miss Abigail Thurston coming up behind me.

"For the love of God, Watson! Don't let her in!"

"Father!" she screamed. "Oh, you must let me pass!"

For all she struggled, I held her fast. "Watson! Do not let her through no matter what happens! It is just . . . too horrible!"

I think that was the only time I ever saw Sherlock Holmes truly shocked, at a loss for words.

I forced Miss Thurston back down the stairs despite her vehement protests, holding onto her until the police arrived, which they did shortly, summoned by the neighbors who had heard the screams and the shot. Only after she had been conveyed away in a police wagon, accompanied by a patrolman, was I able to examine the body of Sir Humphrey Thurston, who was indeed murdered, as I had feared.

Though still seated in his chair, he had been mutilated hideously, almost beyond recognition.

His throat was cut from ear to ear. That was enough to have killed him. But the flesh had been almost entirely torn away from his face, and a strange series of symbols, like the ones I had seen in the letters, had been carved in the bare bone of his forehead. The crown of his skull had been smashed in by some blunt instrument, and—it revolted me to discover—most of his brain was gone.

The final detail was the worst, for it had been deliberately designed to mock us. The still smoking elephant gun lay across his lap, and, carefully placed so that it would be *reflected in the mirrored surface of the polished gun barrel*, was a small jade idol with emerald eyes, a stylized figure of a bat-winged dog.

"Yes, Holmes," I said, "it is entirely too horrible."

* * *

Dr Watson stopped telling the story, and I, the nineteen-year-old American college student, could only gape at him open-mouthed, like some imbecile, trying not to reach the attractively obvious conclusion that the good doctor's mind had gone soft after so many years. It was a terrible thing, just to entertain such a notion. I almost wept.

I would have remained there forever, frozen where I sat, wordless, had not Dr. Watson gone on.

"It was a case which I could not record, which Holmes *ordered* me to suppress on pain of the dissolution of our friendship. It just didn't work out."

"Wh-what do you mean, didn't work out?"

"I mean exactly that. The affair concluded too quickly and ended in abject failure. We accomplished nothing. He would have no more of the matter, the specifics, as he acidly phrased it, being left to the 'official imagination,' which, sure enough, concluded the murder to be the work of a madman or madmen, perhaps directed by a sinister Oriental cult, a new Thuggee. But even the police could not account for the powerful stench of *decay* which lingered in the explorer's study even long after the body had been removed, as if something long dead had invaded, done its worst, and departed as inexplicably as it had come.

"Enormous pressure was brought to bear to prevent any accurate reportage in the newspapers, to prevent panic. I think those instructions came from the very highest level. Sir Humphrey's obituary, ironically, listed the cause of his demise as an Asiatic fever. I signed the death certificate to that effect.

"My own conclusions were profoundly disturbing. The mystery could not be resolved. What we—even Miss Thurston—had witnessed were not merely unlikely, but *impossible.*

"'I *reject* the impossible,' said Holmes vehemently. 'as a matter of policy. Such things *cannot be*—'

"'You and I and the girl saw, Holmes. They *are.*'

"'No, Watson! No! The irrational has *no place* in detective work. We must confine ourselves to the tangible and physical, carefully building upon meticulous reason, or else the whole edifice of my life's work crumbles into dust. Against the supernatural, I am helpless, my methods of no use. My methods *have* been useful in the past, don't you think? And so they shall be in the future, but we must remain within certain bounds, and so preserve them.'"

* * *

Again I, the college boy, was left speechless.

"Holmes made me swear an oath—and I swore it—never to write up this case—and I never wrote it—"

Had he, in a sense at least, broken his oath by telling me? I dared not ask. Was there some urgency now, of which had lately become aware?

"I wanted to tell someone," was all he said. "I thought I should."

King Midas. Ass's ears. Who will believe the wind in the reeds?

I merely know that a week after I returned to school in America I received a telegram saying that Dr. Watson had died peacefully of heart failure, sitting in that very chair by the fire. A week later a parcel arrived with a note from one of my aunts, expressing some bewilderment that he had wanted me to have the contents.

It was the idol of the bat-winged dog.

The Unwanted Grail

He had slain three giants. I never knew their names, so in this tale, in which names are so important, those three must remain anonymous.

On a bitter winter's evening I found them, as the sky faded from steel-gray to purple to black, as the killing wind rattled the ice-coated trees. In the twilight, I beheld the first giant lying face-down in the snow like a dark continent rising above a white sea. The second knelt strangely, impaled on a broken tree as on a spear, his head twisted around so he might look down his own back in blank-eyed astonishment at the enormous splash his blood had made on the snow.

The third rested peacefully, as if asleep with a log for a pillow, his death betrayed only by the frozen tickle of blood that seeped from his eye, where perhaps a poniard had slipped in an pierced his brain.

There was nothing to be scavenged from any of these, for giants are of the fairy kind. Their metal burns the hand, and crumbles like old leaves with the coming of the sun.

Far more promising was the knight, the author of this carnage, who sat frozen where he had fallen amid briers, a fairy spear sunk deep into his side. I could still see where the spear-shaft had dragged in the snow, and the blood trailed.

I grabbed him by the ankles and hauled him ungently out of the briers, then started to work. What I envied most were his thick, hide boots. I had only rags this season, beneath which my feet were no doubt black and bloody. I, a scarecrow of a boy pretending to be a man, a thing of flapping tatters and stinking hides and limbs like sticks, would look ridiculous clumping around in those big, fine boots; but I would have them.

My fingers were too numb to untie the laces, so I got out my knife and started cutting.

The knight's eyes snapped open.

I crouched at his feet, transfixed by his gaze, the knife in my hand a seeming confession of every possible crime. I couldn't understand the feeling. I knew, then, that he was like no other man I had ever met, and I was afraid of him.

"Would you murder a helpless man?"

I couldn't meet his gaze. I stared at the knife.

"I ask you again, would you murder me?"

I cut through his laces and yanked off one boot. Beneath, he wore thick woolen hose. I would have those too.

"I ask you—"

I flashed my knife in front of his face. I trembled, tears on my cheeks, trying to seem very tough. "I've killed a lot of people already—"

He let out a long sigh, then smiled, like a father responding to a child who has just admitted some childishly-heinous crime, *Have you indeed? Naughty, naughty.*

Now his gaze was far away, and he seemed to be remembering or quoting something.

"A third time I say unto you—"

I started working on his other boot. I spat in the snow.

"I could just wait for you to freeze to death."

"Then you would be no murderer indeed, no human criminal, merely a carrion-robbing animal, a beast in the form of a man, which might be an improvement in your circumstances, since beasts are without sin."

He was raving. I assumed his mind was dying, a little bit at a time. I tried not to listen to him as I worked.

"I do what I must," I said.

"And what must you do, Theodorus? That means 'gift of God.' Did you know that? You are a gift of God. To somebody—"

Again I was transfixed. I glared at him with venomous hatred, closer than ever to slitting his throat just to shut him up. But I was too much afraid.

"How do you know my name? Nobody knows my name? I'm called Vermin or Badger or Crow, or Murderer's Get—Yes, yes, I can murder as easily as I can breathe—"

I stood up. Maybe I was going to leap on him and kill him right there. But my knees buckled and I fell over backward, arms flailing, and the knife went flying off into the evening dark.

I crawled back to him, caught hold of his belt, stole his poniard, and lay beside him, with the tip of the poniard beneath his chin.

"You had better explain yourself," I said, gasping from hunger and exhaustion and cold. "Make it good—"

His eyes rolled down to regard the blade, and he *laughed*, but there was sorrow in his laughter, and, I think, a touch of madness, but something more than that: *recognition*. Somehow he seemed to be saying to himself, *Yes, this is the one. This is the answer. It's not what I expected, but this is what I've got.* Only after a long while was he able to speak.

"Your name came to me in a vision. A white bird, with fire circling all around its head in a ring, like a haloed saint, alighted on a branch above a battlefield, while black birds pecked at the corpses. The white bird spoke to me as I leaned on my shield, wounded full sore and weary, and in a voice like that of the fairest maiden the creature bade me seek out God's gift and understand fully the mysteries of knighthood—"

I sat up in the snow, and slid the poniard under my own belt. "I know all about knights. A knight raped my mother and hanged her man when he tried to protect her. He and the other knights slew many men and burned their houses. They did it in the name of God. Therefore I hate God and all his knights."

He laughed again, and I wondered if he even knew why he was laughing. Perhaps it was because the deeds of knights are told in tales, and no poet would ever tell a story that ended like this, with me in it. Here I was, the terminal blot on the page of chivalry and all such pretty lies. So be it.

I wondered if he might have raped my mother, if he might be my father.

He was about the right age.

But his laughter told me something, something mere words could not have: *No, the story is not over. It continues.*

Once more I reached to cut his throat with the poniard.

"Do you suppose," he said, "that we could remove ourselves to a more comfortable place and continue this discussion?"

Maybe I was going mad too. I slid the poniard back into my belt. Then I put on his second boot and lurched to my feet. I took him under the arms from behind, and with every ounce of strength I had, with surprising reserves I didn't know I had, I began to drag him across the snow, his bootless feet trailing. Every once in a while the spear-shaft hit some obstacle, and he cried out in pain.

Once I stopped and made to pull the spear out, but the knight commanded me not to touch it, lest his guts and blood pour out all at once, and he die too soon, as if there were a specific, appointed hour for his death and he knew what it was.

It was a desperate, terrible struggle, and I didn't even know why I was doing it. Some force compelled me, like a wind filling a sail. My mind wandered, and I wasn't even sure any more if I really was that Theodorus who was the get of a knight, or if I'd made that story up just to cause pain or to explain it. Maybe I was a badger, or a crow, or some clod of earth anointed with the blood of warriors and somehow come alive in the mocking semblance of a man.

In full darkness, beneath the starry sky, I dragged him, while wolves howled not far away, and the frigid wind whispered in my ears like ghosts and told me tales of chivalry and monsters and dying knights.

All this while my burden muttered to himself. I think he was praying.

I must have been near to death myself when I reached my hermitage. Call it a hovel and give it glory; a cleft scooped out of a hillside, the opening covered over with mud and stones and dead branches, a little place for a fire and a hole in the roof for the smoke to go out. This was my castle and my domain, the Siege Ridiculous, at which a knight might have laughed.

All I could do was drag the both of us inside. The knight screamed as the spear caught and dragged. I reached for it. I smelled my hand burning as I touched the metal shaft, but my hand was too frozen for there to be any pain. It must have been burning inside his wound too.

I uncovered the fire pit and blew on the ashes and got a little flame going. After a while, pain returned to my hands, and even to my feet inside the knight's warm boots.

I hunched over him, unsure of what to do next, and could only stare at him while he babbled on, about many adventures, and the great King Arthur, who dwelt in Camelot, who had himself done wondrous deeds—

"Are you listening, boy?"

I made no reply.

"Sometimes I feel like I'm talking to the walls," my guest said, and yet he continued on about the Holy Grail, how it had appeared in Camelot at Pentecost, and all the knights had sworn themselves to quests of great holiness, which caused King Arthur to weep, for he knew they were not holy men, and would suffer and perish in the questing; therefore on this Pentecost he saw them assembled together in feasting for the last time; and the Grail fed them, providing each man with the meat he desired most; then it passed out of Camelot and vanished, until such knights could, by their chivalry and worship achieve some fleeting glimpse of it in the course of their adventures—

"Do you understand any of this, boy?"

I shrugged. I was afraid.

The wind rattled in the walls of my poor dwelling.

"The thing about a quest is," the knight went on, "that the author is not the knight at all, but God, and God is like a smith, who works with his hammer, then his tongs, then his pliers, whichever tool he chooses, and then lays each aside to pick up another, even as he has laid me aside, while working to some greater end."

He was silent for a time, and there was only the wind, and the wolves outside.

He closed his eyes. I thought he was asleep, or perhaps, finally, to the relief of all concerned, dead.

But he spoke in a whisper, as if in sleep, "Theodorus, go outside. Then return and tell me what you have seen."

And I got up, and went outside, and came back in to report that I had only seen the stars and the trees bending in the wind, and the swirling snow.

"Ah," said he. "We have a little time yet. I must confess my sins . . . to you, I suppose . . . and beg your forgiveness, since you are my host and have treated me with kindness . . . and I have been lacking in courtesy, being as I am far from home, burdened by sin and filled with sorrow. Those giants, I think, were my sins made flesh, and I overcame them, and may hope for Heaven . . . but they were the undoing of me, and the ruin of my quest . . . and much of what it means to be a knight is that you have a duty, a goal, and *no excuses accepted* . . . Therefore I ask you to forgive my sins, then go outside again, and come back in, and tell me what you have seen."

I muttered some words, afraid and bewildered and certain that I had no business forgiving anybody's sins. Then I got up and went outside once more.

The moon had risen, a pale, dying crescent, flickering through the icy branches, and by moonlight in a little clearing I saw a knight, all in black, with his sword drawn and his visor raised, so to reveal a face which was only a bare skull.

I returned and told what I had seen.

"That is only Death, who has been my companion on the road for a long while. We still have a little time."

Still he spoke on, his tale like a tangle of thread which no one could ever unravel, a muddle of haunted castles and temptresses, of holy men who gave blessings, of demons who led knights astray and to their dooms; of a hundred white knights and a hundred black ones, who fought until not one was left standing, and then all stood up and fought again; and once, on a lonely, dark night like this, in a wilderness, when my own knight, my guest or victim or whatever he was felt himself giving over to despair, he looked up and saw what he thought was a single star shining through a cloud.

But it was not a star, and the cloud settled to earth, and he beheld the Grail, but far away, like a lantern in a window seen from across a mile of darkened countryside.

One of the more confusing aspects of the story was that I didn't even know the hero's name, and sometimes, as he told it, the hero was called Theodorus.

I huddled by the fire, clasping my knees and resting my head on them.

So I asked him, directly, who he was, and he was startled, as if the walls had spoken back to him.

"For this discourtesy, too, I ask you to forgive me."

And I forgave him, for all the good that did.

"I am called Ufilias," he said, "one of the hundred and fifty who were there that fatal Pentecost. I am a knight of the Round Table, if not one of the more famous ones, mentioned only in the chronicles as 'many more were there,' or 'also included,' and I swore a quest with the others, and, well, here I am. I think that is all I have to tell. Therefore, good friend, I beg you to go outside yet again, and return, and report what you have seen."

And I went outside, and saw in another clearing, near at hand, a knight with sword and shield at ready, in armor gleaming golden like the sunrise. His raised visor revealed a face sculpted out of living flame, and I could not look on it.

I reached for my stolen poniard, as if to defend myself. The burning knight turned toward me, and, at once afraid, I ducked back inside.

Crouched down again, I listened to the wind and the wolves and to Sir Ufilias's labored breathing, and I whispered to him what I had seen.

"I think it is the time when God puts down one tool," he said, "which is old and broken, and picks up another, so that his labor might continue."

Then, from outside, I heard many sounds, all of them muted and far away: the thunder of countless hooves, a maiden singing, church bells, trumpets, and clangor of arms, the cawing of crows as they peck at the slain.

"Theodorus," my knight said, "here's what you have to do. You must put on my armor and take up my weapons, and continue on the quest. Win glory for yourself. Become a famous man, a hero, not merely one of the knights who was 'also there.' The labor goes on and on, God hammering away in his smithy of our lives, beating the sins out of us."

And I believed every word he said, and was very much afraid. It was a kind of death that came over me then, for by merely listening, and believing, all that I had been must die.

Angrily, desperately, I shoved the stolen poniard back into Sir Ufilias's belt.

"No! I am *not* a knight! I *don't* go on quests!"

"What are you then?"

"Nothing. I am a rat and a carrion dog and a maggot-worm!"

"Is that what you really want?"

After much hesitation, I finally said, "No, it is not."

"Even a dog or a worm can be a miracle, if God wills it. Go outside, Theodorus, one last time, and see what you may see."

I went outside, and it seemed I was a small child again, running in terror, barefoot through the snow, while all around me houses burned and black knights with demon-masks struck down everyone I had ever known. The snow became fire and swirled up, and formed great castles of living flame, tier upon tier, towers higher than the sun at noontide, windows like gaping mouths, out of which came bewitching songs, which drew me into the fire, and screams, which drove me away. And I covered my eyes and ran, burning and naked through the snow and the winter woods, clothed only in flame, in terrible pain but not consumed; and I heard the hammer of God clanging away on his terrible anvil; and the blood of men hissed as hot metal touched it.

Then I came, at last, to the shore of a lake, where the touch of the waters healed me, and the fire went out. I stood there, shivering, while a white ship drew near, draped all in white samite, with lanterns hung from its masts like stars. And within the ship I saw maidens dressed all in white, and a wounded king, drawn and shriveled with suffering; and a bleeding knight whose name was Ufilias; and likewise another knight who held aloft a bloody spear. Then came someone holding a covered vessel, which shone through its cover so brilliantly that I could not see, and I fell down, dazzled, amazed, and afraid; and a commanding voice called out to me, "Rise up, Theodorus, and follow after."

And I rose, and followed, and ran naked and barefoot on the surface of the water as if over smooth marble. But the ship drew away from me, like a star setting behind a hill, until I was alone in the darkness once more, and the water would not hold me up. I fell, splashing, into the frigid lake, and struggled desperately to reach the shore. Many times I thought I would not, and die here instead, but somehow I *had* to. I *had* to tell Ufilias what I had seen, as if it mattered terribly in some way I could not even dimly understand.

When I got back to my miserable domain, I was indeed naked, and almost dead from cold. Sir Ufilias lay waiting for me, and I knew that he would die very soon.

There was no time to tell the tale. I tried to. He seemed to already know it, and hurried me on about my business as I stripped off his armor and his clothing, and girt myself as a knight.

"But this is a *joke*," I said. "I am a species of carrion-beast, not the stuff of which knights are made."

And he repeated to me again that part of being a knight is that there are no excuses accepted.

"Let me take one more thing," I said, having put on his armor, which did not fit, and his sword, which was too heavy for me. "Let me take also your name." That was the heaviest burden of them all.

I heard God's terrible hammer, clanging.

But Sir Ufilias was already dead. Then I drew the fairy spear out of his side, and no blood issued forth, only a little water. The spear burned my hand, and always as I carried it, I was in pain, but I never put it down while on my quest.

Outside, I battled the two knights. The black knight feigned to yield, and drew off, but circled around behind me and crept into the hovel, to steal away the soul of Ufilias. There was nothing I could do about that.

But the other and I fought all throughout the morning twilight, as the sun rose, and my spear did not crumble away like a fairy thing, but burned like pure flame. Strength filled me, like wind filling a sail, propelling me on, into this battle, as arms clashed on shields like terrible thunder.

And as I fought, I seemed to pass into a dream, in which the boy Theodorus walked through Camelot's halls barefoot, in stinking skins and rags, while all around him the elegant knights and their ladies feasted. No one noticed him, even when he protested that he didn't belong here, and in time his voice faded away, like the wind rattling among frozen branches, growing still.

And I awoke from that dream, into another, which was the dream of Ufilias, which has not ended, ever yet.

When the sun rose and I transfixed the flaming knight with my spear, then smote off his head and saw that his pained, frightened, and utterly bewildered face was that of a boy, of one Theodorus.

One last time, I heard Ufilias cry out, in pain and surprise. I searched for him, but could not find him.

Nor could I find Theodorus.

I searched for them both, through many lands, through many adventures and perils, through much pain, while the hammering of God thundered in my ears and the burning spear seared my hand.

Only once did I ever encounter other knights on the quest. Three of us came together at a crossroads, on a cold winter's evening, and we spoke together there with much longing and sorrow and in endless weariness; yet we did not despair, for all of us had seen the Grail, at least once, that Pentecost at Camelot.

I called myself Ufilias then, and no one questioned me, or asked about Theodorus; and I spoke through my lowered visor, that none would see my face. I suppose the others thought I was fulfilling some sort of vow.

Therefore, when the chronicles are written and the tales told, it shall not be recorded that one of the heroes who met there was an impostor.

Possibly we were all impostors, we, who heard God's hammering.

I Told You So

"There are some things in life you must keep secret," Daddy has always said, "from most people in any case, particularly from that creep you married."

"But Daddy," I always protest, "at least Eddie is *exciting*. He doesn't sit around all day and night shut in with the shades drawn, scribbling numbers and doo-hickeys on charts of astro-astri-nauti—"

"*Astrology*, my dear. It is one of the oldest sciences known to man, if often maligned in our over-confident age."

"Whatever. Still, charts and measurements and little scribbles aren't what a girl wants out of life. At least Eddie can dance."

"I understand that he dances away from bullets very skillfully," Daddy says, giving me that look of his, which is both woebegone and smug at the same time. "Nevertheless, Eusebia, you are my only heir, and as I am getting along in years, I must continue the family tradition which has stretched back for many centuries, and present to you my greatest treasure, or, rather, the *key* to my greatest treasure."

And he hands me a little velvet box like a ring would come in, only inside is this weird coin, with the portrait of this really tough character (with a sissy hair-do, though) on one side, and on the other there's a hand with one finger pointed up, like to wag at you and say, *No, no, naughty, naughty* (and I bet the dude on the other side was very naughty when he wanted to be, and nobody ever pointed a finger at *him* without losing it) and around the rim is—I am not so ignorant that I do not realize that this is what's supposed to be important—the Zodiac, all twelve signs arranged in a circle.

So this is all very nice and worth maybe as much as the old silver dollar my boyfriend gave me once (the former boyfriend, not Eddie, but the one who had the terrible accident ten miles off Atlantic City with the bucket of cement; a fraternity gag gone wrong, Eddie told me later) . . . but I don't get it. So Daddy wants to add to my coin collection?

"This is no ordinary relic of antiquity," Daddy says, "for all it superficially resembles specimens of a series of large coins issued by the Severan dynasty of the Roman Empire in the early part of the Third Century. The portrait is indeed that of Marcus Aurelius Antoninus, better known to history as the tyrant Caracalla—"

(So I was right and he was a tough character, for all his sissy haircut, or maybe *because* of it.)

And Daddy launches into this long, long lecture about the Greeks and Romans and weird gods and occult arts and sciences, and I am looking up to watch the paint on the ceiling dry, but nobody has repainted the ceiling in years, so this is not very interesting. So I make Daddy get to the point.

"Yeah, yeah, but what *is* it and what's it good for?"

"It is the Sacred Key of Emesa, the source of power for the Syrian cult of the cosmos, which backed the Severans—"

"Well what do I *do* with it?"

"For now, my dear, just keep it safe. Only after years of study and meditation will you possess the wisdom to actually *use* it. I think that will come when you are older. For the time being, whatever else you do, keep it out of the clutches of your worthless husband."

I am about to object that Eddie is worth several millions sometimes in a good season, but Daddy talks right over my objection without my being able to get a word in edgewise.

He winks at me, like maybe he's really human after all, and says, "Besides, don't you think every wife should have a *few* secrets from her husband, just in case?"

* * *

So I am a dutiful daughter and I keep the Sacred Whatsit of Whosis in my make-up kit on the nightstand in our bedroom all these two or three years, and when Eddie comes in one evening about nine (*very* early for him when he's out on business) looking kind of rattled, and he holds up the funny coin to me and says, "Zeebie, I think we're going to cash this in," then I *know* that something has gone very wrong indeed, for him, for us, for our marriage and our immediate prospects of remaining on this Earth alive and in one piece, because maybe just now Eddie *isn't* worth several millions and several of his colleagues with names like Mongo Reimer and Luciano the Bat and Charlie Kneecaps and the Fat Man (who is thin; don't ask) perhaps desire to secure the loan or return of some of the aforesaid millions that Eddie hasn't got; and all I can say is, "What the *Hell* were you doing in my makeup kit?"

"Maybe I need a disguise."

"It must be bad." (Because I can just imagine Eddie in eye-shadow, and it makes me sick. He's not the type.)

"I'm afraid so, honey-bun."

Now he only calls me honey-bun when he wants something, but the rest of the drill involves me giving him a tearful, good-wifey hug as I try to grab the coin-thingie, which he holds out of my reach as he says, "Get your coat. We're going."

"Going where? China?"

"To see your old man."

"He doesn't like you, Eddie. I don't think he'll help."

"I don't like him either, and I think he will."

* * *

So we sneak out of Jersey City real careful-like, ducking down below the dashboard at intersections to we won't be recognized should we encounter Luciano the Bat or any of his team mates, but this does not happen and a few hours later, late at night, we are up in the Catskills driving along a winding, bumpy, vine-draped road, from which we turn off onto an even bumpier dirt path which inspires Eddie to say, "Shit, I feel like I'm in *Ramar of the Jungle.*"

But at last we come to rest at the entrance to the *very* overgrown and neglected estate containing the Ancestral Manse, which is what Daddy calls the pile of junk he inherited from his 34th co-linear line of 18th cousins of our great-great-great-great-grandmother who got burned at the stake in Salem for playing with matches.

It is, well, your garden variety haunted house, complete with an iron gate which is always kept chained shut—only now it's open.

"Must have rusted," says Eddie, as he eases down on the gas and we *crunch* along the even worse driveway which is lined with these really *hideous* statues of people and things (there is some preoccupation with seafood, as the subjects include two fishes, a crab, and a big lobster-thingie with its pointed ass in the air) and finally come to the front door where the gargoyles lean over so far you think they're going to drop on you. (And I want to say to Eddie, "Hey, didn't that one used to be *over there?*" Only it doesn't seem a good time for kidding.)

We don't have to knock. Eddie reaches for the bronze knocker (which is made to look like Mister Sun tripping on something and *so happy* . . . I think it was my late Mother's idea and Daddy left it there for sentimental reasons, as it doesn't match the decor one bit) and the door swings open all by itself with a loud *cre-ee-eak!* like in a horror movie; and I do my Scared Female bit and cling to Eddie like a vine and say, "Oh! I don't think we should be doing this!"

"He's *your* father and you're afraid?" Eddie tries to curl his lip and look tough (only he never gets it right and looks like a chimp making faces) and says, "Don't you worry your pretty little head, Sweetheart. We'll be fine as long as we've got the dingus."

He is clearly thinking of another kind of movie. Only he forgot his trench coat.

So we step inside and he fumbles around for the lights, finds a switch, flips it a few times, and nothing happens.

"The power must be out," I say.

"If there ever *was* power in this dump!"

"Oh, Eddie! Look!"

There is another creak (of a floorboard) and we both look up at the ghostly light that is coming down the front stairs, and for a second I think even Eddie is afraid, but then I see it's just Daddy carrying a multiple candlestick and looking like Boris Karloff on a bad hair day. You'd expect him to have on a wizard's robe with stars and signs all over it, but, no, he's just wearing an old bathrobe and slippers.

I do not think we just woke him. I think he was waiting for us.

"Young man," he says to Eddie, "you know that you are not welcome in my house."

So Eddie pulls out a pistol and points it right under Daddy's nose and says, "That's too bad, but due to circumstances beyond my control I must forgo the usual pleasantries, and here I am, and I need your help."

"Oh Eddie! Don't hurt him!"

"If he does what he's told, nobody gets hurt," Eddie says, and I am calmed down a little, because I know that for all he's tough and exciting, Eddie is a man of his word. Some of the time. Particularly when I'm around.

Daddy is unimpressed as if Eddie were a little kid and had pointed a toy gun at him and Daddy didn't have time to play.

"Put that away. If you kill me, I won't be able to help you, will I?"

Faced with such unassailable logic, Eddie puts the gun away. I've always said that Eddie isn't such a bad sort, considering what he does for a living, because if he were really bad he would have pointed the gun at *my* head and threatened to blow out *my* brains unless Daddy did what he was told. In his own way, I guess, Eddie really loves me.

"Besides," says Eddie, "I've got this." And he shows the coin-thingie.

Now Daddy *is* upset, and he looks at me and says, "Daughter, you have betrayed my trust."

"No, Daddy! Honest! I kept it hidden like you told me, only Eddie found it anyway!"

Eddie shoots me an angry glance which means we will settle this later, but for now he pokes the coin under Daddy's nose, then snatches it away before Daddy can grab it, and says, "That's right. I found it anyway."

And I am left thinking that maybe he should have used my eye-shadow and hidden out in Greenwich Village.

"I see," Daddy says with a sense of resignation. Now Eddie is riding very high, like two inches off the floor, because he has outsmarted everybody, even my father, who is rich and a Master of Occult Arts and Sciences, so that makes Eddie a very smart guy indeed.

"I need money," Eddie says. "A lot of it, and quick. And I think I need . . . something more, which I think you can provide." He takes on that real crafty expression he sometimes has when he's getting smarter than smart, like the time he talked Mongo and Luciano the Bat and the rest into floating a life-sized, Styrofoam Statue of Liberty out into New York Harbor so they could switch it for the real one; not because he actually thought this could be done, but because he'd acquired several truckloads of Styrofoam mix in a hijacking and had to do *something* with them.

"Yes," Daddy says, implying I am not sure what, "I command more than mere material wealth. You are quite correct in that regard."

"You will let me have what you got," says Eddie. It is not a question.

"Come upstairs, then."

Eddie turns to me. "Zeebie, you stay *right here* and keep a lookout, while your father and I have our little business meeting, and if I come down and find you're gone, by God I'll bust ya—"

"There is no need for threats, Edward," Daddy puts in. "We are quite far from the nearest road, and farther still from the nearest town. Where would Eusebia go? But in any case, I insist that she accompany us. It will be most educational for her to witness what transpires."

"Yeah," Eddie laughs. "Maybe she *does* need to learn something yet about how things operate."

"Exactly."

So the three of us go upstairs, slowly following Daddy, who lights our way with his candle. There's one landing, then another, then another, and somehow the hallways twist around like in a funhouse, and we pass a lot of doors that are locked or even barred, and a few that are open (but the rooms are dark inside, and only once do I think I hear something moving in there). All this while I am very confused, because Eddie loves me in his own way, but he's just threatened to blow my father's head off and to knock me around a bit too; but I know he only behaves this way because things must be very bad with Mongo and

Luciano and the Fat Man; like maybe they actually went through with the Statue of Liberty scheme and found the old girl just too well known to fence.

So I am not entirely sure whose side I should be on, but I decide that as long as he doesn't hurt Daddy, I'll stick with Eddie.

My father touches his candles to a couple more set in the walls (Did they *ever* put electricity into this place?) and I can see two wide, wooden doors all covered with Zodiac carvings, like the ones on the coin. He swings the doors wide and we go into a big, low-ceilinged room with a thick rug on the floor. I can't take it all in at once. There's shelves of books, maybe something that's a stuffed crocodile over the door (or maybe it isn't), and a skeleton sitting in a chair, holding an hourglass in one hand and a smoldering cigar in the other (and I don't think it was lit recently) and wearing a top hat and sitting with its legs crossed in a position I can only describe as *jaunty*. (So maybe my father has a sense of humor after all, or is completely around the bend.) There's laboratory equipment and stuff, but nothing with crackling electricity like a mad scientist would have (or if there is, it doesn't work because the power's out).

"Now the *pièce de resistance,*" says Daddy, pulling away the rug.

"The piece of *what?*" inquires Eddie.

Daddy pulls away the rug completely and I can see there's something set in the floor. Only after he lights several more candles and places them in a circle around the rim am I able to see it's a tile mosaic which was clearly cut into the wooden floor much later than the house was built, because you can still see the scratches in the varnish. The style is very odd, like what you'd expect to see in a museum where there's mummies in the next case. The pictures are the signs of the Zodiac, just like on the coin.

"What the—?" says Eddie, for once at a loss for words.

"You were expecting a pentagram, perhaps? No, young man. For all you may never be able to comprehend the true significance of what you see before you, I must attempt to explain somewhat. I am, as you probably know, the world's leading esoteric astrologer. I have *no*, I repeat, *no* rivals in my field. Kings and presidents consult with me regularly, if discreetly, because of *this.*"

"Well that's a very impressive floor tile you got there," says Eddie, and I am sure it would look even better in the bathroom, but what do you *do* with it? Look at it when you write your newspaper column? *Virgo:* Tie your shoes today. *Leo:* A good day to clean out the garage. *Pisces:* You will make a million bucks. I am more interested in the million bucks."

I have never seen such barely-controlled rage on Daddy's face as he's got just then. I think he would break Eddie's neck with his bare hands if he could, but he can't, so he huffs a little bit and goes into a lecture of *great* length and complexity (I look up to watch some paint drying, but it is too dark) all about the Sigil of Emesa and how all these ancient guys were in touch with Cosmic

Infinity, and how the Zodiac wasn't just symbols but was actually *forces*—and all this while I am looking for some interesting paint, so I don't follow this very closely—which were harnessed by the Severans by means of this tile-thingie which has been painstakingly smuggled in bit by bit from the ancient Middle East.

Now I want to stop him right there and ask if this means he's got a time machine, because otherwise wouldn't it be smuggled in from the contemporary Middle East? Besides I looked up the Severans in the encyclopedia and didn't most of them come to nasty ends, like the one who got the sword up the butt . . .?

But this is no time for such fascinating historical explorations, let alone revisionism, because Daddy is blathering on about Madame Blavatsky and Cagliosomebody and Eddie can't find any paint to watch drying either; so he whips out the gun again and shoves the barrel under Daddy's chin and says, "Show me what it does. Now."

Eddie's voice is low and tense and scary and even Daddy knows he means business, so Daddy says, "Very well. Place the talisman—the coin—on one of the sections of the mosaic and step back."

Eddie does this and we're all gawking as one of the pie-slice sections of the circle lights up and smoke starts rising, and then there are these two weird characters floating above the floor, dressed like ancient Greek statues, which means they're not wearing very much, and they're both guys and kinda sexy, like you see in *Cosmo*, and I just hope they're not gay, but before I can have any more such thoughts Daddy speaks up.

"Yes. Gemini. The twins. You have summoned the spiritual essence of Castor and Pollux, who were worshiped as gods in the ancient world."

"Oh."

"You will perhaps feel a certain sense of harmony, of being part of a larger whole."

But Eddie just pokes the gun under Daddy's chin in a way I don't like and says, "I don't feel very harmonious. That's a nice hologram you got there, but it's not good enough, and unless I get what I need somebody *might* start getting hurt pretty soon—"

"Eddie, don't—"

Daddy nods to me. I put the coin on another part of the Zodiac and it starts glowing too, and out of the smoke steps a lady wrapped in a bed sheet, holding a balance scale like Justice, only she isn't blind. She looks right through me and I'm scared, I'll admit.

"I *didn't* say I wanted more of the same!" says Eddie, poking with the gun for emphasis like he's going to drive the muzzle right up into Daddy's brain. "I want a million bucks, now!"

"You stupid fool," Daddy whispers between clenched teeth (because who can talk with a gun pushing your chin up halfway into orbit?), "don't you realize that if you can assemble and control these forces, mere *money* will seem as nothing? When you can command the actual *destiny* of mankind—"

"Look," says Eddie, "I got more immediate problems and no time for anybody's destiny—"

And as if to make the point real clear, Eddie's problems become much more immediate when the front door of the house slams open and we see flashlights waving up through the windows like we've been surprised by a whole army, and then there's footsteps on the stairs and somebody's banging in the hall and a voice calls out, "YO EDDIE! WHERE YOU HIDING?"

Then several disreputable types burst into the room, but they just stand in the doorway, gawking, while Eddie whirls Daddy around to face them, as if they should care whether he blows the old man's head off or not; and among these disreputable types is a guy who keeps testing a baseball bat in his gloved hand with a swat-swat-swat sound. I know this is Luciano the Bat, my husband's business partner in the Statue of Liberty venture, and that relations between the two of them are just now a bit strained.

"It *blew over*," says Luciano, hefting his bat. His assorted gorillas raise their Uzis and point in our general direction, marksmanship not being their strong point.

"Uh, what blew over?" says Eddie.

Luciano walks toward him, his bat held steady. He looks at the ghosts or whatever they are floating in the air, but he doesn't blink; maybe he thinks they're holograms too; and he walks a wide curve around the Zodiac circle in the floor and keeps on coming.

"Now Eddie, you didn't think you could just run out on your old friends, did you? That's why we put the homing beacon in your car trunk, because we didn't quite trust you not to fink on us if something went a little wrong . . . like the Styrofoam Statue of Liberty was too light and too top-heavy and it blew over in the goddamn breeze and filled up with water and didn't even sink . . . I had to leave Mongo there to explain it all to the Coast Guard."

"But Mongo's an idiot. It'll take years."

"That's right, Eddie, more than enough time for me to get away and follow you and settle a few scores."

Eddie still backs away, holding Daddy between himself and Luciano, who looks at him as if he were dancing with a paper doll, for all the good it was going to do him.

"Eusebia," Daddy gasps over the top of the gun barrel. "The coin. Put it in the middle!"

For a moment I don't understand and want to say, "In the middle of what?" but I am a smart girl in a tight spot, and nobody is paying much attention to me;

and I know perfectly well that when the bat starts batting and the bullets starts flying, I'm not going to get out of this room alive any better than Eddie or my father will.

It doesn't do you much good to have mastered the forces of cosmic destiny if your face has been turned into spaghetti sauce by eight hundred bullets fired at point-blank range in a fraction of a second.

So my thinking capacity goes into high gear and I have no more questions about whose side I am on, and I make out that where all the pie-wedges come together in the middle of the circle there's *another* circle, just the same size as the coin or sigil or whatever it is.

So I put it there.

That's when the bullets start flying, but most of the targets just keep on coming.

Maybe there's an explosion because light bursts up out of the floor and everything seems just suspended, like there's not time and it's all slow-motion; the noise is so loud I can't hear it, just feel it, and the smoke and light coming out of the floor is like somebody's opened a furnace door, and I can't see a thing; but somehow Daddy's dragged me down onto the floor, into that light and none of the bullets can touch us.

For a while we're just floating in the air, it seems, and everything else is like a dream and kind of vague, as Luciano's bat gets snatched out of his hand by a giant claw and his goons empty their Uzis into various people and things that just won't die and there's this gaggle of shapes and people screaming and I can't make any sense out of it at all.

Then the room is dark again, and there's just the outlines of the Zodiac figures in the floor, glowing like the coils on an electric oven (only not hot, because we're lying on them), and then they go out one by one, as if someone is flicking switches, as the primal forces return to their rest, and up overhead, no doubt, the stars continue in the courses of destiny and the natural world is once again in harmony with the cosmos.

Well, Daddy would explain it that way, but all I can say when I sit up and light a few candles again is, "God! What a mess!"

And it occurs to me that if were in the city we'd have a pretty time explaining to the cops how Luciano got his head snipped off by a giant crab or my Eddie got a arrow right through the heart and hoof marks all up his front, and one guy just bubbled up and *popped* from all the scorpion venom he's taken in . . . just a real, real *mess.*

But Daddy reassures me that there are deep wells and swamps behind the house, and nobody has to know.

I look down on what's left of Eddie and cling to Daddy and sob, "But I loved him—"

"He was no good for you, Eusebia. He may have seemed exciting, but he just wasn't right for you. I knew this was going to happen."

"You *knew?* All of it?"

"Yes. I did."

"But you could have been killed! You were so brave!"

"I wasn't afraid at all, dear, because the stars foretold everything. My destiny is assured. I know when I shall die, and where, and it is not here. When you arrived, I had just finished casting *your* horoscope—"

And this is much more exciting than anything Eddie ever did and I see now that Daddy is *so* much smarter than Eddie and maybe I can be that smart too one day if I work real hard at it. I burst into tears, but they are almost tears of joy, and I try to say all sorts of things all at once, and I manage, "Oh, Daddy! I can't go back! I'll stay with you and study and carry on the family tradition! Oh, Daddy, if you know everything, tell me, what do the stars have in store for me?"

"For the time being, a comfortable widowhood."

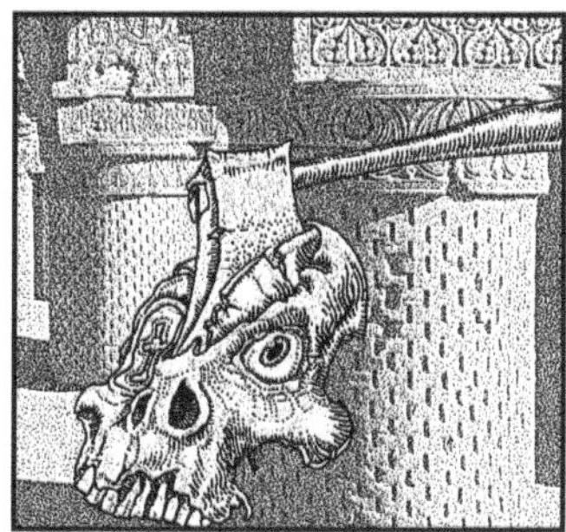

The Murder of Etelven Thios

Out of the darkness of the night, out of the distance of the desert, Etelven Thios came to the house of Oinath the rug merchant. It happened in the early spring, when Oinath had gone north with a caravan and his wife Themara remained home alone, that a magewind rose out of the wastes and dust filled the sky, and the faint flapping of leathern wings was heard. There was a knocking at the door.

Themara answered it.

And Etelven Thios, who moves unseen by the stars, was there.

She knew he was Etelven Thios by his left eye, which had a vertical slit like the pupil of a cat. Huge and green, it glared at her.

By his red sorcerer's garb she knew him also, and by his reputation. Often it had been said that Etelven Thios used his magics for evil only, bringing suffering to men. Was this not why he had been cast out of the College of Wizards, many years ago?

"Woman, bring me food and drink and whatever else I might desire."

Thus he commanded her, and she scarcely dared answer.

"Alas, sir, we are very poor, and have nothing, and my desire is for my husband," she said in a tiny voice.

"I saw a cow behind the house."

And after she had slaughtered the precious cow he had eaten of it, he said, "Woman, prepare me a bed."

She led him to her own bed, the only one in the house. When he was under the covers he spoke again.

"Woman, come join me. Keep me warm this night."

"No ! Ask anything else of me!"

"Get in !"

He defiled her that night, and on the morrow when she awoke she found herself covered with slashes and bruises, as if she had lain with a tiger. She knew that ever after her womb would be barren.

And when Oinath learned these things, he sought the house of Etelven Thios.

He sought it in the first days of summer, when his caravan was newly returned. He went first to a geographer, whose house was filled with maps and charts, and he said, "Show me, sir, where stands the home of Etelven Thios."

But the geographer only wailed and made signs to ward off curses and cried, "No! Seek not Etelven Thios!" And he would say no more.

So Oinath went to a prophet and said, "Tell me, Seer, where hides Etelven Thios."

And the prophet answered, "Between his two daughters," and went away.

Oinath wept in despair, complaining aloud, "By such riddles I shall never find Etelven Thios." But as he spoke a madman chanced by and overheard what had been uttered, and he explained to Oinath that in the eighty-seventh century of his youth Etelven Thios, who is both male and female, gave birth to two daughters named Absithnel and Rotwondel, both of whom were very beautiful. As a woman Etelven Thios envied them, and as a man he lusted after them; but when they spurned him, he enchanted them in a fit of wrath, turning them into mountains, and the mountains stand as yet to the farthest south and are called either the Dark Sisters or the Weeping Hills. Between them lies the Valley of Shadow where the wizard dwelt ever after in an onyx castle.

When this was told Oinath asked his informant how he knew all these things, and the other answered, "I was there."

So the rug merchant rode south to the mountains of Dzim, where he traded his horse for a camel and continued on, across the seven wastes that lie beyond Dzim.

He came to a place where the desert was blasted red by the sun, another where it was scorched orange, and another where it was blue, and another green. And many folk were wandering there, gathering samples of the sands to be used for magical purposes or exported as novelties.

Oinath tarried not.

To his left in the distance rose the holy mountain Cloudcap, where the gods gave the scroll to Obbok long before, but there were no gods there as Oinath passed. And when the mountain was gone behind him, and he could no longer see the slopes where the gods once danced, a great marvel was upon him. In the midst of the desert, where no rain fell and no river ran, there stood a forest, and the trees of the forest had no leaves, and their branches swayed when there was no wind, whispering "Death, death, death." And the moon shone bright in the empty sky, but there was no light in the forest, and Oinath could not see the stars overhead. In great fear and trepidation he rode through that wood, never pausing to look over his shoulder.

On the other side there was desert again, and in this desert, riding atop a great wavelike dune, was a ship without sails. Yet sailors scurried up and down the rigging and stood watch in the masts. So curious a thing was this that Oinath stopped and called aloud, "What is the meaning of this?"

The captain of the ship came to the railing, a thin, ragged man with wild hair, clearly mad.

"We are fleeing Etelven Thios," he said.

"Only in such a vessel can one escape him."

Oinath rode on, knowing his destination to be near, and as he left, he heard the captain behind him turn and shout to his crew, "Yo! Tiller to starboard! Sweat for your souls! Away! Away!"

When he saw two. mountains before him and the constellation of the Toad peering between them, Oinath found what he had sought. He approached the towering black gate of the wizard's outer wall and shouted the words he had rehearsed so many times.

"Sorcerer come forth!"

Etelven Thios appeared on the battlements.

"Go away, little man, before you cease to amuse me."

"O great one, I have found a splendid thing in the desert."

"What sort of thing?"

"A fountain, from which flows all riches. For a price I shall lead you to it."

"You shall have my favor."

"Agreed."

"I will come."

The vast gate of the fortress opened and a tomb-cold breeze blew out into the desert darkness.

Etelven Thios rode a hairless black thing, half like a horse, half like a camel, half again like neither. It had no eyes or ears or tail. It made no sound as it moved.

Together the rug merchant and the sorcerer journeyed all the night across the sands. Many times Etelven Thios grew impatient and said, "How much further is it?" And each time Oinath would reply, "Only a little further." And the wizard would add, "I have no patience with tricks." To which Oinath would say, "Lord, I fear you too much for that."

When dawn was beginning to glow on the horizon, they came to a place in the middle of the desert, featureless except for the dunes that rolled uniformly in all directions.

Oinath caused his camel to sit.

"This is the spot."

"I don't see any fountain," said the wizard.

"It is buried in the sand. You must help me dig it out."

The legs of the black thing telescoped, and Etelven Thios dismounted. He didn't leave any footprints as he walked.

"Where is your fountain hidden?"

"At your feet. Look closely, Lord."

Etelven Thios crouched down, and, as soon as his eyes were turned from Oinath for an instant, the vengeful rug merchant drew from the folds of his cloak a small hatchet, which he had carried hidden all along. He struck one blow, and the blade crashed down through the wizard's skull almost to the jawbone; struck another and the face was ruined; and another and the head fell from the shoulders. The green eye bulged and glazed over.

"Behold," said Oinath, "a fountain of limitless riches. Your blood I have desired above all things."

He buried the corpse where it had fallen, climbed atop his mount, and rode off. The black steed stared blindly after him.

The day was dawning fast but—curse his luck—a sand storm rose almost at once. Oinath pressed on, and the winds howled, and the dust stung his eyes. He sought to put as much distance between himself and that accursed spot as he could, but he knew not how far or in what direction he went.

At last he saw a dim shape ahead.

"Hail friend!"

There was no answer. He perceived what looked like a horse, unmounted.

Some traveler has met distress, thought Oinath. He drew nearer, only to confront the black beast of Etelven Thios. Perhaps it had followed him. Perhaps it had never moved. Waves of sand swept over the ground.

Recoiling in disgust and horror, he turned his mount at once and faced the wind. The wind seemed to come directly at him no matter which way he turned, blowing from all directions. The storm grew even worse and the sky was as black as midnight. Oinath drew his hood forward over his face, but it did no good. Still sand caked over his eyes and poured into his clothing. He couldn't see the nose of his camel. He had to stop.

Again he caused the creature to kneel, then got off and crouched down beside it. On either side there seemed to be no relief from the wind. The storm increased in fury, if such a thing were still possible. After a time Oinath shifted his position a little, and felt something beneath him in the sand.

It was a human hand. The arm wore a sleeve of scarlet.

Above him stood the unseeing thing.

With a scream of surprise and terror, all but certain that sorcery was upon him, Oinath scrambled atop his camel. Had the storm beguiled him, or was it something worse? He knew not; he cared not; he rode.

Yet again he saw something before him in the sand, and it was Etelven

Thios. His camel tripped over something and it was Etelven Thios. The wind uncovered something, the green eye glared hideously up at him, and it was Etelven Thios. Finally, when it had happened an uncounted number of times, and the green eye blinked, Oinath cried out in rage and despair.

"By the gods! There is a whole army of them!"

"Only one," said Etelven Thios.

* * *

Again on a dark night there was a knock on the door and Themara answered it. The one who entered wore a cloak she recognized.

"Welcome husband."

The other did not answer.

"Why do you not speak?"

Silence.

"Husband, why do you hide your face in your hood?"

The hood fell back.

And Themara screamed.

The face revealed was slashed to the jawbone, a mass of pulp and blood. Only the green eye remained whole.

Themara screamed and screamed, tore her hair and screamed more, ran mindlessly about the room like a headless chicken.

And screamed.

"Verily," said Etelven Thios, "the man has led me well. This is indeed a fountain of riches, for above all things I prize the terror of others."

The sorcerer's corpse collapsed to the floor. The head departed from the shoulders, rolled a short way and stopped, its one eye left staring at the ceiling.

Some time later the neighbors burst in, and they found Themara alone with the remains of Etelven Thios, and by the way she screamed and the blankness of her face and the whiteness of her hair, they knew she was mad.

Oinath they never found.

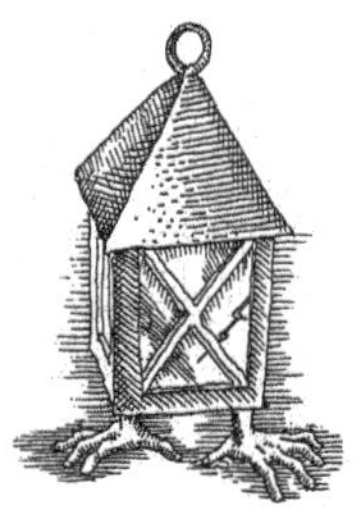

The Other Murder of Etelven Thios

The evil mage Etelven Thios had been murdered by Oinath the rug merchant, as was already well known in the lands surrounding Dzim. Minstrels were beginning to sing of the deed, telling how the vengeful husband, whose wife had been foully molested by Etelven Thios, had lured the wizard out of his castle on a pretense, into the desert, and there slain him with a hatchet, only to meet a frightful and doubtless magical doom shortly thereafter. The details of his fate were not known, and since by and large people prefer to hear pleasant songs, no one cared to expound upon them. But the rest of the story rapidly grew in complexity and detail, and, resplendent with bold struggles, midnight terrors, and implacable courage, it began to drift, slowly, like a poorly moored ship dragging its anchor, into the realm of myth.

Meanwhile, in the city of Garnathrion by the inland rivers, on the outskirts of which stood the cottage of the late Oinath, there was a matter of more immediate concern. The beheaded corpse of Etelven Thios had been found within, and beside it the shrieking wife, Themara, driven completely mad by what she had seen. The city fathers took her gently to their temple, where along with other lunatic persons she was worshiped as one touched by the gods—for such was the custom of their country—and the body and ruined head of the sorcerer, with its still malevolent green, cat-like left eye, they buried in hallowed ground, amongst their most revered ancestors, while chanting petitions to patron divinities, in hopes that all this accumulated goodness would make the grave lie quiet.

Alas, they did these things in vain. On a night when rain drizzled silently out of a gray sky, while fog filled with ghosts drifted over the land, every single mound in the cemetery began to stir, and all the dead arose, from the oldest and most brittle skeletons to the beloved Urga, mother of the town's mayor, whose funeral robes had yet to gather mold. An unliving army walked or limped or crawled to the place where Etelven Thios lay, and removed the signs the priests had placed over him—the sign of the earth and stars, inverted with the stars on the bottom; the sign of the thunderbolt transfixing the asp; the sign of the dry fountain—and they drew out the long silver sword which had been driven deep into the ground, piercing the wizard's heart. Then they began to dig with their ruined hands, their broken limbs, and their teeth, even stillborn babies clawing at the earth, until the coffin of Etelven Thios was completely uncovered.

The next morning there were discovered a pit, a heap of shattered planks, and a trail of corpses leading out of the city, across the plains, and even to where the desert began. No one cared to find the end of it.

A council of prominent citizens and the ruling elders was held. Said one: "Lords, soon Etelven Thios will plague us with renewed fury, unless we swiftly dispatch him once and for all." Said another: "One must not impugn the courage of Oinath the rug merchant, or his righteous quest for vengeance, but it must be admitted that he had no prior experience in wizard-killing. He was hardly qualified to deal with the likes of Etelven Thios. In short, he was an amateur."

So it was decided. This time they would send for a professional.

There was a man called Eom of the Shadows, for all his deeds were done after nightfall and out of the gaze of the bright moon, who dwelt across the sea in the city of Kosh-Ni-Hye, about which much is written elsewhere. There he kept a shop, above the door of which swung a hand-painted sign showing a man with a sword killing a nine-headed sea monster. This was all that was needed to advise passersby of his trade, but if they cared to hear more, he often was to be found seated beneath that sign, telling of his exploits to any who would listen. This was good for business, he said. It spread his name about, till eventually it fell upon the right ears.

"My father was a maker of jugs," he told his audience once. "When I was a boy he had me sit by his side all my waking hours, spinning the wet clay on the potter's wheel or painting designs on the finished products. You can scarcely imagine how tedious my life was. I began to dream, first of running through the streets and playing with the other boys, caught up in frivolous games, and then, when I was a little older, of far lands and the heroes whose images I painted on the baked clay. I wanted to be as brave and as famous as Ganhuil, who wrestled with the Bull of Fire on a cliff by the edge of the world, finally casting the beast into the abyss. You can still see it flaming there, in the sunset, an everlasting memorial to Ganhuil. Definitely I wanted something more exciting out of life than jug-working, and when my father died, dishonorable to his memory as it may have been, I sold the shop and assumed my present occupation, about which you already know much."

One day as he was speaking thus, Kamdok his apprentice came to him, saying, "Master, we are wanted," and he excused himself and went inside the shop, into a room which was always kept locked. There he searched among his collection of enchanted and empowered swords until he found the one he wanted, a huge, silver broadsword forged by a godling who dwelt in the heart of a sun. It glowed in the dark and gave off slight heat. To complement this he took a shield made of arctic ice, frigid and permanent by virtue of the runes carven upon it and the magical light entrapped within its center. On his head he placed a helm of coral and the bones of dead mermen. He selected also a dwarfish dagger for Kamdok, and then, dressed in ordinary street cloaks, the two of them went to the docks, bought passage on a ship, and sailed over the Middle Sea to the other end of the world, coming at last to Ptnarnir, then passing overland to Garnathrion, where the city fathers welcomed them with smiles, open arms, and promises of much gold.

They followed the route Oinath had taken, as well as they could reconstruct it from the accounts of eyewitnesses who preferred to say nothing. On camelback they crossed the desert beyond Dzim, past the place of colored sands, past the mountain Cloudcap where the gods no longer danced, and into that dreadful forest of leafless trees where branches swayed without any wind and had whispered "Death, death, death," to the terrified Oinath. This time, since there were two intruders beneath its boughs, the wood was distinctly heard to say "Death-death, death-death, death-death." Kamdok was uneasy, but whenever he looked into the calmly determined face of his master, his fears were still a while.

Emerging into the desert once more, they came upon a ruined ship, half buried in the sand and tilted to one side, so that the yardarms of the leaning masts nearly touched the ground. This too Oinath had seen, and he had conversed with the captain of the madmen who sailed it, never moving from that spot, convinced that only by such a paradox could they escape Etelven Thios. Now the rigging dangled loosely. Silence lay upon the decks like a sated beast, and all over there were deep gashes cut into the wood, as if from nibbling.

At last, in the middle of the night, they spied the two mountains called the Dark Sisters and the constellation of the Toad peering between them, and knew they had found the lair of Etelven Thios.

Eom and Kamdok stood before the massive ebony gates of the sorcerer's castle, wondering how to get in.

"Could you not take your sword and cut away the gate in great ringing slices?" asked the apprentice. "I could," said the man of Shadows. "There is precedent for such a thing, set of old by the hero Leothric, but I think this particular instance calls more for stealth and finesse than the magic of a blade and the sheer strength of the wielder's arm. Behold."

And the boy beheld as his master walked into the darkness before the gate, and straining his eyes to the utmost, he perceived Eom stooping to whisper something to a seated figure. Cautiously Kamdok came closer, and saw that there were two persons sitting in the sand, both mummies of a very ancient sort, which had remained unmoving for so long that the desert caressed their laps as the sea does rocks at high tide. Between them was a chessboard on a stand. They had been playing for aeons, each unable to defeat the other, by the design of Etelven Thios.

When Eom spoke into the ear of one of the mummies, the creature rose. Sand fell from bandaged legs, and joints creaked like dry wood. Unsteadily it walked to where the two gates joined, and made before them a sign. There was a deep rumbling, and lo! the gates spread apart, leaving a space wide enough for a man to slip through sideways if he were not too fat.

Then, returning to the game, the mummy moved a single piece, checkmated its opponent, and crumbled into dust, having been bribed with the promise of victory and won the privilege of oblivion. The other sat forlornly in the sand, regarding eternity.

Inside was a courtyard filled with sand, out of which grew metal flowers. The master bade the boy not touch them, for he saw how their petals glinted like razors in the starlight. The two of them came to a black ivory door, through which evil dreams pass into the world from the imagination of Etelven Thios. This hung open, as it always did at night. Beyond it was a vast room, floored in shining black stone, held up with pillared arches. Above them in the darkness, the ceiling invisible, lay a nesting place for vampires; around them in darkness, yellow eyes drifted like sparks from a campfire. Somewhere unearthly voices tittered. In front of the intruders, leading upward, was a stairway of what looked like glowing red marble. Eom and Kamdok examined this more closely, and saw that it was in fact a clear substance containing a bubbling red fluid.

The Shadow Man put a foot on the first step, and a little scream rose up, fluttering like a moth until lost in the distance above. He mounted the second, and another scream ascended. Kamdok was quivering, nearly ill from fright, when the master finally understood. Each of these steps was a prison, holding some wretched soul bound there by Etelven Thios.

And taking his sun-forged sword, he thrust the point deep into the first step, at the same time whispering, "Peace, friend, your deliverance has come."

The step died in silence, blood spurting onto the floor. The second one did likewise, and by saying to each as he slew it, "Peace, friend," Eom was able to climb the flight of stairs without any further alarms. Kamdok followed closely behind, knees shaking and eyes wide. When they were at the top, the stairway behind them was a pale, delicate thing, like a row of shattered glass coffins. All the gore had drained out, forming a pool on the floor below, to which hunched shapes from the gloomy corners of the room came to drink.

The stairs had brought them to a room filled with the Essence of Night, a blackness so unfathomable that no earthly light could penetrate it, and against which the star-sword was reduced to the barest hint of a glow.

Carefully, guiding his apprentice with one hand, Eom made his way through this room. The Night seemed to welcome him. He was in his own element. He groped for the metal knob of another door, opened it, and emerged into light (which somehow did not pass beyond him to illuminate the previous room), and found himself in the lair of a dragon, without which no evil wizard's castle would be respectable in story or in song.

Before he even saw the beast, he knew the nature of his foe, for the room was not well or often cleaned; the rushes were stale, the air thick with the odor of the dragon droppings, which seemed to be everywhere. Then the monster unwound itself from the top of a pillar and came slithering down. It was a magnificent specimen, a hundred feet long and more, lined all along the top of its body with barbed spikes, and with a two-edged plate like an executioner's axe on the end of its tail. Its mouth was too dreadful to contemplate for long; out of that cavern lashed a tongue like a leather whip, and-the teeth lining it were like an armory of swords set aside for an especially strenuous war. From within came the drum-like throbbing of the dragon's heart, and occasionally a low moan from some poor soul swallowed perhaps ten years before and digested slowly. When it moved, the creature made sounds like huge trees being felled with each step, and like laborers dragging those trees, bound in chains, across the smooth floor.

With his first blow Eom struck off the end of the tongue which sought to ensnare him. The dragon let out a bellow of rage and pain, and twin clouds of burning vapor burst from its nostrils. With another blow he chipped one of the teeth; with yet another he parried the awesome tail. But he knew he could not slay his enemy, for all the scales of the upper body were of polished steel, stronger than his sword, magical as it was. Only the tender belly, protected by nought but thin bronze, was vulnerable. He had to get the dragon onto its back, a seemingly hopeless task, since dragons only roll over when sleeping, and only then when having discontented dreams. (So Keothak the Traveler says in his Bestiary. I take his word for it.) There was only one thing to do. He retreated back into the room filled with Night, with Kamdok scurrying before him. He stood to one side of the door, and when the dragon had gone within, he closed it behind him.

Now the only light was that of the sword, and the occasional glowing snorts of the beast. Eom hid the blade under his cloak, and he and Kamdok stood flat and absolutely still against the wall, on either side of the door. Utter darkness. The dragon wandered about, dragging its tail noisily, but was unable to locate the two humans.

At last, tiring, it lay down and slept. Because of its failure to catch Eom and

Kamdok, it went to sleep hungry, and its dreams were discontented indeed. After a short while it rolled over, its armor against the floor making a noise like rocks being ground in a quarry. When it was still again Eom inched in the direction of the sound, then, when he was sure he stood almost near enough to reach out and touch the bronze scales, he uncovered the sword. By the light of it he saw he was correct, and swiftly, before the dim glow could make the shiny eyelids flutter, he drove the blade with all his might into the gigantic mass before him, reaching deep, until the tip pricked the dragon's heart. All its life blood spouted from the wound, and the body seemed to deflate like a punctured water bag until it lay in flaccid ruin on the floor. Again the two left a lake of gore in their wake, and things came to sip from it.

"Someday you'll be doing that by yourself, my boy," said Eom.

"Y-yes, master. Maybe I should have been a pot maker."

Eom of the Shadows only laughed, and led Kamdok through the befouled lair of the dragon, down a corridor decorated with murals celebrating the wickedness of mankind, and into the roof garden of Etelven Thios.

Moonlight shone through a crystal skylight on many marvelous plants and the gleaming stones of the pathways that ran between them. There was a thing as tall as a sunflower which whispered something distressingly like, "Food," over and over, and lashed out with leafy mandibles as the two passed. There was a toadstool the size of a fat woman's rump, on which sat a twisted thing vaguely suggesting a toad. Even as they watched this thing quivered, made a feeble attempt to hop, and exploded into a cloud of spores. As Eom and Kamdok watched, miniature versions of the first, complete with tiny toads, began to grow out of the soil, the pavement, and their clothing. They hurried on, then stopped to scrape the things off with their knives, gagging at the putrid odor they gave off when pierced. As soon as the blades touched each one, it wiggled, fell to the stones, and died. Next the two of them came upon plants which bore a strange, heavy fruit on the ground, hidden among shadows and twists of vine: vegetable women, which were becoming more human, more beautiful, and less attached to the parent stalks even as the intruders watched. One plant, which seemed to be diseased from the way its foliage drooped, bore a shriveled hag.

There were lovely plants, too, among the horrors. One spread golden petals three yards across, and sang when moonbeams touched it. Another shone of lace and silver, like the aftermath of an ice storm in winter.

Eom and his apprentice suddenly found themselves in a square, where all the paths converged, with Etelven Thios. The wizard did not look well. He moved stiffly, as if just barely able to control his limbs. His frame seemed shrunken and bent beneath his red cloak. And they were not exactly face to face with him, because he had no face. His head was missing.

A voice thundered from somewhere.

"Ah, botanists, I presume, here to admire my humble garden."

"Yes," said the master, stalling for time until he could spot the inevitable traps. "How did you know?"

Laughter echoed through the garden. Eom still couldn't tell where it was coming from. Kamdok looked six weeks dead.

"You have many . . . unusual specimens here," Eom continued.

"Yes," said Etelven Thios. "Here is an especially remarkable one."

He led them a short distance, to the edge of the square. Half buried in the loam, just beyond the end of the pavement, was a man, or what had been a man. The naked, pale gray skin showed here and there above soil and leaves. One arm stood crookedly upward, the wrist limp, the hand twisted, and young vines growing in place of the fingers. The chest was exposed, and the upper legs, but from the knees downward they were either missing, or covered. Eom couldn't tell, and Kamdok was in no condition to try. Etelven Thios wasn't telling.

There was part of a face. The head was bent far back, chin up. The eyes and forehead were buried, but the rest was clear. Out of the mouth grew a perfect red rose.

And Etelven Thios, taking a pair of scissors from his pocket, cut that rose. At once blood spewed out of the mouth. In a spasm the body nearly sat up, dirt smeared eyes rolled in mindless terror, while a scream in the throat died in a gurgle. Then the thing lay still, and out of the bloody mouth another rose grew.

And Etelven Thios held the first one up above the stump of his neck, as if invisible nostrils were sniffing it. The blossom wilted.

"You are right, sir," said Eom of the Shadows. "I have never seen a plant like that before."

"It bears an uncanny resemblance to a certain purveyor of cheap carpets." The voice seemed distracted, and Eom had a hint of where it was coming from. But he didn't wait to find out. As the wizard stood there, momentarily off guard, he slipped a hand under his cloak and drew forth Rumor, a dagger famed for being swifter than its namesake, and with a single, silken motion slid it between the ribs of Etelven Thios, deep into his ancient and thoroughly black heart.

The result was instantaneous. There was an explosion of wind blowing in all directions from the body, sending Eom and Kamdok sprawling in opposite directions, to either end of the square. Then a wall of flame rose from the stones, encircling the corpse but not touching it—a wall of protection.

Phalanxes of flaming soldiers, with long red-hot spears lowered, appeared in the pathways converging on the would-be assassins. The plants around them stirred hungrily.

The hand of Etelven Thios removed the knife, and the body remained standing, even if it swayed unsteadily. The voice laughed, louder, louder—and suddenly Eom knew its source.

On the far side of the square, behind where his assistant was flow standing, in a patch of innocuous, broad-leafed shrubs, lay what looked at this distance like a melon.

A melon? How could something so tame, so mundane, be in the garden of Etelven Thios? Of course!

"Kamdok! There! Behind you! Grab it !"

The glowing spears were only a few yards away, advancing steadily.

The apprentice turned. His training overcame his fear. Without even a flash of thought he obeyed his master's voice, and snatched the thing from beneath the leaves. It wasn't a melon. It was the head of Etelven Thios, still mutilated from the blows of Oinath's hatchet, but healing. The green, cat-like eye glared balefully.

Again instinctively Kamdok moved. He drew his dagger, called Terror, the brother of Rumor, and plunged it into the green orb before it could blink, bursting the iris like a rotted grape, the tip reaching up through the skull into the brain.

At once the flames and the soldiers were gone, and the headless remains of Etelven Thios fell limply on the stones. The realization of what he had done came to the apprentice, and in dumb shock he let go of the head. It too fell and lay still. All was quiet in the garden for an instant, and then Eom of the Shadows, the master assassin, began to laugh, out of joy for his victory and the irony of how it had come about.

And like an echo came the laughter of another!

Kamdok screamed, and pointed. There, standing over what had been Etelven Thios was—Etelven Thios! He was tall and slightly stooped, as he had been in life, his face a white mask of hate, entirely unscarred, his green eye a beacon of doom.

Eom paused, startled, but then casually advanced, drew his sword, and slashed at the apparition. The blade passed through without meeting resistance, rippling it like the reflection on the surface of a pool.

"You see, my boy? It's only his ghost. A mere insubstantial wisp. It can't hurt us. Remember this adage, which has been known for countless ages: *Anything you can't cut with a sword isn't material enough to worry about.*" He laughed again. Karndok forced a smile.

And, laughing also, the spirit of Etelven Thios drifted into Eom of the Shadows, superimposing itself over him, cutting him off from air, suffocating him as smoke can.

When the master was dead, Etelven Thios turned to the boy, who cowered before him in helpless, babbling terror.

Before he did anything, he waited, giving Kamdok enough time to go mad.

The Final? Murder? of Etelven Thios?

Little is known of the early life of the student Guetheric. It is said that he was born in one of the teeming slums of some fishing and trading city along the coast of the Great or Eastern Continent, perhaps in Irtash or Clarisdruil, and that as a child he knew much of hunger, deprivation, and death. By one account he had an elder brother who was blinded for thievery at the age of fifteen, when Guetheric was twelve, and shortly thereafter his father ran off, his mother died mad, and his hapless brother was sold to a doctor of physick. In any case, there can be little doubt that his beginnings were unhappy.

Somehow Guetheric gained the rudiments of an education and the patronage of the wife of a Tarasian noble, and with such credentials sailed across the narrow sea from Irtash to the Isle of Sorcerers, enrolling in the university there.

One of his teachers, the Windmaster Aelgemark, remembers him:

"Guetheric was a frail youth. One felt he should have been stocky, but he was lean, almost skeletal. He had a gaunt, expressionless face, and deep-set eyes which struck most as mysterious . . . oh yes, that sounds strange. Mysterious. Even as a would-be sorcerer he was mysterious. Showed lots of promise, he did. I remember also he had the beginnings of a red beard, pointed, as the young men were wearing them in those days. Was he a good student? Yes, he most certainly was. The best I ever had. I never, saw anyone grasp the fundamentals of name-wrestling or summoning as quickly or as thoroughly as he did. He worked hard, but that was his downfall, I suppose. He was obsessive. Never mixed much with the other students, never gamed or went to festivals. They complained he was a miser, but he had one extravagance. Burned midnight oil like a lighthouse, up every night all night, poring over eldritch tomes. I don't know what he did for sleep. Perhaps he found a spell to suspend time in one of those things. Read even more than the Masters, he did. Brother Librarian, may Lerad gaze upon him forever, used to insist he went through every volume in the place, covering them systematically by section: first Forgotten Lore, then Forbidden, then Blasphemous, then Nameless—fiendishly hard to find anything there, because none of the books have titles—and finally Eldritch. I haven't even been through those myself. I think Guetheric was looking for something. And I'm afraid he found it. Did he have any friends? No, not really. He stayed to himself. Of course, there was Tzano, with whom he shared a room. A harmless sort of boy, possibly not very bright, and certainly not good for much. The complete opposite of Guetheric, always at the dice or drowned in his cups. On trips to the mainland, he used to conjure in the streets, just to show off. Deep learning wasn't for him, and I knew he'd never last out his first year. Of course he didn't, but it was because of the terrible tragedy. . . ."

The tragedy began on a spring evening. The week-long Festival of Light was drawing to a close, and the entire population of the university, except for Guetheric, laid aside routine cares and celebrated. Illusions were not frowned on for this night of nights. It was the time for all things unseen and never before seen. A huge crystalline bird, aflame with pale blue light, soared over the island and vanished into the sea like a second sunset, its image caught by one quick-thinking soul in a recording glass, that it might overawe succeeding generations of students.

But throughout all this, Guetheric sat alone in his dormitory tower, annoyed by the noise and the sparkling flashes beneath his window, staring at a repulsive object.

He had just taken a human head out of a leather sack, and placed it on the table at which he was seated. Perhaps it was the head of a man. It was too grotesquely mutilated for anyone to be sure. The skin had long since dried into a hard, leathery brown, its surface slightly powdery to the touch. Contracted muscles drew the remnants of the upper lip back to reveal broken, nearly black teeth. The lower jaw was gone, ragged flaps of tissue hanging where it had been. But it was the upper part which was the most severely ruined. The whole crown of the skull was shattered as if by a tremendous blow from an axe or sword, down to the top of the nose. The left eye socket, which was twice as large as the right, held traces of a rubbery green substance. In the right was an eye, probably once yellow, now shriveled and the color of an olive. The back of the head wasn't recognizable as anything.

Guetheric had paid a considerable sum for this grisly relic, and if it was what he thought it was, no price would have been too much. He had found the thing in a certain shop in an alley in a very disreputable section of a disreputable city, in a country depicted by most geographers as a blank spot on the map. The person from whom he had purchased it could no longer vouch for its authenticity, for shortly after the transaction he had been found, or more precisely *not* found, sprawled over and around his counter—much blood, a trace of brain, a few small bones, and a tooth or two, which, admittedly, could have belonged to anyone. Another person, an importer of the most unusual sorts of novelties, with whom the first sometimes did business, was similarly and untidily missing. All this bothered Guetheric only a trifle. Death, he knew, was the most common coinage in many places never mentioned in polite society.

His intent now was to discover if the charnel souvenir was in fact the head of the famed and most malignant sorcerer, Etelven Thios, whose many centuried career had come to an end about a hundred years before Guetheric was born. He knew the standard tales, how Etelven Thios so brutally abused the wife of Oinath the rug merchant, and of the horrors that followed his "death" and burial. In the Valley of Shadow, between two weeping mountains which had once been the daughters of Etelven Thios, still stood the mage's violated fortress, perhaps even yet haunted, but certainly with its major terrors long gone. About this was whispered a more secret tale, of the earth opening up to reveal wealth beyond the most fevered imaginings of mankind—the treasure of Etelven Thios.

Guetheric gazed at the head in the starlight, hoping to discern mystic patterns in the face not visible under the sun's rays, which might reveal the presence of magic, but before long Tzano came noisily up the stairs.

Hastily Guetheric put his prize back in the bag.

"Hello! It's me!"

The youth fumbled with the lock on the door. Guetheric rose and let him in, his face an expressionless mask to hide his anger. Not that it mattered anyway—the other was drunk beyond caring.

He nearly dropped the taper he was carrying.

Before he accidentally burned the whole university down, Guetheric took it from him.

"Gueth—Guetheric . . . ? Where have you been? You missed all the fun."

"I had more important things to do."

"Wha—? How can anything be more important than . . . *wine!* . . . *women!* . . . We had some girls brought over from I dunno where . . . and s—"

With that he passed out. Guetheric caught him before he hit the floor, bundled him over one shoulder and dragged him up into the sleeping loft. Soon contented snores filled the room.

Guetheric got the head out again and tried to resume his work, but couldn't concentrate. Soon the smoke from the taper made his eyelids heavy, and the regular snoring of Tzano seduced him also into sleep. Some hours later he awoke with a start.

The courtyard was below, the study totally dark. The taper had long since gone out, and not even a trace of its smoke remained. In the dim starlight from the window he could see that the head on the table before him was gone. Frantically he leapt to his feet, fumbling for a candle, but just then there came a scraping sound from above, then a surprised cry, a kind of gurgling, and one brief terrified scream. Tzano.

Something small dropped to the floor on the other side of the room, near the ladder to the loft. By this time Guetheric had found a candle and a flint and steel lighter, and he struck a light.

There revealed in the gloom before him, creeping across the floorboards, was the ruined head, perched atop a three-legged footstool. The wooden legs bent and moved as if alive. All over it, and dripping from those abominable teeth, was something which even in the dimness was clearly blood.

Quickly he grabbed the leather bag, and muttering a spell of power, seized the head from off the stool. It became a dead thing again, just a weight as he pulled the strings tight over it. He was not afraid, but joyful. He had never found Tzano more than a nuisance anyway. He was delighted because now he knew his money had been well spent. He had in his possession the genuine article, the head of Etelven Thios.

Lights were coming on throughout the tower and in surrounding buildings, but before anyone could come up to investigate, Guetheric had packed a few essentials, taken up his prize, and slipped down the back stairs. By this time there were cries of alarm. Someone had discovered what was to be discovered. With all attention attracted there, it was no problem for Guetheric to make his way undetected to the university's storehouse. There he whispered a sleeping rhyme to the cat-like familiar of Brother Watchkeeper, the only thing resembling a sentinel he encountered, and then an unbinding spell into the lock of the door he wished to open. He entered the main storeroom and found the chest he sought, beneath a heap of stuffed crocodiles. Within were various lengths of knotted rope, each constraining a wind. The one he took twisted and stirred as he picked it up. He then proceeded to the island's wharf, stole a boat, and was off, loosing the knot enough to let the wind fill his sail. He knew that soon his absence would incriminate him, but he cared little. He had gambled everything and won. He was not coming back.

The captive breeze propelled him over the sea for three days and nights. He never once put ashore, but followed the coast of the mainland southward, passing at night the three great cities there, each to him no more than a glow on the horizon. Once beyond the headland of Dzim, he came closer to the shore, and into the morning wind uttered a word. Far away a camel snorted, cast off its startled nomad rider, and ran away, following the path of Guetheric's command to a certain cove, where it knelt on the wet sand, ready to serve him. He arrived late one afternoon, changed his boat for concealment into a pile of stones, mounted the camel, and was off.

He knew what to expect from tales earlier told—a forest of whispering trees, a place of multi-colored sand, unmoving ships awash in desert dunes. But none of these things were encountered that night beneath the stars. Instead he found only a limitless plain of fine ash, without feature, which curiously did not stir in the wind, but which fell back into place so quickly when disturbed that his camel made no tracks in it.

Onward he persevered, the constellation of the Toad before him, and one evening, just as the stars began to appear, he spied the Toad squatting between two mountains, the Weeping Hills, also called the Dark Sisters, the former daughters of Etelven Thios. All this had been foretold, and all had come to pass. But the Valley of the Shadow remained as silent as the desert beyond. The Sisters wept not a tear when he passed between them, nor even an avalanche.

Before him stood the huge basalt castle of Etelven Thios, its walls still firm, its black gate slightly ajar. He gazed upon it for a while in final confirmation of his hopes and speculations, but ventured no closer. Instead he bade his steed kneel, dismounted, and sat down in the sand. He took the brittle, ruined head out of its bag and held it in his lap, waiting.

Four hours passed in silence. Then the camel became uneasy, first turning its head this way and that, then snorting and wheezing in displeasure. Finally, about an hour before dawn, Guetheric spied a dark figure approaching, not from the direction of the castle, but out of the desert. The camel saw it also, lurched to its feet, and galloped off. Guetheric made no attempt to restrain it, knowing he could call it back by magic any time he chose.

Thus he was alone, still seated, with the head in his lap, when the specter drew near. He addressed it calmly, as if it were another traveler, even though he knew otherwise.

"Greetings, stranger. I trust your midnight walk was a pleasant one."

In reply came only a faint hiss. The figure stood where it was.

Guetheric held the head up, so the other could see it clearly. The thing began moving again, in a motion half like walking, half like the drifting of mist. He spoke a word of power. "*Elam.*"

The thing recoiled like a man from a viper. Angrily it stalked around him in a circle, its footfalls now making a definite pad, pad, pad. It drew closer, as he turned to face it, still not rising. Now he could see the outline of a thin, bent man, with face entirely covered by a hood. "*Olam.*"

And again the thing recoiled, but not far, and still it circled, coming ever closer, like a great fish being slowly reeled in. "*Aelam.*" It loomed over him now. There was a stifling odor of decay about it. "*Thhoh!*" All human semblance fell away. The creature became a cloud of dust. Guetheric held up the head, turning it so the empty left socket was nearest the spirit. Like water down a drain it was drawn through the place where the eye had been, into the head of Etelven Thios.

Flesh and soul were united once more. Guetheric had captured the ghost of Etelven Thios. Quickly, before it could discern what had happened, he took a large cork out of his pocket and shoved it firmly into the eye socket, passing his hand over it afterwards, whispering a spell of sealing. Likewise with the crumpled leather bag he blocked the opening where the head had joined the neck and sealed it, and with a handkerchief he stuffed up the hole in the top where the axe had gone through. Now Etelven Thios was his prisoner. The head trembled in anger, but he held it firmly.

"Hear me," he said.

"I hear you," came a voice from within.

"Do as I say, or I shall bind you forever within a stone and cast that stone into the deepest part of the sea."

"I hear and obey." The grim trophy shivered again, with uncontrolled rage and humiliation.

"You have a treasure beyond all imagining."

"Beyond your imagining in any case. It is vast ."

"Take me to it."

"Arise."

He stood up and went where the voice directed him. They came to the massive gates of the castle and passed through. Nothing stood guard there but sand. They crossed the equally empty courtyard and came to the ivory door of evil dreams, which also hung open and untended. Within was a room of once shiny black stone, now faded with the slow invasion of the desert. It had not been licked clean in quite a while. All was noiseless and still. No vampires tittered in the rafters. The castle was empty.

They passed a stairway going upward made of what seemed to be shattered glass coffins, continuing until they came to another door richly imbedded with the skulls of rodents. As the head approached a bar slid back on the other side, and the hinges began to creak for the first time in aeons. The door swung wide.

Within was more gold than could be hoarded by all the kings of Earth from the beginning of time till the end. Precious stones stood in heaps to the vaulted ceiling far above. Brilliant ornaments filled countless open chests. At the sight of all this Guetheric let out an involuntary "Oh!" and nearly dropped the head. But still he grasped it.

"Mere baubles to please barbarians," sneered the disappointed Etelven Thios. "I have a greater treasure than this."

"Greater?"

Overwhelmed by greed beyond all reason and description, caution fled.

"In the middle of the room is a trapdoor. Open it and descend."

Clearing aside thousands of perfectly round pearls, Guetheric found an iron ring, pulled on it, and raised the door, revealing a narrow stone stairway into the earth. Down he went for what seemed like miles and must have been thousands of feet. Etelven Thios let out a kind of snort or cough, and torches set in the walls flared, revealing an altar of white stone, atop which lay a long silver sword, intricately decorated from tip to hilt. "With this sword all victory comes. With it you can conquer all men. With it you can take all the treasure in the world."

Guetheric reached for it.

"The perfect gift," continued Etelven Thios, "for some mindless mercenary. But for men of learning and intelligence, I have something even greater."

"Greater?"

"Beyond the altar is the head of the glimich. Press it."

Indeed, there in stone was the head of the most feared of all beasts never wholly seen by man. Guetheric was at first loathe to touch it, but greed drove him on. It slid easily back into the wall. Counterweights dropped. Stones rumbled, and a passage was opened into another chamber.

Within, a simple writing desk, a quill pen, an inkwell, and a sheet of parchment.

"Are you sure this is the right room?"

"*Yes,*" thundered Etelven Thios. "With this pen you may write all the secrets of all the worlds. With lore from this inkwell, with the pronouncements on this parchment, you may make yours even those things the sword can never conquer or the treasure buy. It is a far, far more potent thing than either of them."

So Guetheric made to take up the pen and write.

"Mighty and wise one, you have forced me to reveal my final, greatest treasure."

In truth he had done nothing of the sort, and thought only of writing a mighty rune with the pen, using it to carry off the sword and the gold, and to bind Etelven Thios forever, so he could never be revenged. But all had gone well so far, so he was willing to extend his scheme to a fourth phase. '"Yes? What now?"

They went through another door, and Guetheric was surprised to find himself outside the castle, in the bottom of a vast gorge. He glanced up at the battlements. He had never seen the place from this side before.

Believing still that Etelven Thios was in his power, he went as directed, until they came to a ledge overlooking a flat expanse of sand.

"Now raise your wand and repeat the words you used before." A pause. Silence. He did nothing.

"What troubles you?" jeered Etelven Thios. "Are you a wizard or are you not? Your wand!"

"Modern sorcery eschews wands as a useless encumbrance—" A sigh.

"Just do it. . . ."

He raised his right hand—the left held the head—over the flat space, fingers outspread, and he spoke the words of summoning and binding.

"Elam. Olam. Aelam. *Thhoh!*" The spell worked, and a long-standing theoretical argument was set to rest.

Before him the earth was rent apart, revealing not an abyss, but a boiling mass of protoplasmic slime, without form or shape or intelligence. Noxious vapors nearly suffocated Guetheric, and as he reeled the head of Etelven Thios flew from his hand, either of its own power or flung by a command from elsewhere than his brain. It dropped into the seething stuff but did not splash; instead it was absorbed instantly, and the face of Etelven Thios, not the dried wreck, but the *full living face, with the cat-like green eye glaring malevolently,* spread across the surface like a film, a thousand times larger than it had been in corporeal life.

"Behold! Behold! My greatest treasure. You have brought me back to my true body, that which I spawned and from which I was spawned, in the days before the earth had any shape. I stretch beneath all the seas and lands of the world, primordial and powerful, ready to rise up and make them mine. I am my own greatest treasure, next to which the parchment will do you no more good than an autumn leaf, the sword is a toothpick, and the jewels a heap of bird droppings. *Behold! In every deep place of the earth you shall find me!*"

And screaming, near to madness, Guetheric fled the Valley of Shadow, all thoughts of riches and power forgotten. It was only as he struggled across the desert three days later that exhaustion and thirst slowed him down, and he was able to think coherently enough to recall the word he had used to summon the camel. Then he rode, never resting, never dismounting, until he came to the sea where his boat still was, in the form of stones. He changed it back, but as yet there was no opportunity to relax. As he was loading the supplies from the back of the camel into the boat, he chanced to look behind him into the mouth of a cave by the shoreline. There, staring back at him was the vertically slit eye of Etelven Thios, large enough to fill the entire opening.

With a hoarse shriek he tumbled into the boat, untied the knotted rope almost all the way, just able to prevent himself from letting the wind escape altogether. He was off, with no idea of where he was going.

Days of delirium and nightmare followed. Steadily the vessel glided over the choppy sea, into colder waters where pieces and then mountains of ice drifted by. At last the chill air and his hunger brought him to his senses, and he looked blearily ahead. The dim shape of a coastline appeared out of a bank of mist. He took the tiller in hand and steered toward it. Landfall came in the middle of the afternoon. He walked a short way over the bare rocks of what turned out to be the tip of a peninsula, and discovered on the other side a massive tomb, once covered with carvings but now all but rubbed plain by the waves and the weather. At this sight he was relieved, for he knew this to be the final resting place of Grimgril, a very great hero of ancient times, who, it was said, rose from the dead eleven times to aid mankind against the primal darkness. This was his twelfth and last abode. Surely his lingering power would ward off any evil.

Surely here Guetheric would be safe.

He went back to the beach and prepared a meal. There were clumsy, flightless birds tottering over the desolate landscape. He summoned one with a simple spell, raised fire out of the sand with a snap of his fingers, and roasted it.

Then he took from the bags of the trader who had owned the camel a wineskin and a brass goblet, and poured himself a drink.

This was his ultimate mistake, for as he raised the cup to his lips he saw staring up at him—*Etelven Thios!* Before he could cry out to the spirit of Grimgril, or even drop the cup, he was gone. A limb of the seething mass reached through and dragged him bodily, in defiance of all laws of perspective, into the very goblet he held and out of three-dimensional space altogether.

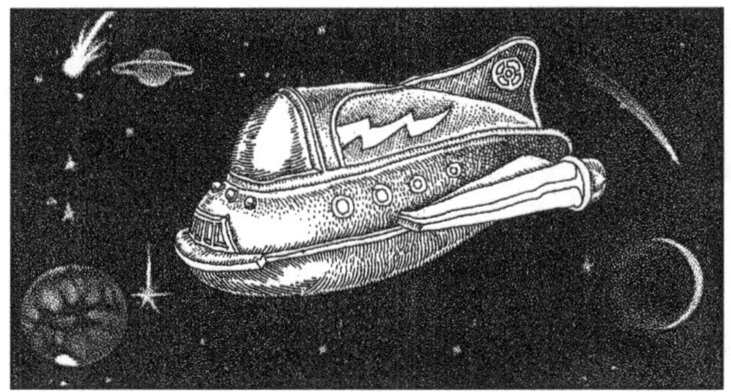

Wanderers and Travelers We Were

To outrace Time, Age, and Death, to walk the shores of unseen worlds, to outlive and outlast any and all—

Thus:

She stood in the observation dome, watching the starbow doppler into ultraviolet.

A decade/instant passed.

"Ellie?"

She turned, and a generation of young men grew old.

"Franz, darling, how good of you to drop by." I walked toward her, and a century passed outside the ship.

"We're landing soon."

"Oh?"

"I forget which planet. They said it was Earth-like."

"Oh." (Yawn.)

We went back to the curved window and looked out at the other spaceships in our little flotilla, the *The Wind in the Willows*; the *Take Her, She's Yours*; the *Stanley, I Presume*. Beyond them, a dozen more cigars of light. Our vessel, the *Aquitaine*, seemed to be at the edge of the group.

She tickled me. We both laughed, and children grew into adulthood between our breaths. It's at times like that when I really believe that God made man in his own image and likeness. Or maybe the other way around.

"Hey you two, don't just stand there! We're having a party. A landing party!" Laughter.

I hadn't heard the door slide open, and Patchwork X. Quilt, formerly a distinguished anatomist (he claimed) and now an oddball even among oddballs (definitely) had crept up behind us. Centuries or even millennia of planetside years old like the rest of us, he had never told anyone what his real name was, where he came from, or what he had looked like originally. The present version was blue and warty down one side of his face, with an extra eye above his (flaring, reddish) nose. Spiky white hair on head, chin, and chest glowed in the semi-darkness. Black fur glistened on his legs, and behind, a tail twitched. Genitals like the branch of a tree hung in unshocking nakedness.

Patch was a collector. He accumulated tissue grafts and stray genetic material as a hobby. On every planet he visited, he was sure to pick up something from something and put it somewhere. No one dared speculate what his insides were like, although it was common knowledge (or at least well-founded rumor) that his piss was blue and he had odd dietary habits.

A good way to pass the years. I'd considered it myself at one time, but by then Patch was already doing it, and I didn't want to seem unoriginal.

"Know anything about the planet?" I asked.

"No, but the sensies at the party are first-rate."

"I think I can do without this round."

"Franz!" said Ellie. "It would be poor form to stay away. People would think you *anti-social!*" (Barely suppressed giggles.)

"Aren't we all?" I said.

"Run along, Mr. Quilt. We'll be down in a minute."

"Must we?"

"Yes."

I put up token resistance as she dragged me. The corridors were filled with clocks showing the time and date on every known world, and choked with people who ignored them.

Wanderers and travelers we were, from out of space and time, from off the starry sea, and we came that day to a world with an entirely unoriginal name, New Home. After a while, you encounter dozens of New Homes. Maybe some of the ones I've seen don't even exist anymore. This one had been settled for a hundred and fifty of its own years, and the colony was small, the world untouched. Twenty-five self-renewing, hydrogen-gobbling silver needles filled New Home's only spaceport. Crowds and officials waited to greet us, at least half the population of the planet, it seemed. They treated us with muted awe, as supernatural beings must have been regarded in the ages of magic. They considered only what we were, not *why* we were what we were. Men and women (and a few questionables) older than history, but really just fleas clinging to the hides of magnificent, immortal, galaxy-roving beasts.

They should have worshiped the ships.

On New Home the sensies continued to be first-rate. Parties and receptions last a month, interspersed with interviews in the media, surprise visits by anyone of note or pretense, exchanges of priceless artifacts from distant worlds for new gadgets we could hardly understand; plus sex, new additions to Quilt's collection, more sex, guided tours, buying sprees, more sex. I rather liked the tours. The New Homers were quite backward by galactic standards, their methods and machineries so outmoded I could almost follow what they were doing. When one is in space, progress goes on, and you miss most of it. New Home was comforting.

Ignorant of our ignorance, they asked *us* the questions. Not just historical ones, first-hand accounts of happenings long ago (yes, those too), but profound, probing ones. Meanings we had allegedly learned.

And we answered them, profoundly of course, knowing that generations of scholars would ponder what we said in what would be to us the blinking of an eye.

Ellie loved every minute of it.

New Home once had another name which had been lost, given to it by a culture which died out long before the first human colonists came. No records, no pictures were left. No bodily remains were found. Most people guessed the original inhabitants hadn't been humanoid, but no one could ever be sure.

Ancient cities still stood, slowly crumbling masses of geometric shapes out of which archaeologists had never managed to make any sense. Perhaps it was anthropomorphic to call them cities at all. I had slipped away from the others, borrowed a tear-shaped aircar of thousand-year-old design, and drifted alone over the miles and miles of circles, squares, and curiously elongated triangles, the exact proportions of which were repeated in large structures and small, I was told, all over the planet. Here and there domes rose above the low, flat-roofed stone buildings. It looked like a set of children's blocks scattered at random.

Beyond the city lay the sea. I sat the car down on the beach, got out, and walked a short distance along the water's edge. Phosphorescent snakes leapt in the fading light. A while later darkness came, followed by a second twilight, and billions of stars poured splendid over the horizon. New Home was at the edge of a globular cluster, and when that cluster rose, it was almost as bright as a second sun; and so, for half a year, the true night was very brief here. It was a strange world with a strange sky, but the sea, God, the sea, reminded me so much of Earth. I met her there, by sea.

"Uh, hello."

"Have you been waiting here for me?"

"Not long. I knew you come here."

"So much for privacy."

"Wait! I didn't mean to—"

"Of course you didn't!" Snakes danced. The tide seemed to be coming in rapidly and I looked around for a moon. There wasn't any. I wondered vaguely if the globular cluster could be responsible.

She was young, pretty, and nervous. "I—I wanted to ask you a few questions. I'm writing a book."

"You know, I wrote a book once. It was called *The Timeless Dream* and it was about this guy who lost his way in time. I called it a fantasy. Funny that I should have written something like that."

Her eyes widened. "You mean you're *the* Franz Gilbert?"

"Is there more than one? I'm surprised you've heard of me."

"But, *The Timeless Dream* is a classic! People have been reading it for centuries. It's one of the greatest romances in human literature!"

"Oh, really? Madame, your flattery will gain you nothing, except perhaps an interview. I assume you have a recorder hidden somewhere."

It was dangling between her breasts on a chain.

"Sight and sound," she said. "You mind?"

"No."

We sat on the sand. Waves died a few feet away. The interview began.

"Why did you, uh, start—?"

"Why did I hop in a spaceship and race around in circles longer than anyone could keep track of?"

"Yes, why?"

"Because it was fashionable. Everyone was doing it."

"Was that all?"

"Don't forget status. You had to have money, and class, and a name, or no Group would take you. Very strict rules they have. A lot of people read my book, and, quite frankly, read a lot more depth or profundity or whatever into it than is actually there, and suddenly, that did it. I was in."

"But—?"

"It was also a great way to get away from obnoxious neighbors. Outlive them. Outlast them. Every one of them an old wreck in what seemed like a few days to me. Time dilation is *the* best method ever devised of maintaining social exclusivity."

"There must be more to it than that, um, more to it than just that."

I stopped toying with her. She seemed genuinely sincere, and I realized that I wanted to talk. It's comforting to confide in strangers. They always believe what you tell them.

"Seriously, I think every one of us succumbed to a temptation. We all saw Death closing in on everybody and we wanted a way out. Our contemporaries might be good for a hundred and fifty years, tops, but onboard the ships we could hang on for a thousand. Or more. But the catch in this arrangement, the one flaw in this glittering little scheme, is that *you have to keep on going.*

Otherwise you find Old Man Reaper waiting in your oh-so-luxurious suite when you stagger home after a hard night's orgy. Or a quiet evening of contemplating the infinite for that matter. It doesn't matter."

My interrogator scratched behind her ear.

"What would happen if you, or anybody from your Group, decided to quit? What if they just stopped?"

"They'd be gone, just like that. *Pffi!*" I snapped my fingers in front of her face. "In the eyes of the Group they'd cease to exist. So we all have to keep on going. In a terminology far older than you are, my dear, I'm a junkie, an addict of space travel."

I leaned back on my elbows and let her think. A little flying thing with trailing hairs buzzed around my ears.

"Uh, tell me Mr. Gilbert, don't you find it inspiring, maybe I should say exhilarating, to go around the universe like that? You're a living witness to the progress of the human race."

"Oh, I am, huh?" I laughed. The Chief High Something had asked a question like that the other day.

"Well, aren't you?"

"No, I'm just old-fashioned, and the farther and farther I go in space—and time—the more things change and the more of an antique I become. Progress? We miss most of it in transit, and I don't think we appreciate what little we do see very much. Look, I found this planet once where there should have been a colony like New Home, only something went wrong, *very* wrong. I don't know, maybe their equipment got wrecked or something, but a couple generations later, when the Group dropped in, the survivors were savages. Their planet didn't have heavy metals, and that might have had something to do with it. You know what they did when we landed? They ran and hid. *That's* what it means to witness human progress. It's scary."

"Well then, why don't you stop?"

"You already asked me that before. Hey, you don't strike me as a real journalist. They rarely say `uh' and they *never* say `um' and in general they talk like a simulated newsholo announcer. Am I being had? Have you ever written a book before?"

"Actually, no."

"Aha! Interstellar fraud revealed!"

"But I want to. I really hope to."

"That's not good enough."

"Please don't be angry."

"I'm not angry. Just tell me why you're really here." She drew a deep breath, held it in, paused.

"I guess it's because I'm an incurable romantic. I look to the stars, and that's where you come from."

"How strange. I'm an incurable romantic too, and I look to the earth, because that's where *you* are." Now both of us were smiling.

Her name was Tanereth Kim, which means Sea Flower in some language I'd never heard of. She turned her recorder off and we rambled on about trivial things for hours, and maybe some things not so trivial. It was a good talk, the first I had had in an extremely long time that meant anything.

The vast globular cluster sank into the west, and in the darkness preceding dawn I drew Tanereth Kim to me, and tide ran out until the noise of the surf was so faint it sounded like someone softly breathing, sliding off into sleep.

I began to suspect that I loved her. There were fireworks off to the west, in the fading darkness, projections of strange shapes in the sky, darting aircars. I imagined Ellie in the midst of it all, in full hedonistic splendor, Mr. Patch showing off his newest member, all the others doing their quirky, individualistic things. Performing rituals they had repeated so many times before.

All this happened but a week before liftoff. A week, that was all. Then the Group was leaving New Home behind in a wake of centuries.

Leaving Tanereth Kim, who would be no more. First, it was a race to see all and do all. The aircar was always aloft, streaking to new destinations. I had to cram everything in, with her.

Monday the mountains, Tuesday the sea, with Death's soft footstep padding after—

One night we sat high in the hills, alone beneath tall white cliffs. A small fire burned before us, the aircar parked hidden behind.

Shoulder to shoulder, leaning.

"Tanereth, let me ask you one thing."

"What?"

"What do you want to do or see more than anything else? Name your miracle and I shall perform it."

"What?"

"Anything." Silence. She looked to where the cluster was rising. The sky faded from night into starry twilight.

"I think I'd like to go into space. We don't send ships from New Home often, you know, and then only official ones."

"Into space. Done." Wednesday morning we flew to the spaceport. I borrowed one of the *Aquitaine's* shuttle craft and lifted in lightmotor, easing into orbit over New Home's equator.

In a darkened cabin. With the viewports open. New Home swam blue in a sea of black.

"There you are. In space. Now give me a big kiss." Silence.

"That wasn't big enough." Again silence.

"Better."

We sat and watched New Home's ocean pass beneath us, then saw the planet's solitary continent slide across the face of the world. Tanereth began to cry.

"Hey, what's this?" I asked.

"I was thinking, Franz. In a couple of days you'll be gone. I'll never see you again. I know you've been very nice, spending all your time with me, but it'll be *pfft!* like you said and I'll be an old, old hag."

"I'm sorry, but there's nothing I can do. Oh Christ, what a lame thing to say! What can I do?"

"Take me with you!"

"You want to leave everyone you ever knew, forever, for me?"

"Yes! Yes!"

"Well, I can't. You'd have to pay your way. I don't think you have that kind of money."

"But you do! Oh Franz, I love you. I don't want to be without you."

"Let's try and think of something else, okay?" Fuel was low and we had to get back, but before we did I unbuckled our safety straps and the two of us drifted around inside the shuttle.

Sex in free fall is a lot different.

Patch was waiting for us back at New Home Port, and a very unfortunate thing happened. The shuttle came down on the pavement, and the crowds of awed and slightly frightened New Homers who had been standing around him drew back as Patch came to meet me.

"Franz! I haven't seen you in ages!"

"Only a few days." I stepped down the ramp.

"Well it seems longer. You haven't seen my latest."

"Your what?"

"Look at this." A thin, brownish tentacle the length of a man's arm shot out of his navel, twisted, and coiled in the air. Screams, and a few unnerved people turned and ran.

"You ought to know better than to show something like that in public! What is it anyway?"

"From one of the water critters. It's an organ for an entirely new sense."

"What kind of sense?"

"Touch it and see. Go on."

"I think I'll forego the pleasure." I felt a little squeamish.

Just then Tanereth emerged from the spacecraft, slowly, as if a little dazed.

"Patch." I turned and took Tanereth by the arm. "Have you met—?"

"No," he interrupted, "but I heard about her. You've been collecting too, I see. Good boy!" Tanereth went white. I was furious. Even Patch could tell he had said something wrong.

"I've got to be going. Ellie invited me for lunch. I'll give her your regards."

More embarrassment. After saying the most inappropriate thing imaginable, he'd gone on to second best. The last person I wanted my regards sent to was my wife, who so far had left me alone in this matter. Maybe she thought it was another affair I was having, the short, sweet kind so easily buried in time and lightyears. Maybe she hadn't even noticed my absence, but I didn't want to push my luck.

Involuntarily, Tanereth drew her arm from my grip. I turned, and she turned away. That hurt more than anything else. I knew what she was thinking, as much as I knew it wasn't like that but she'd never believe me if I said so.

"Come on. Stay with me." She didn't reply.

Thursday I met her parents. An old, old, shrivelled man and a fat lady who hadn't had her body tailored in years, both of them conventional, rather stupid, asking me the same tired questions all over, exclaiming how rare and valuable an experience it was for their daughter to make my acquaintance. If only they knew what any of it meant. I was glad when we left them.

Friday, Saturday, Sunday, I had all planned out, but Tanereth said, "Let's not go anywhere. Stop running for once. I can see all New Home in my own time."

So we stopped, and went to our favorite spot, where we had first met, a fitting place to end what we had begun there. Sunday night, both of us were barely able to look one another in the eyes. Our time was nearly over and we both knew it.

"Want to interview me again?"

"No. Please, just sit by me. I want to think."

I did too. Tomorrow at dawn.

Stay/leave/stay/leave/stuff Tanereth in my luggage/what? Sex until both were exhausted. That didn't help.

At last, as if with great pain and deliberation, the cluster set and darkness returned. It would soon be dawn. The last day. I was desperately aware that I couldn't bring myself to say goodbye.

Finally she did. "Franz, it's time."

"Time?"

Her lower lip was quivering. She fought to hold back tears.

"Time . . . for you . . . to go back to *that!*" Arm and finger shot out in the direction of the million stars sinking into the sea.

Then her control went, and she dropped her head down into my lap, wrapped her arms around my waist and cried. And I bent down over her, chest on her back, and cried also.

She struggled out from under me.

"Hurry, or you'll miss your ship." I let her drag me to my feet. We ran along the beach to the aircar.

"Hurry!"

Anti-gravity motors whirred. I put the throttle all the way forward, and we rose over the ruined city.

Tanereth's face was intent, worried.

"Why are you so eager for me to get back?" I said.

"Because you'll die if you don't. It'll be like a week for the rest of them, and you'll be dead. *Pffi!* I shouldn't have expected you to stay here on New Home. Thanks for everything, but your life is with them."

"Tanereth?"

"What?"

"Did you notice that you're thinking of me, not yourself? You really love me."

"Look out!"

The aircar lost altitude fast, banked to the left. Ruins towered to smash us. We brushed the top of a wall in a flurry of dust, dodged a pyramid, whirled crazily down narrow streets, came to an open space, sped across it, and smashed into a wall, which collapsed.

"Tanereth? Are you all right?"

"Yes? How could this happen? We'll have to call for help."

I flicked a few switches. "Speaker's down."

"We'll have to run!"

I let her lead me through the winding streets, trying to find the edge of the city. She didn't know her way out of the maze any better than I did.

We were still deep inside when the ground shook and twenty-five suns rose into the sky, shrank, and vanished.

"They didn't wait for you!" Both of us dropped exhausted against the side of a building. "Oh Franz, you've lost so much." Her voice broke into a sob.

"Hey, don't worry. Everything is all right."

"No it's not all right! You'll only live as long as the rest of us. No more. No hundred thousand years. *Think about it.*"

"What makes you think shipboard people actually *live* all those years? We don't. It's an illusion. We skip most of them. We age just like anyone else, cut off in our own private time-stream, able to visit the real universe only on occasion. That's no way to live. It's all subjective. You see, I have thought about it."

"You don't mind?"

"No. You must have wondered what happened to the aircar. I did that. It didn't malfunction. I just never learned how to drive."

Wide-eyed disbelief.

"Tanereth," I said. "When we go *pffi!* we'll do it together. Okay?"

"Okay."

Together. Tanereth, I have come to you by tangled paths and devious ways, and I shall never leave this place.

Somewhere above, my Ellie, my dragon lady of the stars, flies forgetting and forgotten.

Below, love burns white hot on the ground.

Silkie Son

There was a fisherman of the Shetlands named Peter Asmundson, a man of long lineage, whose forefathers came with the Vikings. Yet he was no mighty lord. Poverty forced him to wrestle with the waves for his living, like all his neighbors.

Still he remembered who he was and was proud of it; a large, fierce man, broad of frame and strong of limb, so skilled in every aspect of his trade that there was no greater boatman anywhere in his day.

But not even the greatest can control the wind and the sea. Did not the tide come in against even Canute's command? So it happened that one day Peter Asmundson's craft was caught in a storm and blown far from his home waters, to the south, and wrecked on the wild shores of Ireland. He alone of the crew survived, and after nearly a year of hardship returned to his own country, only to find his wife with child.

That was how it started.

* * *

Christina stood alone on the beach, watching the dark clouds and they gathered over the horizon like a blanket drawn slowly over the sky. She watched the waves as they foamed against two massive rocks that stood on either side of the tiny harbor. She tried to distract her mind with the tales she had heard concerning those rocks, how they were monsters from the sea, grown old with time, or pagan giants frozen there by the curse of some wandering saint. Once, when she was a girl, a stranger had come to the island, the only grown man she had ever seen whom she had not known all her life. He had compared the rocks to the Pillars of Hercules. His words were strange to her.

Off to her right her small son Olaf played among the sand and shells, sometimes chasing after butterflies, sometimes wading into the water when he spied something that seemed of particular interest.

This is the day, she repeated to herself over and over. *Three years are now passed, and on this day he will come. "I will feel my son's birth in my mind," he had said, "like a lamp newly lighted, and for three years it shall burn ever brighter, like a beacon. Then I shall come for him.*

The boy found a large and brightly colored shell. He ran to show it to his mother.

"Look! Look what I found!"

"That's very pretty, darling."

He doesn't know. He must feel the truth, even if he doesn't know it. He and the waves are cousins. Today he will be with his true father. It's better that way, for him and for me. It will hurt just as much, though. For me, and for him.

The gazed out over the choppy, gray sea, waiting.

* * *

"You didn't have to *beat* him so!" she screamed, slamming the bowl of stew onto the rough-hewn table. "You are a monster. Only a monster would strip a child naked and whip him till the blood ran. I hope the Devil takes your soul for that, Peter Asmundson, if he doesn't own it already!"

He cursed and threw his mead cup at her. It missed and landed in the fireplace, sizzling.

"Silence, you faithless bitch, or I'll flog you too. The only monster around here is *your* son, not mine. The Devil is in *that thing*, not in me. I beat him to drive the Devil out. He'll bring bad luck."

"Monster!"

It seemed for a minute as if he would rise from his place and throttle her, but he held himself back. He gripped the edge of the table so hard his huge, reddish hands went white at the knuckles. His face seethed. Spittle formed at the corners of his mouth.

"Do you know what *your* brat told me this morning? Do you? He said the sea was alive and beautiful. He said that fishes talk to him and we shouldn't eat them because they're our friends. Well, fishes don't talk unless the Devil makes them, and the sea is just a lot of water. And if it were alive it wouldn't be beautiful. It would be a filthy, stinking bitch. Like you."

"Children dream. Can this be so wicked?"

"*Is he just a child?* Is he?"

She felt herself going slack with horror. It was just too much to bear. Her mind, her body could muster no defense anymore.

After a while she managed to whisper, "How could he be anything else? He's my son."

"Yes, yours. *Satan* is his father and you are the witch the spawned him. I should have denounced you to the priests long ago."

She wrung her fists helplessly. She bit her hand to hold back a scream.

Then she spoke once more. "Denounce us then. Stop torturing us and let them do it. Or do you just enjoy it too much?"

He bolted up from the table, wordless with fury, striding toward her, herding her into a corner. With one shove he had her on the floor. He stood astride her, a raging giant, more a thing of personified, malevolent, elemental fury than a mere man. He swallowed her in his shadow and just stood there. At last he spoke in a low, deliberate tone.

"I ought to kill you both. I ought to drive stakes through your hearts and burn you in a great pyre. That is the only way to deal with your kind."

"No! For the sake of Jesus, no!"

"What do you care about Jesus, witch?"

* * *

He did not kill her that night, though for a while it seemed that he might. She slipped between his legs and ran. He lunged after her and they circled around and around inside their tiny cottage. She fought him with anything she could find, pots, stools, his own harpoon. This last he merely snatched out of her hand when she tried to stab him with it. He laughed and tossed it aside. Finally he trapped her in the corner again, taking an added precaution so that she could not get away this time.

He stood on her hand, crushing it with his boot, hard enough to make her cry out, not quite breaking bones. Then he stared at her for what seemed an endless time, shrugged, and quietly went away.

He sat down on one of the few stools they hadn't broken in the course of the battle and glared at her for an hour without making a sound. All this while she huddled in the corner like one dead. Finally he yawned and went to bed.

She waited until she was sure he was asleep, then rose, and slipped into the loft where Olaf had screamed in unnoticed terror throughout the fight. Now he was on the threshold of sleep, feverish, whimpering softly from the wounds her husband had dealt him.

She took the boy quietly in her arms, wrapped him in a blanket, and hurried from the house.

The sky was overcast and low, like a ceiling pressing down, the wind harsh and cold. Bending against the wind, she wandered over the island a ways, across desolate, rocky slopes, until she came to the main part of the village. There she found a boat dragged up onto the beach, a boat small enough for her to handle.

She laid the boy gently into the prow, then pushed the boat out into the water and climbed aboard. After some further struggle, she had the sail raised and was on her way, unseen she hoped, and unheard.

Christina sailed over the sea that night, the boat leaping from wave to wave as if of its own volition. She knew little of navigation, but that didn't matter since she didn't know where she was going. Just *away*. She thought vaguely that she should go East, lest she wander aimlessly in the western ocean. Norway, Germany, any country in the world would do. She didn't care.

Away.

It would be hard. The roads were filled with robbers and trolls, the seas with devouring leviathans; and if men heard her story they would probably turn against her. Who would shelter a woman who fled from her lawful husband with a child that was hers but not his?

At such a time she could expect no mercy, no forbearance, even from God.

Still she pressed on, clinging to the tiller of the boat, trying to guide the sail with her hand. But in the first twilight of dawn the ocean itself rose against her, huge waves thundering for all the sky was clear and the wind had died, driving her back the way she had come with blow after unrelenting blow. The mast was soon gone, the tiller snapped from her hand as the rudder tore away. She whirled about and it was all she could do to hold her son against herself while clutching the side of the boat.

A voice spoke to her, out of the green depths, out of the wild, dark sea, whispering impossibly in her head. *"I feel him like a beacon in my thoughts, and I shall come, soon. Go back. You cannot betray me."*

And for one dreadful, eternal instant, she thought she saw a familiar face gazing up at her, but before she could be sure foam washed over it and the face was gone.

As the sky began to lighten, the boat was cast up on the very beach from which she had departed. The waves ceased as suddenly as they had started. The sea was calm. Gulls shrieked overhead. The wind blew gently, heralding a day of fair weather.

Christina staggered across treeless fields, her son quietly miserable in her arms.

She thought of God again, of the White Christ who drove out demons, and of his Mother, who loved, and said a prayer to them, but got no comfort from it, no confidence.

Finally, in the broad light of morning, she stumbled into the house, haggard with exhaustion, her clothing clinging to her body and smelling of brine.

Her husband lay awake in bed. He stared at her and seemed to appreciate something of her predicament.

And laughed.

* * *

The clouds were drifting closer. *He* always came with the clouds, she knew. Only when it was dark and the waves pounded against the shore would he come.

Only when the North Sea roared.

"Can we go home now, Mama? It's cold and it looks like it's going to rain."

"No, darling. Not yet. Your mother likes to sit and watch the sea when it's this way. Let's wait a little longer. You can sit by me and keep warm if you like."

Olaf climbed up onto a boulder beside her and pressed close. She wrapped her cloak around the both of them.

* * *

On the day her son was born she had screamed aloud in her agony, yet no one came to help her. All the village knew she was about to give birth, and midwives came to her house, but Peter drove them away. He stood tall and unconquerable in the doorway, threatening to bash in heads with a shovel. Men came by later, bidding him let the women pass, but he repeated his threats and hefted his shovel, and no one dared fight with him, for he stood a full head taller than any one of them.

At last they all went away, and he walked inside, barring the door behind him. He glanced at Christina as she writhed and sweated on the bed.

"Now we'll have a look at your bastard, huh? Maybe we'll even learn who your filthy lover is. Will the brat have red hair like Snorri the smith? Or black, like your brother Thorstein? What is a little incest to one like you?"

For many hours he sat beside her. Not once did he raise a hand to help her. Not once did he whisper any words but curses. It was only when at last the infant came forth and began to cry that he said anything more, and then only two words:

"Ugly thing."

He spat on the floor beside the bed and left the house. Some while later Christina was aware of gentle hands touching her, and voices she had known all her life, but couldn't quite place. The midwives had returned. They took the baby from her. She didn't remember anything after that.

* * *

She named her son Olaf, after the saint and king, and took him to be baptized as soon as she was well enough to walk. The boy throve, despite Peter's hatred. He seemed endlessly cheerful, even in the presence of that dull-witted brute. There was something clearly out of the ordinary in this child. Anyone, even Peter could see that. Christina knew what much of that strangeness was, too, or where it had come from, though she dared not speak of it, lest Peter kill them both. At the best of times he only half believed the story she constantly told, how she had come upon a band of ruffian strangers by the edge of the sea and they had raped her.

Peter Asmundson couldn't possibly have known the truth, but he suspected more than he could understand, and hated the thoughts that constantly nagged him. Hate was all he knew. Hate was all he could deliver. He was good at it.

So he made life agony for Christina, and, when he could, for her son. Many times he wondered why he did not put her away as most men would a faithless wife, but always she came to the same, terrible answer. He would keep her with him always, so he could torture her.

* * *

The storm clouds were overhead now, and a light drizzle began to fall.

"Mama, let's *go.*" Olaf squirmed beneath Christina's cloak.

"No wait. We must wait."

"What *for?* We'll get wet."

"For something much more important than not getting wet. For something I've known would happen since before you were born."

"But *what?*"

"Think for a minute. If a bird were kept in a cage all the time and never allowed to fly, would that be right?"

"No, Mama! There aren't any birds here! I don't understand."

"You will, very soon."

* * *

Long ago there had been a time when she had found life with her husband at least bearable, even if she never loved him. When news came of the loss of his boat, she had actually grieved, and had even longed for him. One morning, a few weeks afterward, she had gone down to the harbor to watch all the boats set out. It was a cold and windy day, the sky deeply overcast, and there had been much argument among the men about whether they should go out at all. On such a day as this Peter Asmundson had sailed, never to return.

Finally they did go out, but not beyond the Out Skerries, so they could get back quickly if a storm arose.

She walked out to the two great stones, the ones the stranger had called Pillars of Hercules. After all the boats had passed from sight around the edge of the island, Christina stood for a while, gazing at the rocks and little islets which rode the rough waves like ships. Once or twice she thought she saw something moving out there, sliding into the sea.

She scanned the horizon, hoping against all hope that she might spy a sail and it might be her husband's.

The open ocean was rough and slate-gray, flecked with whitecaps, but within the harbor behind her, the water was relatively calm, and green, then brown, then almost blue beneath the cloud cover and variable light.

She turned back toward the village. The houses were within sight, but the village women had gone about their daily tasks. Among the crevasses and boulders she could only hear the sounds of the sea and the wind. She might as well have been on the Moon.

A dark shape, perhaps a large seal she thought, flashed through the water about ten feet from shore, then vanished.

Curious, she waded out a little ways, to get a better look. She was sure it wasn't a shark or any other fish. It had to be an animal of some kind. A seal. Yet seals seldom came into the harbor or near the village. Men hunted them. Boats and human voices were to be feared.

She saw it again, in the water but so close she could have reached out and touched it. She felt a tinge of dread then, a terror that this was no natural thing at all.

It *was* a seal, a huge one, and stouter and darker than any she had ever seen before.

This seal was the size of a man.

It swam closer yet, almost brushing her legs, then passed her, circled, and came back. She stood perfectly still, horribly afraid now for reasons she didn't quite understand. She remembered old pagan stories she had heard as a child, about demons that came from the sea—

The outline of the creature began to fade, and for an instant it seemed an irregular stain on the water. Just a region of blackness, not a shape.

Then a naked man stood up, dripping. He was tall and immensely muscular, his wild hair and beard thick and tangled, like kelp.

His penis stood firmly erect.

"I am the King of Skule Skerry," he said.

* * *

All her memories faded now, but the pain of them remained. Christina wept softly. The wind blew ever fiercer; rain whipped down on the two of them as they huddled atop the rock. Olaf said nothing, somehow sensing the urgency of something his mother could not put into words. She knew he trusted her. She tried to be worthy of that trust, to protect him this final time.

She held him close.

Not much longer. She closed her eyes and merely felt the presence of the half-human child of rape she had come to love as her own. Soon Olaf would know his real father and his heritage. He would be what he truly was, gone forever as he had to go. *Because* she loved him, she knew, she must cast him from her, as a mother casts her child out of a burning house that it might live, even if she is to die.

They waited a half an hour more as the storm worsened and the ocean seethed before them. Then she spied something long and dark swimming in to the mouth of the harbor, heading directly toward her.

He had come.

"Take off your clothes, Olaf."

"*What?*"

"Take off your clothes. It is time for you to go."

"Mama, why?"

"Because you must."

She helped him undress as the Silkie rose out of the waves and walked onto the beach. Christina saw her son's eyes widen with wonder as he beheld the seal-man, and beneath that wonder there was something else. *Recognition?* Did he understand his dreams at last, his visions, the voices he heard from out of the water?

"He is your real father, dearest. Go with him."

Olaf shivered, naked. Christina kissed him on the forehead.

"Mama—"

"Go. Try to remember me. You will never see me again."

The boy sobbed. He clung to her fiercely. "I will! I will! I'll come back!"

"No you won't. It will be enough that you remember that I loved you. Goodbye."

The Silkie placed his hand on Olaf's shoulder.

"Come," he said. "I will teach you how to change."

At the last minute he gave Christina a small leather bag. Her fingers worked the drawstring loose of their own volition. Several coins spilled out onto the sand and stones. They were faded and almost green, as if they had been underwater for a long time.

A nurse's fee.

* * *

Two black shapes, one large, one small, sped out to sea. Neither paused.

"Where do I go now?" Christina said, whispering first, her voice getting louder until she was shrieking to the waves and the wind and the distance. "What about me? Don't go away and leave me. There is nothing for me here!"

She ran into the surf, wading into the bitterly cold, heaving water, struggling as it rose to her waist, to her shoulders, to her chin, half staggering, half swimming finally as she shouted, "Take me with you! I want to come too! Please!"

She kept on going.

They didn't look back.

It was a new ending to a very old story.

Just Suppose

Hey.

Just suppose that when you were six years old and heard branches scraping at your window one winter's night a little too insistently, and you got up in your pajamas and stared wide-eyed at the discovery that the huge oak tree outside your bedroom window as swarming with what you could only describe, in your limited experience, as fairyland lights, like candles inside paper bags, but drifting in the air among the branches; and there were *people* inside the tree, with glowing faces, some of them very strange, some of them children like you, not to mention a few with wings like you'd seen on a TV show not long before.

Suppose, too, that you opened the window, feeling the damp air, all too afraid that your mother would burst in screaming, "You'll catch your death!" But she didn't, and you had that special moment all to yourself, and you heard the voices of the people in the tree, inviting you to come to them.

Let's suppose, further, that you *did*, and your parents found you in the snow the next morning, half dead from hypothermia, with an odd criss-cross cut on your wrist, but supremely happy, because you'd had a *wonderful* time adventuring among the knights and wild Indian boys, battling giants and discovering pirate treasure . . . and after several more such episodes you were committed to psychiatric care and convinced, reluctantly, that it had only been a series of dreams, which was clear by the way the imagery changed as you got older, like the naked sirens that appeared after you hit puberty . . . and you couldn't really be seeing the ghost of your grandfather rocking sadly back and forth in the wind, as if he wanted to tell you something and had forgotten how.

But maybe it was really contact with the Other World, whose inhabitants sometimes help human folk, particularly their allies, like you, who cut your wrist and commingled your blood and became one of us.

Suppose further that after a largely unsatisfactory adult life you are lying in bed again *in that same room*, because your parents died and left you the house, and the branches are blowing against the window again, too insistently.

Suppose . . .

But you put away your dreams as a grown man puts away childish things, and eventually married a nice girl, who wasn't very nice after all; and the barrage of her complaints sent you retreating into the minutiae of your profession, which is antique coin dealing, so that you can blather on about the fine points of the *Fel Temp Reparatio* series of Constantius II, and show off your monographs, but haven't had a happy moment in twenty years, unless you want to count the time you flew into Paris, rushed from the airport to an auction, and rushed back to the airport again an hour later with fifteen absolutely perfect gold *histamenon nomismae* of Michael V Kalaphates in your briefcase. You didn't even visit the Louvre while you were in town because you are, in fact, a boring, pedantic little man without the time or the sensibility for that sort of thing.

But let's suppose you could go back to being a child and grow up *better* here, in our world, and forget about your wife and your partner Fred who is cheating you in more ways than one, and even forget about Michael V Kalaphates who was a son-of-a-bitch anyway.

Because you know perfectly well that they want to be rid of you, and she's downstairs humping Fred on the sofa right now, with the TV on loud so you can't hear, and the two of them are planning for you to hit your head in the shower and accidentally drown in two inches of water.

You're getting fat. You could happen, right?

But suppose that instead you crept downstairs and bludgeoned them both to death with some sharp, heavy object, like the National Numismatic Society trophy on the mantle. You wouldn't have to worry about the evidence, because you *wouldn't be around anymore*, if you were merely to climb out the window afterward and join us here in the tree, which is actually a gateway to other places, a new life.

We'd catch you if you started to fall.

Just suppose we're really here.

It's not the wind.

We're all waiting for you to make up your mind.

We Are the Dead

What Mrs. Dwyer and he had in common from the beginning, Jerry decided, was that they were both of indeterminate age.

He prided himself on this sort of conclusion. He was always the observer, the analyzer, the one who stood outside of his own life and looked in.

There were a lot of things he knew about himself: that at twenty-two he could still be taken for seventeen. He was smooth-faced and slender and lacked that assertiveness most people had by his age. He was still very much the adolescent and he knew it, and it was somehow less painful to know it. He was away from home for the first time, already making his mark as a scholar, completing his Ph. D. program at an accelerated pace, with articles to his credit and his notebooks full of fragments of what was to be his book, *The Byzantine Genesis.*

So he needed a quiet place to stay, so he showed up on Mrs. Dwyer's doorstep with a copy of the university newspaper in his hand.

"Um . . . I've come to ask about the room you have for rent."

The old lady stood there for a moment, peering out through the half-opened door. He thought she was going to slam it in his face.

"If it's already taken, I'll—"

But her reply startled him.

"You do."

"I'll what?"

She opened the door all the way and retreated into the house. He followed, dubiously, closing the door behind himself.

His first impression of this woman was that she was enormously old, and he joked to himself, silently, that here was someone who had known Justinian and

Theodora as contemporaries, or at the very least Leo the Third.

She walked unsteadily, with a slight stoop, and her hands were covered with liver spots.

It was very much an old person's house, the inside more a matter of years' long accretion than design, dark, the curtains drawn, antique furniture not always in the best repair. The lamps were electric, but modeled after 19th century kerosene ones, their glass shells almost black with dust. Lace seemed to be everywhere. Faded photographs stared at him from darkened walls. Great heaps of worn and tattered books leaned on shelves, or just piled on surfaces. Here and there was a flash of color: flowers in a vase, some silver knickknack, or a jade statuette. In a quick glance around the downstairs parlor, he made out a framed medallion of a dignitary who could well have been George V or the Kaiser, and a few more modern pieces here and there—though for this place modern meant Art Deco, 1920s at the latest.

And he noticed that faint odor of age which has nothing to do with untidiness or uncleanliness. When he was five, he had been lifted up to give his great-grandmother a kiss, and she had smelled a little bit like candle wax and a little bit like, as he had imagined it for years afterward, a mummy. That same, unmistakable smell was here, in Mrs. Dwyer's house.

She turned to him again and said the surprising thing over again.

"You'll do."

"I don't understand."

"You're about the same age as my son, and you look a little like him too. That's fine." She smiled gently.

He didn't know what to say. It was one of those awkward social situations he knew about analytically, but had no idea how to handle now that he was actually in it. He felt an intense urge to just run away and be done with it. But sheer embarrassment kept him where he was, and silent.

She grabbed him by the arm and dragged him out of the parlor, into a hallway, toward a flight of stairs. Her grip was surprisingly strong.

"Come on," she whispered in an amused, conspiratorial tone. "Let me take you upstairs."

Light flooded the stairs from a skylight. He noted, as they went up, the sealed off stubs of gas-jets in the walls. He noted, too, that here Mrs. Dwyer seemed much younger, maybe in her upper fifties. She climbed the stairs quickly, without any difficulty.

"Is this your first time away from your family?"

He stopped halfway up the stairs, not sure what to say.

At the top, she turned around and grinned broadly. "Oh, come on, young man. I won't bite." She laughed. Somehow, at that instant, he trusted her completely, as if she'd just cast a spell or broken one.

"Well, it's more that my family moved away from me," he said. "My Dad got transferred to New Mexico, and I needed to stay behind at the university, so here I am." He shrugged and joined her on the second floor landing, then followed her up another flight.

The room she showed him ran the whole length of one side of the house on the third floor. It was spacious and well-lit, and modestly furnished with a bed, a writing desk, two chairs, and a stand-up closet. It was more than enough for his needs, he realized, almost luxurious by the standards of what he had been expecting, and the price was so unbelievably low he was astonished the place wasn't as crammed as an opium den with impoverished undergraduates.

"This was my son's room," Mrs. Dwyer said. "I think he'd like you to stay here."

Again the acute embarrassment. She seemed to see his difficulty.

"My son has gone away," she said.

And he felt, once more, complete trust, and gratitude for having been spared the difficulty of phrasing a tactful inquiry.

* * *

That was how he came to stay with Mrs. Dwyer. The same evening he got a great deal of work done, sitting among the suitcases and boxes he'd had brought over by cab. He was up very late, poring over texts of degenerate medieval Greek, parting spider webs of rhetoric until he came to a scene which had fired his imagination so many years before when he'd first read Bury's *Later Roman Empire*, in which the soldiers of the Christian emperor of the East, at the height of their death-struggle with the Persian foe, took a town and burst in upon the Abomination of Desolation itself—a blasphemous idol of the mad Persian king surrounded by symbolic figures of the sun and moon and stars all bowing at his feet in adoration. Jerry imagined the soldiers standing there, in shocked, silent awe, and even the hero-emperor Heraclius speechless before the thing. It was one of those moments when time seems to stop.

He sat in a reverie, the turgidity of the ancient text forgotten. History had always had this vividness for him, a culmination of lives rather than dry names and dates, more real than the world outside at times, as if the past were an open door only waiting for him to step through forever.

Then he heard a noise. He thought at first that it was a footstep outside his room. Something shuffled, scraped. A murmur came from below, as if Mrs. Dwyer were talking to someone—on the telephone perhaps?—in hushed tones.

He went to the door, opened it, and gazed down the now darkened stairwell. He listened for several minutes more and heard only the faint ticking the grandfather clock downstairs in the parlor. Once a police car went by outside, rattling softly on the cobblestones, the rotating red of its roof-light flickering through the house.

He glanced at his watch, saw that it was past four in the morning, and went to bed.

In was indeed strange lying in an unfamiliar room in a strange house, far from his family for the first time in his life. Tired as he was, he couldn't sleep immediately, but stared at the ceiling and the faint shape of the window at the far end of his room, listening for that sound again, vaguely afraid the place might be crumbling or riddled with rat-tunnels.

He reached out and touched the wall. It seemed solid enough.

When he did sleep he dreamt that he followed the sound downstairs into the parlor and somehow there were hundreds of people surrounding him in the darkness, a shadow here, a pale face glimpsed for an instant in the periphery of his vision. He turned, again and again, and they remained in the periphery, whispering in medieval Greek. They followed him along one hallway and then another, turning, turning as in the labyrinth of Daedalus, until at last he came to a huge room filled with ticking clocks and old pictures and crumbling books; and the others cried out and covered their faces; but Jerry gazed straight ahead, guileless as a child at the idol that stood before the canopied bed, the huge, stone image of the Persian king who somehow looked like Mrs. Dwyer and spoke to him in a voice that was not hers, but deep, almost thunderous, yet muted as a distant wind in a mountain pass.

"We are the dead," it said.

* * *

He awoke, sweat-soaked for all the room was cold, merely puzzled rather than afraid. The dream had not frightened him. He had been no more than an observer, like a camera eye riding on the shoulder of the main character.

He wasn't rested, but the clock told him he had a class in two hours. So he got up, showered, dressed, and stumbled downstairs.

Mrs. Dwyer had breakfast waiting for him.

"Oh, you needn't bother yourself," she said, heaping pancakes and eggs on his plate. "I like having someone to cook for. You don't mind, do you?"

"No," he said.

"You see, I've gotten into the habit, and now that my son has gone away and . . . well, you understand."

"Yes, I understand," he said meekly, for all that he didn't understand at all. There was, as a professional historian would put it, something wrong with the chronology. But there was nothing to be done now except to humor her.

"I dreamed about my son last night," she said suddenly. "It was amazingly real. Like he was right here with me."

All Jerry could say was, "Oh," and an awkward silence followed.

But as he ate there she became quite talkative, and spoke of places she had been and famous people she'd either glimpsed from afar or actually met. There were a lot of them, places and people. She vaguely alluded to "the old country," and recalled how, when she was a child, her mother had taught her to be wary of Gypsies, "because they kidnap children, blind them, and put them out to beg. But that's not true. I traveled with the king of the Gypsies once. He looked into his crystal and saw my future clearly. But he wouldn't tell me what it was. He only said I was very, very special."

Perhaps it was obvious that he didn't quite believe her, because as soon as he was done eating she led him into the parlor—leaving the dishes behind on the table, shushing him when he made to clear them away—and there, with the lights on and the curtains drawn, layer upon layer of her past was revealed. He saw movie and theater posters from the flapper era, most of them framed, some hanging, some just stacked against the walls. There was even a photograph of Noel Coward signed, "To Vanessa, darling." The regal-looking medallion he had seen the previous day was indeed George the Fifth. Lying in an open desk drawer was a Victorian tintype in an oval frame, of a young man who did resemble Jerry slightly, standing uncomfortably before the camera with his hand stuck in his waistcoat in the familiar Napoleonic pose.

The chronology made less sense than ever. It was a problem, a puzzle to be worked out in his detached mind.

He examined the books. Most were very old, many in calfskin with boards falling off, but others were fashionable novels from the '20s—Ellen Glasgow and Michael Arlen, and a whole shelf of Joseph Hergesheimer—accompanied by, surprisingly, a City Lights paperback of Allen Ginsburg's *Howl.*

There were piles of sheet music. Mrs. Dwyer started leafing through them.

"I used to sing these. I was the rage of New York."

It occurred to him for the first time that she might have once been genuinely famous, now retired in obscurity. But before he could ask her, she winked and said, "I used a different name in those days, dearie."

He remembered his class.

"Will you be back for lunch?"

After some hesitation, he said, "Yes."

* * *

It was so easy to go on like that. His life had always followed a certain pattern, which had been broken when his parents moved away. Now there was a similar one. He followed. It was incredibly easy, for all some part of his mind rattled clichés at him: *Get a life. Grow up. Get out into the world on your own.*

It wasn't good for him, he knew. He was like a smoker taking just one more puff before quitting.

Easy.

Mrs. Dwyer lived on one of the oldest streets in Philadelphia, where the 20th century had touched but lightly, and the narrow pavement was still cobblestoned and the house fronts were Colonial. It was only fifteen minutes from the university by subway. So he came home for lunch most days. When Mrs. Dwyer knew he'd be a long time in the library, she would pack something for him. She also did his laundry and made his bed, cooked his breakfast every morning, and, when autumn came and the weather grew harsh, she always saw him off, puttering with his scarf to make sure he was wrapped up properly.

So easy. He let her do it. He told himself he was humoring her, that it was for her—he was letting her exercise her maternal instincts one last time.

Easy.

His world was there, in that little house on a back street, when it wasn't in his books and on the plains of Asia Minor as Heraclius drove the Persians into the dust. The other students were faces in a corridors, voices in the classroom. He couldn't remember their names. What mattered was that the faculty regarded him as the most brilliant and devoted novice historian they'd ever seen. *The Byzantine Genesis* progressed.

("But you should get out more," his graduate advisor said once, turning from matters strictly academic, "or you'll turn into something of a Byzantine icon yourself." Jerry shrugged. "I'm not joking," the man said.)

It astonished him that Mrs. Dwyer understood his work and even discussed it with him. She was certainly the only non-academic person he had ever met who knew who George of Pisidia was, much less had actually read some of the *Heracliad* and actually had her own theories of what the more obscure parts were about.

Again, it didn't make sense. She might have been an actress once, or a singer, or some sort of social gadfly, but social gadflies are not supposed to read Byzantine Greek. At times it seemed to him that, for all her brilliance, she were not a real person at all, but a reflection of himself; and his thoughts were hers and her thoughts were his, with all the chasms of age and gender and social background between them completely covered over.

But then, one afternoon in early December, as they sat side by side on the sofa sipping tea, she leaned over, put her hand gently on his wrist, and said, "Jerry, there is something I have to tell you. It's about my son."

She hadn't mentioned her son in over a month. Now she spoke with real urgency.

The adolescent fright returned. Jerry put his teacup down on the coffee table and said nothing at all.

"It's my son's birthday soon. He always loved his birthdays."

With a kind of desperate courage he managed to ask, "What happened to your son Mrs. D? Is he . . . dead?"

"No. It isn't like that. I think he changed. He wasn't my boy anymore, after a while. I suppose you could say that I sent him away, without really wanting to."

"Well, where *is* he?" Jerry's heart was racing. He sat rigid, staring directly forward, at the coffee table, at the curtained window. For an instant he had a vision of Mrs. Dwyer's son as severely retarded or hideously deformed, raised here in complete isolation until he got too big to manage—

"Perhaps, somehow, I forgot him." The terrible silence returned. It seemed like an eternity before she finally said, "I've told you too much. I'm sorry. I shouldn't have."

* * *

He worked late that night, but could get little done. His mind returned again and again to Mrs. Dwyer and her mysterious offspring, who, he was now half-convinced, was some sort of lunatic or escaped murderer who was likely to show up on his birthday and carve the two of them into dog food with a meat cleaver. He was very close to packing his bags just then, and slipping out into the night, never to be seen by Mrs. Dwyer or her son again.

But he couldn't. He told himself it was because it would hurt Mrs. Dwyer.

He nodded off at his desk, then woke at the sound of something in the corridor outside. At first he thought it was breathing, someone gasping, out of breath, just outside the door. No, the wind. Then footsteps, definitely footsteps, tap, tapping down the stairs in the darkness.

He considered that this might be some kind of lucid dream, but didn't really believe that. He felt the cold floor beneath his stockinged feet, the draft from under the door. He heard the house creaking against the winter wind.

He slipped out, and down the stairs as quietly as he could and stood outside her bedroom door.

Mrs. Dwyer seemed to be sobbing, pleading with someone. He couldn't make out a word. Something answered her, its reply a slur of gibberish at first, almost a mewing sound, and the thought came to him, *Jesus God, has she got some sort of animal in there?*

Glass shattered. Something heavy crashed to the floor.

And the other voice spoke, more like a string-pull doll than something alive, "*Ma . . . ma . . . ma . . .ma.*"

He closed his hand on the doorknob.

The voice changed, faded into a whisper, then rose, and became distinctly his *own* voice, like tape-recording of himself, babbling on about past times and events he did not remember.

Something else fell.

Jerry burst into the bedroom. Mrs. Dwyer screamed and was suddenly in his arms, her nightgown rustling, her cold, thin arms clinging.

He struggled partially free and flicked on the light switch.

The two of them were alone in the room.

"Oh," Mrs. Dwyer sobbed. Merely that. "Oh."

Jerry looked around, over her shoulder. It was the first time he had ever seen the inside of her bedroom. He felt like a trespasser.

The room was like the rest of the house wildly exaggerated. The bed was a four-poster with a dusty golden canopy. Three stand-up closets stood around it, one draped with a feather boa. The doors of another hung open to reveal a faded wedding gown. The walls were covered with prints and posters of Broadway shows from long ago, and there were even crossed scimitars and a boar's head over the fireplace, the boar rather the worse for wear.

The clutter on the surfaces was awesome, like the inside of the most jammed, bizarre antique shop he had ever seen.

What surprised him more were the occult objects—a statuette of an Egyptian god, a metal hand with astrological disks on the fingertips, and even—signed to "Anna of the Light"—a photo of Aleister Crowley in magician's garb, with *666* written across his forehead.

Jerry gently led Mrs. Dwyer around the room, to reassure her, and himself, that there was no one hiding anywhere.

The source of the crashing sounds was obvious enough. A glass-fronted cabinet lay smashed across the edge of a trunk, its contents—antique china, odd Oriental figurines, porcelain dolls, silver—spilled over the floor and mostly broken.

He let go of Mrs. Dwyer. She sat on the edge of her bed, her hands over her mouth as if she were a bad child who had said too much. She stared at him with wide eyes.

He righted the cabinet. It was so heavy he could barely lift it, even with the contents dumped out.

"You've got to tell me what is going on," he said.

"I wish I could. But you'd just think me a batty old woman."

"Please . . . was it your son?"

"No, it was a dream."

"Dreams don't knock over furniture."

"Maybe mine do." She got up and nudged him toward the door. "Now scoot. Upstairs. Everything will be better in the morning."

"Don't you want me to help you clean this up?"

"Scoot."

He left reluctantly, bewildered, more than a little afraid for her—and for himself.

* * *

He got no sleep at all that night, but lay in bed with the light on, listening to Mrs. Dwyer sweeping up the broken china downstairs, and then, later, to the silence of the house, to the ticking of the clock in the first floor parlor, to the faint rattling of the pipes, to the wood creaking as the house settled. The wind had died. There was nothing more.

That morning, they gazed at each other bleary-eyed over breakfast. Neither said a word.

When the dishes were cleared away, she said suddenly, "I have to go out. I won't be back till this afternoon."

He was too numb to be suspicious. He saw the opportunity and took it.

As soon as she was gone, he started searching her bedroom, as a historian would, examining the evidence and trying to piece a story together out of the bits and scraps.

But the evidence led only to more questions. The posters and playbills dated back to the 1880s. He found a copy of *Pearson's Magazine* from 1895 with an article about one of Sarah Bernhardt's appearances in Paris checked off on the table of contents. He turned to the article. Someone had written *A memorable evening!* across the top. He discovered a sheaf of letters in a trunk, most from people he had never heard of, including a passionate proposal of marriage from a German count. There were also what seemed to be a handwritten note from George Bernard Shaw and another, addressed to "Miss Annette Dwyer," from President Ulysses S. Grant. Then again, a photograph showed a thirtyish woman who might possibly have been Mrs. Dwyer sipping drinks with Gary Cooper on a verandah overlooking Hong Kong harbor.

The chronology made no sense at all. Fascinated, he delved further and further, opening the large trunk the cabinet had fallen over, digging through heaps of jewelry—strings of pearls, a necklace of Byzantine coins, a pendant that looked pre-Columbian—and clothing until he found a bundle of notebooks tied together with ancient ribbon.

The ribbon broke in his hands. The books formed a diary. He opened the first volume and started reading, with no sense of invading someone's privacy, as if he were an archaeologist entering a tomb.

Some of the handwriting was virtually illegible: tiny, written with a quill pen, almost Elizabethan. But he skimmed through the more legible parts and concluded that the text had to be fiction. Mrs. Dwyer could not have met so many people, gone to so many places, or *lived as long* as the diaries implied.

It was quite impossible. The chronology. Everything.

He put the diaries back where he found them, wrapping them as best he could in the broken ribbon.

He felt something else underneath.

It was a scrapbook, far more convincing and terrifying for its lack of elaboration.

The first page showed a table with a high chair set at it. A bib was laid out, a baby's rattle, and a cake with one candle on it. The caption read simply, *First birthday.*

He turned the page, and again found a photo, labeled *second birthday.* A third followed, and a fourth, and so on, each of them changing as the "boy" grew older. She bought him a very old-fashioned bicycle for his fourteenth.

Then the pictures stopped.

He went back and looked at them again. Nowhere in any picture was anyone present. Just cakes, tables, gifts.

Suddenly the door to the bedroom opened and Mrs. Dwyer was there. She dropped a shopping bag onto the floor.

Jerry let out a startled squeal and jumped to his feet, spilling the scrapbook and the photos.

"I—I'm sorry. I'll just go, okay? I know I have no business here. You don't have to bother throwing me out. I'll—"

He couldn't control himself. He started to cry.

She took him gently by the hand.

"No, Jerry. Don't go. I wanted you to find all this. I wanted you to understand. Do you understand now?"

"Yes," he said, lying desperately.

She hugged him hard, and for the first time ever, kissed him on the cheek.

"It's my son's birthday tomorrow. But you know that, don't you, Jerry?"

"Yes," he said, lying again. She had never told him when her son's birthday was.

"I want you to be there."

It was one more situation, one more intrusion into the comfortable pattern of his life that he had no idea how to handle. All he could do was lie.

"Okay. But I have some things I have to do at school. Maybe if I leave real early, and take care of them in the morning—"

"That would be fine, Jerry."

* * *

Another night passed in hopeless paging through books, in even more hopeless attempts to sleep, in listening to the house, to Mrs. Dwyer talking to herself in the room below. Sometimes she was singing. The tone was wrong. It was like a string-pull doll. Sometimes she seemed to be terribly, terribly afraid, sometimes merely sad.

He finally did sleep and dreamt of the Greek soldiers in the labyrinth of the house, in the clutter of Mrs. Dwyer's room, searching for that terrible idol of the Persian king. He was pushing his way through them, desperately trying to get out, but the corridors went on and on and he could never find the door. Sometimes he heard voices through the walls, his parents speaking to him as if he were a small child, or people he knew at school; sometimes it was only the traffic noise of the city. He tried to follow those sounds. After hours of exhausting struggle, he came to a window, and his father's voice, just then, was very loud.

He opened the window and climbed through, irregardless of what storey he might be on, how far he might fall.

But there was only more corridor on the other side, and he was all but buried by Mrs. Dwyer's amazing accumulations, the books, the pictures, the dolls, jewelry, the moth-eaten boar's head.

He heard her voice now, wordless, soft, like the cooing of a dove. She was with him, right beside him. He could smell the old-age smell, and the tea steaming in her cup.

But he couldn't see her, not quite. He turned, turned again, and she was always just beyond the edge of his vision.

After a very long time, it was simply easier to remain there and listen to her.

At the very end, he was face to face with the idol, and the stone mouth spoke. But he shouted and broke the spell of the dream, and awoke before he could make out the words. Somehow he knew that if he did hear those words, he would never awaken.

He left at dawn, without showering, without breakfast, grabbing his coat and a few books to make the pretense look right. Outside, the wind was blowing hard along the narrow street and tiny specks of sleet rattled in the semi-darkness.

He wandered for a while, only barely aware of where he was. Then, later, when the day had completely dawned into bitter gray, he stood in a phone booth, fumbling through his pockets for the one plausible scrap he'd found among Mrs. Dwyer's papers.

It was a letter, dated six months previously, from someone who genuinely seemed to be her brother. There was a return address on it.

After some arguing with Information, then with a switchboard operator and a receptionist, he got through to a retirement home in the Germantown section of the city.

"Mister Dwyer, you don't know me, but I rent a room from your sister, Vanessa—"

The answer was gruff, angry. "My sister's name is Jocelyn—"

"Please, Sir, don't hang up on me. She says she used another name once. But there's this problem about her son—"

Jerry heard a sharp intake of breath at the other end of the phone connection.

"Young man, you had better come and see me right now."

* * *

Mr. Dwyer must have been in his eighties at least. He was shriveled and hunched-over, almost completely bald, and liver-spotted not merely on his hands but over most of his scalp too.

Jerry pushed Mr. Dwyer's wheelchair out onto an enclosed porch, an observation deck on the roof of the retirement home closed over with glass like a greenhouse. Before them, Fairmount Park was a black mass of leafless trees revealing the contours of hills. Far away, sullen beneath the gray sky, another castle-like mansion rose out of that dark sea, no doubt converted, like the retirement home, into some lesser use.

Beyond that, television towers stood like needles.

"What you have to understand about my sister," Mr. Dwyer said, "is that she has never gone anywhere or done anything. What you have described is merely the accumulation of a lifetime of fantasy. Those mementoes, they're all fakes. Admit it—you don't know what Noel Coward's handwriting looks like. She could easily have signed that picture herself."

"I guess so, Sir.'

"She was a dreamer as a girl, but she didn't grow out of it as she got older. She wasn't, as the kids put it today, *all there*, ever. She preferred to imagine glamorous adventures for herself rather than go out and take any risks. So she didn't do anything for real. She never dated and was an old maid by the time she was twenty-five. For a while, our parents thought of putting her in an institution, but they couldn't bring themselves to do it. So they let her dream on. It is an intensely *destructive* thing to dream like that, a soul-destroying cancer—"

"Well, yeah. Complete escapism," Jerry started to say, then hesitated, unsure of what he really was trying to say.

"No!" The old man slammed his fist onto the armrest of his wheelchair with startling vehemence. "It is *not* escapism. Someone like my sister doesn't escape. She has spent her whole life in a prison she has constructed for herself. She has buried herself alive in her own mind. I don't think you can really comprehend what she has done to herself."

"No, Sir. But I don't understand either about her son—"

He sighed and said softly, "My sister never had a son. She never married."

"Excuse me, Sir, but that's impossible. I saw—*something* knocked over the cabinet. She couldn't have done it herself. I mean, how do you explain it?"

Mr. Dwyer closed his eyes and was silent for so long Jerry thought he had gone to sleep. He gazed down at the old man with growing alarm.

"Sir?"

Mr. Dwyer opened his eyes suddenly and said, "I can't explain it. Unless you want to believe in ghosts and poltergeists. Maybe my sister is such a powerful believer that it was just what she said it was—her dreams knocked the cabinet over. Maybe she . . . *created* something with her mind."

"I can't believe that," Jerry said.

"Can't you?"

* * *

He left the retirement home slowly, walking down the stairs instead of taking the elevator. He wept for Mrs. Dwyer, for her insane, wasted life. He wept for himself.

Hours passed somehow. He remembered, vaguely, walking through endless streets, trying to reach a decision, to set himself on some definite course.

Nothing made sense. The detached observer, the historian, was at a dead end. There was only pain.

The sleet had become snow. It fell heavily, smothering the sounds of the world, closing off the city to him, little by little, as if behind curtains.

It was late in the afternoon by the time he returned home. The sky was turning a dark, metallic blue.

At last he thought he knew what he had to do.

He found her upstairs, in the bedroom, sitting on the edge of the bed.

"Mrs D?"

She didn't seem aware of him at first. She was, perhaps, listening to something faint and far away.

"Mrs. D?"

She looked up.

"I was afraid you wouldn't come."

"But I promised."

"It's . . . your birthday."

Jerry stood over her, gripping one of the bedposts firmly.

"Look. I went to see your brother. He told me everything."

"I can imagine. There would have been no surprises for me in your conversation with him."

"How can you know?"

"Jerry, do you think I *don't* know what has been going on all throughout my life? I'm not that oblivious. My brother told you that I've built a prison for myself in my mind. He used to say that a lot. Well, it's true. And if you've built a prison, brick by brick, you can't lay that many bricks without being aware of what you're doing."

"This is crazy," Jerry said. He helped her to her feet, then rummaged through one of her closets until he found a suitable winter coat for her.

"Come on. You ought to go out. I'll take you to a movie. Just get out of the house. It's time for a jailbreak."

She only muttered as he led her down the stairs, but when they neared the front door, she pulled back hard. He stopped.

"Do you know why I laid all those bricks, Jerry?"

"To avoid pain. To avoid living."

She smiled. Somehow that gentle smile was more terrible than the expression of the idol in his dream.

"We are the dead, Jerry," she said softly. "That's the whole truth of it. We were never more than half alive, you and I. We were never really born. We only entered the world part-way, then retreated, and built our own little prisons. You did. I did. You understand because you're just like me."

He took her by the arm again and dragged her toward the door.

"No. That's crazy. You're just as alive as I am."

"Exactly, Jerry."

"We have to go. Today. Now."

"Jerry, I gave birth to my son in my dreams, and raised him in my dreams, but somehow I lost that dream and he went away for a time. An old woman forgets. You can't imagine how horrible it was for me, to realize suddenly that I had inexplicably *forgotten* my dear boy. But then you came. I brought you here. I dreamed you into existence, to make my dream whole again."

They stood before the door. He fumbled with the lock. She shook her head sadly.

He spoke with desperate deliberation, to avoid tears.

"My father is Joseph Gardner. He's an electrical engineer. My mother's name is Eleanor. She teaches school. I remember—"

"I remember a lot of things, Jerry."

He considered of heaving her over his shoulder and hauling her out of the house in a fireman's carry.

"Come *on!*"

"I can't go out anymore, Jerry. Nor can you. We are the dead. There's nothing out there for us."

He let go of her and flung the door open. The cold air blasted his face. But beyond the doorstep there was nothing to be seen, not even snow. The city was gone. He stared out into gray, empty space.

He blinked and rubbed his eyes, and reached out into the void, feeling only the air.

Mrs. Dwyer was pulling in his arm. He caught hold of the doorway with one hand and held on there, just briefly, while she spoke to him softly, soothingly. He knew he was somehow drowning, dying, but in the end he let go, because it was so much easier, and he fell back with her into the endless labyrinth of the house, among the shadows and the thousand whispering voices. His death came silently. He couldn't even scream.

"Happy birthday, son," the Persian idol said.

"I love you, Mother."

Tom O'Bedlam and the King of Dreams

I

From the hag and the hungry goblin
That into rags would rend ye,
And the spirit that stands
By the naked man
In the Book of Moons defend ye.

—Traditional

If that doesn't work, alack, alas,
and something nasty comes to pass,
the sole advice that I can tell
is you should surely run like hell.

—Somewhat less traditional

Tom O'Bedlam awoke: His days were always like that, beginning with a flash, a crash, like a sunburst, in the discontinuity of his muddled mind, his diseased wit, having lost track of his five senses before he ever learned to count to four.

It was getting a bit tiresome.

For Tom O'Bedlam had been mad for many and many a year, and madness was the glory of it, yet still he had begun to feel the weight of those years, the number of them, and he heard the chattering voices of all the memories they contained.

But only just a little. Ask a madman and he will explain that mad folk do not age as do the rest of us. They are almost deaf to the stealthy footsteps of Time.

It's not enough. For stealthy Time is not entirely deaf to *them.*

And in that year when King Harry of England was resting from the arduous task of beheading wives; though he might do it again and he might not; and the ghosts of headless ladies howling through Hampton Court were becoming tedious—*ahem!*—in *that* year, King Henry rested, England rested, the headsman got a day off, but Tom O'Bedlam awoke.

He saw things clearly. That was the terror of it.

The scales fell from his eyes, and when he groped around to find them in the dazzling sunlight, he could not.

Thomas of Bedlam and his friend Nick the Gaoler, who had been Tom's keeper in Bethlehem Mercy Hospital for the Knocked-a-Brained some years before (and there was no mercy there!) until madness had liberated them both—this Tom and this Nicholas still danced in the streets of London mid-day and midnight. They stood upon their hands and ran around in circles, their toes sticking through their soleless shoes to catch the money people tossed to them. They stood like posts against gales, their colored tatters trailing like so many pennons. Their bells jangled. They spoke portentous prophecies to which, of course, no one listened.

Thus things were as they had long been, for he was *the* Tom O'Bedlam, the genuine archetype, the standard, the legend, against whom all other lunatics were measured.

But Tom's joints ached. He sprang to his step less springingly than before.

And, in one tiny corner of his mind, like a pebble dropping from the ceiling in a vast cavern, its faint sound growing and growing as it echoed, Tom O' Bedlam began to doubt.

The magnificent edifice of his lunacy cracked, just a little bit.

And One came to him, bearing an hourglass. This was in the springtime, amid the songs and festivals of May. The crowds tossed pennies. Madmen leapt through their accustomed contortions, and no one but Tom seemed to notice the terribly, terribly thin fellow with the hourglass, like a bundle of sticks come alive, his cloak so gauzy you could see right through it, though in his passage all the color seemed bleached out of the day.

This One came, in a cloud of grayness.

Tom and Nick stopped gambolling. The onlookers shrugged and went off after other amusements.

Now the houses all around seemed to nod like giants in their sleep, and shadows seemed to rise, like the bedclothes of those nodding giants, in time with their gigantic snores.

Tom and Nick were alone, in the gathering darkness at noon, and bony hands held up an hourglass, and a voice like a creaking coffin-lid cried out, "Look, look, and look well. I'm afraid you're running out of sand, as any sensible person can see."

The eyes of the speaker gaped at them, like open graves.

Tom laughed, a little nervously, and replied, "But we are *not* sensible!"

He reached out and spun the hourglass, so it tumbled end over end in its frame.

The bearer, snarling, whirled his cloak around himself and vanished in stages, like smoke from a cannon shot, slowly dissipating.

The shadows retreated. Colors returned, but grudgingly.

And people came back into that narrow street. Tom and Nick rattled their bells, but no one gave them anything.

"Just common beggars," someone said.

And Tom sat down in the mud and dreamed while he was awake, or awoke, from waking, into a higher state which cannot quite be described. A vision came to him, of the two of them struggling up a slope of pouring sand, inside an hourglass, which tumbled end over end.

He told Nick what he saw.

"I can't see it, Tom, but I believe you. I'm so afraid."

And Tom looked into Nick's eyes and beheld, not the haired-haired, wrinkle-faced person who was there now, but a child who suddenly awakened because a nightmare came galloping through his dreams.

Tom said, "Be comforted."

But Nick was not comforted.

Tom sent forth his dream, like a tide across flat sand, to touch on brighter, stranger things.

Meanwhile, a common beggar nudged him out of his reverie with an outstretched hand and said, "Give me some money."

Tom saw at once that the beggar was not mad at all, but merely wretched, one who went hungry more often than not, who slept in the gutter when he'd been chased off doorsteps, who shivered in winter's cold and would likely die there.

He took a stick from the ground and a little mud, and drew a map on the beggar's palm, where X marked the spot beneath which an old Saxon king reclined in a ship inside a mound.

"Here is gold more than you can count or carry," said Tom. "Only beware of the what sleeps with the one who sleeps," for he knew that the dragon of the king's avarice lay coiled on his dead breast like a serpent.

The beggar went away, scratching his head and staring at his palm.

Tom realized that the man was to no degree less sane than he had been before their meeting, and so was unlikely to understand the gift Tom had given him.

"Do you suppose I'm losing my touch?"

Nick looked at him, again afraid, like that child staring up out of the deep well of passing years.

"Oh Tom! Don't say such things!"

And silently, then, the seasons turned, Spring into Summer and Summer into Autumn like the shadows of turning pages of a book; and Time's footsteps were left a little ways behind; and silently Tom got up out of the mud, for all the pain in his joints or shortness in his breath; silently Tom stood, and Nick went with him, and they walked away from London until they came to a place of ancient stones.

The leaves of autumn lay all about, covering the stones and the ground. Tom and Nick stood still, their toes crunching down through the leaves into the soft earth.

The leaves stirred. A whirling wind shaped them. The Autumn King revealed himself, like a whale rising out of the sea; all red and yellow and golden were his beard and cloak in the masses of leaves.

"Haven't we met before?" said Tom.

"Aye, and this is possibly our last meeting."

The Autumn King's soldiery rose out of the leaves, their burnished armor gleaming. They moved, rustling and creaking like scarecrows made out of the husks left behind when the harvest is long since taken away. Beneath their visors were only leaves.

They lurched toward Tom and Nick in the chilling of the air.

Tom took off his hat and bowed low before the King, making a sweeping, grand gesture with his hat, and he said, "Majesty, yes, we have met before, and this may indeed be our last meeting. I cannot be sure, for, true I've felt an autumnal humour of late within me, but there is no time for us to continue this audience, alas, for it's time for Winter."

And Tom blew hard and Tom blew cold, and in the blast of his breath the

Autumn King and all his minions were blown clean away.

Tom felt smug for an instant. He held his chin in his hand and nodded sagely, muttering, "I'll miss the old bugger, you know, but he always was such a bother. Maybe this is the last time, and maybe it isn't, but I am more a windbag than he even yet."

He laughed. Nick afforded a cautious smile.

Only a madman would have believed in such things. Tom looked at Nick. Nick looked at Tom. They tried very hard to believe.

(And somewhere in the vast and haunted cavern of Mad Tom's mind, another pebble fell, rattling.)

Barefoot and wretched, shivering in the winter's snow, they made their way back to London, where no one knew them, no one turned to the sound of their jangling bells, and all the doors were shut, the windows shuttered, bolts bolted firmly in place.

"Oh Tom," wailed Nick at last. "What has all this got us?"

"It's got us where we are, not where we are not."

"And what might *that* mean?"

"Nick, I fear for you, for your madness is flaking away like ill-kept plaster, like pebbles rattling down from the ceiling in a cave, if you pause to ask what something *means*, for *mean* is for *mean*-spirited folk who take little accounts in huge ledgers and waste their souls away trying to make the numbers add up. We madmen do not *mean*. We utter cryptically and let someone else figure it out. Thus do we escape the ledgers, the figures, and hear not Time's winged chariot when one of the horses throws a shoe."

Nick hopped up and down in the cold.

"Just now all I hear is my teeth chattering."

Somewhere, in the darkness of London, a dog barked; a maiden sang; a pikeman tramped through the icy streets in iron-shod boots, thinking only of warm beer; a villain died with his throat cut and his face drowned in his soup; a poet heard the chimes at midnight and thought that'd make a good line; but where Tom and Nick were, in the empty street, beneath the shuttered windows and leaning rooftops, nothing happened at all.

And Tom began to doubt. A flash of sanity came to him, like a knife to the heart.

It came to him that the insane are merely in pain and not amusing at all, that the two of them were just dirty old frauds who would soon die in the winter's cold, that there was no transcendence in their songs, their babblings, their antics; that in all the world *things made sense* when written down in careful ledgers, in neat columns; and all dreams and fancies were like snowflakes in the dark, which may blow up against a lighted window for an instant, then drift away and are gone.

And One bearing a scythe approached them, like a smudge spreading across the snow.

Tom tipped his hat. "We have met before, Lord."

The other, all in black, his scythe gleaming, whispered. "We have, but never before have you deigned to tarry and chat. I'm flattered."

"Nor can we now, Dread Alas."

"I think you can. I pause. We converse like sensible gentlemen."

"But you have a schedule to keep. You've written it all down in neat columns, in your ledger. I only seek to remind you, Your Deathfulness, of the vast importance of your work, which cannot be stayed or delayed or frayed."

Snow whirled in the air, though the sky was clear and uncaring stars gleamed far above. Dread Alas drew back his scythe for a swing and said, "Just hold still, the two of you. This won't take a moment."

Tom, at this critical juncture, didn't know what to do. Inspiration failed him. He could only grasp at the thinnest of straws.

"But wait, Sir."

"That I cannot."

"Already speaking, you have—"

"So?"

"Now that the moment has passed, *you're behind schedule!*"

This sort of thing had worked before, for Tom knew that all the Dreads and Alases and Deaths were exacting creatures, obsessed with neatness and with schedules. There had been Cousin Snip, whom he and Nick had left in hopeless confusion by asking him how he could possibly tread too and fro in the world and up and down it if he didn't know in what order to put down his feet.

That worked, once. Tom, his invention failing, sanity pressing in on him from all sides, pebbles rattling like rain within the cavern of his mind, could only hope it would work again.

But Dread Alas merely planted his scythe in the snow, took out a notebook, flipped through the clacking pages (for they were made of bone or stone, certainly not paper), and said, "Well, there's a plague I'm supposed to be doing soon, and the numbers are plus-or-minus a few thousand, so I could work both of you in."

He snapped the book shut.

"Then again," he said, hefting his scythe, "I have an *extra* moment just now, because someone else took care of a villain I was supposed to deal with—"

It was Nick who saved them, Nick who suddenly somersaulted onto his hands and wobbled in the snow. He shouted. He gobbled like a turkey. He garbled bits of old songs. He intoned hideous prophecies, backwards so they wouldn't come true.

Dread Alas paused, puzzled.

"No time!" said Nick. "No time at all, Dreadfully, Alasfully! We cannot linger. We cannot chat or stand still for even a moment, for a *geas* is upon us, which is like a *wyrd* only weirder; and we are the two of us the bold and trusty servants, the messengers and paladins of the King of Dreams, who outranks you and your whole family—Great Auntie Death and Cousin Snip and Uncle Slice, not to mention Clotho, Lachesis, and Atropos—for do not dreams soar beyond the reach of mere fate and time and death and meaning?"

Dread Alas, who was actually just the third cousin twice removed of the youngest nephew of Lord Pluto, King of Hades, and who was only allowed to collect souls because, with all the wars and plagues going around, the family was short-handed—Dread Alas wasn't entirely sure who outranked whom. There was nothing in his notebook to clarify the matter.

He clacked through the pages forlornly.

"Well, I, uh—"

"And while you're figuring that out," said Nick, "my friend and I must be on our way, for we are on a special quest for our master the King of Dreams—"

He somersaulted backwards onto his feet, not as gracefully as he once had; in fact landing with a splash in a half-frozen puddle, but he caught hold of a post and hauled himself up and grabbed Tom by the arm. He drew him near and whispered, "Run!"

"That sounds entirely too sensible," said Tom.

"Just *run!*"

They ran as they had not run in years, through the streets and squares and courtyards of London, vaulting over fences and walls, past the tramping pikeman, who merely turned to watch as they passed; leaping over the throat-cut, soup-soaked villain who had been tossed out a window into a lane; all the while glancing back to see if they were pursued.

When they could run no further, both of them fell to the ground panting. Tom clung to Nick's shoulder and gasped, "Bless Momus and Bacchus and Gooble-Gobble-One-of-Us and all the ridiculous gods, Nick. *My* madness may have faltered, but, that was *pretty good.* You raved magnificently. I am impressed. Take cheer, Nick. Take cheer!"

But Nick took no cheer.

"What do you mean, 'faltered?'"

"I have been plagued by tremors of mundanity of late. I'm not as mad as I used to be, I fear."

"Then I fear indeed, for we are lost."

"Lost, how?"

"Found."

"What?"

"Oh, Tom, I did not rave at all. I *lied.*"

"What difference?"

"Any sane person can *lie.*"

"And they do, every day."

"Tom, all I did was stitch together a tatter of your old routines, speaking words you've spoken in the past. 'Twas but an imitation, a lifeless, strutting phantom—"

"I thought it strutted nicely—"

"Upon this stage of life, a poor player, soon to get the hook—"

So the conversation went on some while, as they shivered disconsolately, and Time's Winged Chariot completed its repairs and drew ever nearer. Once they spied a black, hooded figure with a scythe slipping in and out of the crack around the door of a house; but this was some other Death or Dread who followed a different schedule, and it did not pause to note them or to converse.

Near to dawn, as Nick was weeping for the futility of chasing after a madness which recedes like a tide over flat sand, Tom tried again to comfort him, and put his arm around him and shook him, saying, "Well, what about the King of Dreams?"

"*Is* there a king of dreams?"

"There seems to be a king of everything else."

"It's a crazy idea, Tom."

"Exactly."

It was, in fact, the thinnest of straws, but all they had to grasp at.

II

Forth from my sad and darksome cell,
Or from the deepe abyss of hell,
Mad Tom is come into the worlde againe
To see if he can cure his distempered braine.
—Traditional

Or maybe not.
—definitely a later interpolation

These were the dreams of the Saxon king, asleep beneath his mound, with the dragon of avarice curled on his breast.

These were the dreams of giants, hurled from England's shores by Brutus the Trojan long before London was born, giants who now lay grimacing in the depths of the sea, their golden teeth gleaming.

These were dreams of beggars, maidens, madmen, villains dead in their soup; of soldiers, sailors, candlestick-makers, old men in their beds and babies in their cradles, of corpses in coffins. These were the dreams of fallen leaves. Of stones.

And the King of Dreams opened his eyes, in the dark depths of that secret sea on which the world of waking men, of sane men, floats like a thin scum.

He gazed upward, intently.

He caused Tom O'Bedlam to dream once again, and he caused Tom and Nick to rise up, whether waking or dreaming they knew not; walking, waking, dreaming, they ascended, as if climbing stairs, and only a madman could have explained it, but no madman would ever try.

A miracle then.

Tom and Nick walked through the fading darkness, in the first light of dawn; and they thought they saw a King rise up beyond the edge of the world and put on a silver mask, which was the Moon, and then change it for a golden mask which was the Sun. London stirred, awakening. A wagon creaked. A dog barked yet again. The maiden, who had been singing now poured slops out a window.

Tom and Nick leapt aside nimbly enough.

They nearly tripped over the throat-cut villain yet again.

Stumbling backwards they came into street which was still dark, which was Day of Doom Street, and retreating further into the darkness, they came to a courtyard, or a Close, which was Day of Doom Close, and Tom and Nick did not doubt it.

They came to a door, whereon was painted a grinning, bone-faced harlequin.

"I think we belong here," said Tom.

He pressed the door open. It creaked like a coffin-lid. The two of them made their way down cold, stone steps onto a rough wooden floor. The room around them was dim, shadowy. Dust motes danced in flickering candlelight. Boards creaked. Nick jumped back, startled at some sound or some movement. He bumped into an array of glass bottles, which crashed to the floor.

"Now look what you've done!" someone shouted. "Look! Don't just stand there! Help me clean up the mess!"

The speaker was an old man with a long, tangled beard. He wore a robe like a wizard's, with moons and stars embroidered in it, but stained and in worse repair than any wizard would tolerate. In his hand he held a thin, clay flask. Something steamed in there. It might have just been tea.

Tom looked around for a broom or a mop. Nick started to gather fragments of glass in his hand.

"Oh, never mind! The work of centuries ruined! Elixir vitae, the universal solvent—which dissolves itself and so transcends matter—the fluids of transmutation and transfiguration and transmigration, all wasted, spilled down through the floor to make the mice drunken. What does it matter? I was hoping for maybe a couple of Salamanders of Eternity to come traipsing through that door."

"Sorry," said Nick.

"You two don't happen to be Salamanders?"

Tom touched himself here and there, as if to make sure he was still who he had been the last time he checked. "No. Sorry."

"We thought, because of the sign on the door, that this was a haven for the mad," said Nick.

"Oh, *that.* That's just to scare off obnoxious tradesmen and peddlers. I can't stand such tiresome, mundane folk."

"Oh."

"But sometimes I think I *am* mad."

"There's a great future in it," said Tom. "Very promising." (And as he spoke he thought he was lying, as Nick had lied, just repeating snatches of old routines. But somehow he couldn't quite *dis*believe everything he said, and he clung to that single straw.)

"But you're not exactly, quite, *mad*, are you?" said Nick.

"No, I am the next best thing. I am an alchemist. Fred the Alchemist, at your service. Afeared Frederick, my detractors call me. As long as you're here, you might as well have some breakfast."

Though madmen such as Tom and Nick were widely reputed to live on air, the bread and broth and beer the alchemist offered them were most welcome. (Though Tom had a vision of a tiny version of himself floating face-down in the soup, a thin stream of a darker fluid leaking off to one side.) They sat around a wooden table. Fred pushed aside books and bottles and assorted clutter to make room for them. A homunculus wriggled out of a flimsy box and flopped off the edge of the table, onto the floor. A stuffed crocodile suddenly came to life and followed after.

Tom noticed that the floorboards where the bottles had spilled earlier were now gleaming gold.

"That's an old trick," said Fred. "It fails to impress after a while."

"I know some who'd be impressed," said Nick.

"A vulgar thing for vulgar minds."

"Not to mention vulgar purses," said Tom.

"Exactly," said the alchemist. He put his hands on Tom and Nick's shoulders, and drew the three of them together into a huddle. "I see, gentlemen, that we are all of like minds, not the same, but similar enough. I think you are sent to me for a purpose, there being a destiny that shapes our ends, transplant them, water them, put white picket fences around them as we may—"

"Uh, Tom—" said Nick.

"We are sent by the King of Dreams," said Tom, not entirely lying, as a certain inspiration came to him again. "It is our quest."

"For what?" said Afeared Fred.

"We're not sure. We're getting to that."

"Uh, Tom—" said Nick, with rising urgency.

"No matter," said Fred. "We three are brothers, like knights on an adventure. We will share this quest. Oh! How wonderful!"

"I'm wondering," said Tom.

And Fred the alchemist told them, at great length, with much explication and consulting of arcane volumes, pointing to illustrations and strange woodcuts, how he was on a quest of his own, through his alchemy, for the Ideal, that perfect beauty which exists beyond all mortal things, beyond time and eternity. He had seen her once, from afar, in his youth, but glimpsed her in the form of an ineffably beautiful maiden, and now, many years later, after much hardship and poverty and sorrow, he was no closer than ever to regaining that vision. ("What a crazy thing to do," said Tom, and he too saw the alchemist as a brother.) But the alchemist hadn't given up. Even if the Salamanders of Eternity he had been attempting to conjure hadn't shown up on schedule, there was always tomorrow, always the night after that, always a page to be turned, a concoction to be concocted, a casting to be cast—

"We shall swear our souls to this end!" cried Fred. "Yes, yes, like one of those knights at Camelot when the Holy Grail came floating into the room during the Pentecost feast and everybody got second helpings. Yes! Yes!"

"Yes!" said Tom, and he was much heartened, and hopeful again, for this was genuine madness.

"Uh, *Tom!*" Nick yanked at Tom's arm and turned him around and pointed.

There at the bottom of the stairs, standing in the middle of the golden floorboards like an enormous copybook blot, was One in the familiar black, hooded robe, with regulation scythe, hourglass and notebook. Only this One was taller than the rest, more massive (though you could see through him, like a wisp of dark cloud), and Tom somehow knew that this wasn't any junior cousin three times removed, or elderly auntie or doddering Great-Great-Grandfather Rigor Mortis, but the King of Reapers ("I'm always meeting royalty," Tom said to himself), Catastrophicus Maximus, the boss, the one in charge, to whom even the Four Horsemen of the Apocalypse referred their more difficult cases.

"I have come for you all," spoke a voice like an earthquake. Plaster and small stones rattled down from the ceiling as the room shook.

"He's been around before," said Fred. "Such a bother." He got up and struck at the newcomer with a broom. "Shoo! Scat!" The broom passed right through, as through a shadow.

"I don't think that's going to help," said Nick.

The alchemist sat down slowly, despairing.

"I guess not. It's not fair. I was *that* close—"

Catastrophicus Maximus put his hourglass down on the table. Within, Tom could make out tiny figures of himself, Nick, and Fred the Afeared swimming desperately against the sand, which had almost completely drained from the upper chamber of the hourglass.

Holding his scythe under one arm, Catastrophicus Maximus paged through his notebook. The pages crashed together, like muted thunder, each of them a gravestone with a name and date already written on it. Tom had seen such a thing before. He suspected it was standard issue. The pages turned, one by one. He looked for the one with his name on it.

"Ah, here we go." More plaster fell. A large piece fell directly through the specter's head and hit the floor with a crash. Catastrophicus Maximus glanced up, irritated, then resumed. "Yes, here. A blank page. I can write the three of you in immediately. No delays, no excuses, no frills. *Now!*"

And the creature's skeletal forefinger began to glow, and he started writing.

"But our quest," said Tom.

"We have dreams to dream yet," said Nick.

"I'm still waiting for those damned Salamanders," said Afeared Fred. "They were supposed to help. I had hoped to attain the Ideal."

"I'll add a footnote to that effect," said Catastrophicus Maximus, who continued writing.

Tom looked at Nick. Nick looked at Tom. Tom shrugged. There was nothing left for it, nothing he could do, but one reflex, little more than a spasm.

He flipped over the hourglass and set the double-chamber tumbling. Sand poured up, and down, and up. The tiny figures within vanished.

"STOP THAT!!!" The whole house trembled and swayed like a thing alive. A heavy timber snapped and came crashing down through the table. It was all Catastrophicus Maximus could do to snatch his hourglass out of harm's way. He dropped his notebook. His scythe went clattering through a shelf of bottles and jars. Wriggly, glowing things with half-human faces, misplaced eyes, and voices entirely innocent of key or harmony flopped onto the floor, singing an insipidly cheerful anthem, which enraged Maximus all the more. He stomped ineffectually, his footsteps too light to be heard or have much effect under the circumstances.

Tom looked at Nick. Nick looked at Tom. They both looked at Fred, who grabbed them both by the arms and hauled them out of there. "Run!" he said.

They ran, Tom and Nick following Fred. Catastrophicus Maximus had recovered his scythe. One long swing cut through the walls of the room. The rest of the ceiling caved in. An enormous bed with a fat lady in it dropped into the room. "Ooh! I'll raise your rent for this!" she squealed, but by then Fred and the others were out the opposite end of the room and struggling up a narrow, twisting passage to a cramped landing which afforded no refuge, then up another stair, and another, until at last they burst out onto the roof, from which there was no place to go.

A wooden tub with a mast and sail set in it rocked on swaying sawhorses at the edge of the roof.

They could hear the footsteps of Catastrophicus Maximus drawing nearer now, stamping furiously up the narrow stair.

The wooden tub had a name written on it: *H.M.S. Folly.*

Tom and Nick looked at Fred, who said quickly, "We *are* all fools, aren't we?"

Without further ado, the three of them clambered aboard.

A familiar, hooded figure emerged onto the roof. The great scythe swung back.

Fred unfurled the sail, which filled with wind. "Heave to, boys! Heave to! At times like this I think I'm losing my mind."

"That's good!" said Tom. "Very good!"

And he dared to hope even more.

They heaved, all three of them throwing their weight to one side. The *H.M.S. Folly* tottered, then fell over the side of the roof.

And only a madman could have expected what came next. They didn't crash into the street below. Instead, a burning golden cloud seemed to fill the whole world. The *H.M.S. Folly* rose, slowly, through the cloud until the light above them was almost too much to look upon. Tom shaded his eyes, and could barely make out the huge mask of the Sun which was worn by the King of Dreams, and he more imagined than saw the vast eyes behind that mask gazing down on him, with benevolence, even with fondness.

He knew then that he was healed, that his madness was once again complete.

He sang for the King of Dreams in the special language of lunatics.

Nick joined in.

Fred remarked, "I think I can make some of that out."

"Good!" said Tom. "Very good!"

The King of Dreams set aside his mask of the Sun and put on the tarnished and spotted silver mask of the Moon. The *H.M.S. Folly* sailed on a sea of swirling stars, beneath a moonlit sky.

There was a faint thunder, far behind. Tom turned once, and saw a black-robed figure swimming in the stars, considerably encumbered by his scythe and his hourglass. A wave of stars washed over him, and he was gone.

The wooden tub came to rest on a glowing shore. There, as heroes of old, Tom and Nick fought and slew a dragon, whose name was Doubt or Dread or

Reason, or perhaps all three. They came to a cottage where an old lady was scrubbing all the color out of people's lives, making them dull, drab, and melancholy, storing the colors thus pilfered in clay jars, carefully sealed and numbered. Tom, Nick, and an increasingly less fearful Fred rushed in, shouting, and spilled a shelf of jars. They left bright smears and handprints everywhere, while Mother Sereda shrieked and chased after them with a broom, which passed right through them as if she were trying to beat away the light that streams in through suddenly opened shutters.

There, in the Land of Dreams, which is beyond the reach of Time, the place of the marvelous, the impossible, the mad, they met an honest politician, a generous rich man, and a merciful judge, who led them up a hillside, as a young girl fell from the Moon. As they neared, they saw her descending, like a shooting star at first, then more gently, like a luminous leaf settling to earth. They came upon her as she lay amid the grasses, her face like a perfect pearl, her long hair trailing in the wind like finest silk.

And Fred the Alchemist knew her, for she was the Ideal, some village girl he had known long ago when he was a boy and had loved from afar. But of course this was not the girl herself, only the perfect image of her he had formed in mind and memory and dream.

The alchemist became that boy again, his youth regained. He and the girl sailed away over the star-sea in the wooden-tub ship, and vanished from sight as the King of Dreams in his lunar mask began to set below the horizon, until only his eyes and forehead were still showing.

Now the others were gone. Tom and Nick stood alone on the shore.

The Moon continued to set.

Nick suddenly shouted, "Hey! What about us?" but Tom hushed him.

A wind blew between the stars, over the rippling sea, and on the wind came the voice of the King of Dreams, who said, "I am a lie, but you have dreamed me, and so I am also true. Therefore, be rewarded."

He reached up with his golden hands and broke an hourglass as if it were an egg, and golden sand came raining down.

Tom and Nick fell, down through the stars, the golden sand swirling around them. It seemed they viewed a thousand years at once, and saw many things even a madman could not put into words. There was an impossible version of London where gleaming towers seemed to float above a layer of soiled clouds, and great metal birds roared overhead. Though this was the sort of vision madmen might properly have, they turned away, and swam back through the centuries toward the London they knew. Once they passed Catastrophicus Maximus, who was completely helpless without his hourglass. He fluttered his arms uselessly.

They paused once to save England from a great, lumbering fleet of ships, like dark castles under sail, sent forth by a monarch who knew not dreams or fancies or joy, only misery and fear, which he wanted to share; but Tom and Nick borrowed lanterns from the Man in the Moon and walked upon the waters of the North Sea, and they directed the ships as one directs traffic, pointing to say, *You, that way!* and *You! Over there!* and so the ships of Philip of Spain were scattered.

They saw an England which became great, ruled by one called the Fairie Queen.

But this was not the place for them. Not quite.

The King of Dreams spoke to them one last time, saying, "Be not aged. Fear not death. For you are impossible yourselves. You are dreams. Therefore exist as dreams."

And they regained their youth and found themselves back in the London they had known when they were young, before King Harry had whacked off even one queen's head.

They landed with a thump in the middle of a crowded street.

Some sort of procession was passing by. There were richly-clad nobles, guards, bishops. Then, in a fine carriage, the King, with his first queen, who, at that time, he still loved.

"You!" someone shouted. "This is no place for beggars. Be off."

But Tom bowed low, with a grand, graceful sweep, and then explained himself, blurting out all at once of his adventures and how he had, incidentally, saved an England not yet born. Not that he expected any reward for that. It was all in a day's work.

"Oh, I see! You're *mad!* Here's a penny for you!"

Tom stood on his hands. He caught the penny between his toes.

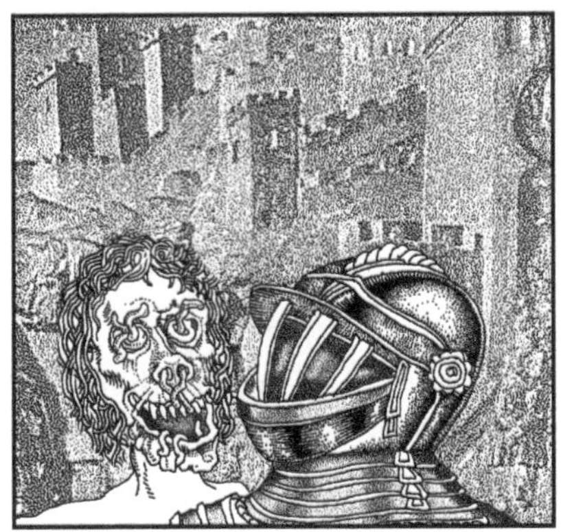

The Invisible Knight's Squire

When he came in the night, crashing through the door of my humble abode amid howling wind and freezing rain, I thought he was a thief after my cloak or my shoes. The loss of either would have meant death: pain, then numbness, then black rot. But I didn't have time to explain all this.

"Silence, boy!" he thundered at me, and his voice seemed to shake the earth; and I started to choke on my own words even as he seized me and shook me and I never got to explaining that he had no business calling me a boy because I, look, look, I had a scraggly something that could pass for a beard—

He yanked on it, as if he knew my thought, and said, "Ha! It takes more than chin-hairs to make a man. Therefore I command you. Silence!"

But there was no silence as he shook the splinters of the door off himself and advanced, like a victorious army into a doomed castle, and my hovel echoed with words I couldn't understand.

I fought. My fists bounced uselessly off his iron self like stones rattling down a mountainside.

My fingers found his visor. Then iron fingers crushed my wrists.

"Don't you *ever—*" he said without need to finish.

He forced me to sit on a stack of my priceless books. I fell over, in a heap. He crouched beside me, armor creaking and groaning. He rummaged among the books and tossed a heavy volume aside as if it were trash.

"What are you?" he said.

"What are *you?*"

"I asked first," he said. "Answer." His sword slid from his scabbard, rasping.

"For God's sake, let me light a candle first," I said.

"For God's sake, I command you, do not."

I was very afraid then, fearing for my worthless life and soul. What kind of devil was this, who would strike me dead if I beheld him?

I heard him sigh and settle down, as a man might, and for an instant dared to hope that he wasn't a devil at all, just a madman, and we could all be madmen together, he and I and whoever might listen to our story, and we might weep and laugh, trilling snatches of wordless songs, beyond all hope and pain.

But he merely said, "What are you?"

I was angry then. I didn't care if he cut me in half.

"I'm just a poor student, studying to be a misanthrope. These are my texts. The one you have so barbarously handled is called *On Hating Mankind* by Isaac of Edessa. I have here also *The High and Holy Romance of Sir Flibberdeygibbet—*"

He grabbed me by the collar, from behind. Maybe he was a phantom after all. He wasn't where I expected him to be, and I hadn't heard him move. I felt his blade slide gently across the side of my neck.

"That tells me nothing—" His breath was hot, but not sulfurous. He was, then, more likely a madman than not. Of course, with the knights of the Round Table traipsing all over England in search of the damned Grail these days, madmen in armor were as common as starlings.

"A hermit, then, let us say."

"A *holy* hermit, who will cleanse the wounds and heal the soul of an errant and erring knight, who will point me in the direction I have to go if I am to achieve my quest?"

I gulped, and said slowly. "I'm afraid God hasn't had much to do with me of late."

"*Boy!* You blaspheme! But I forgive you. For in blasphemy you are human, capable of sinning and therefore of redemption."

I didn't try to follow the theological acrobatics of that argument, but I was relieved when he put his sword away.

Rain and sleet rattled on the remains of my door. Water poured down. I scrambled to put all my books into their leather bags, to protect them. As I did, I heard my visitor stirring, creaking in his armor. Once he was whispering something. Possibly he was praying, as madmen often do with such intensity.

He grabbed me again and hauled me to him as if I were a rag doll, and said, "*God* sent me to you. *You* appeared to me in my vision, and I was led to this place. But it is a condition of my vision, or curse, or quest, or whatever you want to call it that I must remain as one invisible until my soul is healed of its grievous wounds. Now you may think this amusing, or the intriguing premise for a really good romance of chivalry full of poetic flourishes, but *I assure you*, that it is more than that, it is a hard, miserable affair, filled with suffering, a purgatory on Earth. *Theophanes*, you must swear to serve me as my squire. *Theophanes*, I am sent to you by God."

I was afraid again, for I had not told him my name.
And all the while he was with me, he never told me his.
I could only say, "What does God want with me?"
"You'll have to ask him."

* * *

That was how it all began. I swore to serve him as his squire and broke my word as soon as I could. That night I shared with my knight a meager repast, bread as hard as wood and cheese not much better, and a little wine, and he bade me clean his armor for him; so he took off that armor and withdrew a little ways off, while my hands did their work and my mind turned and turned and my anger grew.

He had intruded on my private suffering. He would not allow me to be miserable in my own way. I hated him for that.

I cleansed his sword, too, and thought of killing him with it.

Then, in the darkness, he showed me how to strap his armor back onto his body, piece by piece. I felt that he wore a hairshirt. I said nothing about it. In that hairshirt, in that armor, he slept.

In the first gray light of dawn, I looked at him, all in a heap against the wall, beneath my ruined roof, and I bethought me, *This is not a man, much less a devil, but a pile of junk.* And I violated, first, the secondary part of my oath to him, that I would never look on his face. I couldn't resist the temptation. I crept over to him and raised his visor, then drew back, not entirely amazed when I saw that there was no one there.

It was a pile of junk.

I thought to gather up his armor, take it into the nearest village, and try to sell it, but I was afraid to do that. I did not touch the armor again. Instead, more sensibly, I gathered up my books and my blanket and stole out into the morning drizzle.

I robbed my knight only of a jeweled poniard and of a purse of coins.

I walked for hours. I must have lost my way. I didn't want to go back to any village anyway, for, I told myself, a misanthrope is one who despises mankind, and I was a misanthrope, wasn't I? Not a holy hermit, not someone blessed or cursed or capable of stumbling into visions.

It is said that fools and sinners sometimes turn into saints, but I wasn't about to let that happen. I had that much control over my life still.

If I could find one deserted charcoal-burner's shed, I could always find another. If I found one still inhabited by a charcoal-burner, I could always read poetry at him and drive him away, for base mankind cannot bear the sound of true beauty.

I walked, and my adventures began in the cold and the rain.

First, wolves gathered around me, their eyes burning, their breath like smoke, and the wolves spoke among themselves, saying, "*Behold, here is the false squire, through whom we can work his master's destruction.*"

I tried to tell them that I wasn't a squire at all.

The wolves followed me, like hounds after a huntsman, and we came to a clearing where white doves rested upon a stone. The wolves looked to me, as if for a command perhaps, but I said nothing to them, and the wolves leaped forward as one, seizing the doves in their teeth, rending them, until their snouts were covered with blood.

And I saw that the stone in the clearing was carven with the image of a knight, lying as in a tomb. Then, though it seemed but an hour or two past dawn, again the sky was fully dark, and sleet rattled through the trees. Wolves crouched all around, feasting. The tomb opened up, grinding. I couldn't see, but there was a combat in the darkness, as if many knights contended together. Metal clanged, and the only light was the occasional spark, by which I glimpsed a huge man in battered armor fighting against many foes, whose helmets were shaped like the snouts of wolves.

I tried to run away, but it was like pushing against an avalanche; and one of the wolf-knights bore me down and tore at me with fangs and claws. I rolled and swatted him with my book-bag, and felt my cloak torn away. I cried out for help then, and I am sure I would have died had not some immense force ripped the wolf-knight away. I heard a yelp, and bones crunching.

Then there was silence again, in the darkness.

And in the darkness, my invisible knight and I made camp. He sat far back beneath an overhanging tree while I struggled to get a fire started in the rain, couldn't do it, and prepared our supper cold.

He would not eat of it until I was finished. That was odd. We two sat in absolute darkness, in the cold and rain. I could smell his sweat and the almost sweet odor of wet leather and iron.

"You could not have found your way out of the Endless Forest by yourself," he said at last, "for it is made anew by the sins and errors of mankind and races before us like a tide."

I launched into a geographical discourse, about the absurdity of having an Endless Forest here in the isle of Britain, but he said to me, in a voice of infinite weariness, "Just shut up, Theophanes. Be instructed by the silence. If you cannot do that, at least tell me the tale of your own deeds, and how you came to be where I found you."

For once I had very little to say. I told him that Theophanes was not my real name, just a literary affectation.

"I knew that already, Petrus, son of Dagdanec," he said.

And I told him how I was the youngest of five sons to the Duke of a country so small no one has ever heard of it.

"It is called Aquilae," he said, "the Country of the Eagle."

I, the youngest and least favorite son of the Duke Dagdanec of the Eagle Land, who failed at chivalry through clumsiness or cowardice or a bit of both, who was filled with pride nonetheless, who sought fame as a poet, who composed exquisite verses I fed into the fire nightly out of sheer mean-spiritedness—

"Are you sure they're as exquisite as all that?" he said.

In my pride I appeared before the whole court and told them I was leaving them, whether my father said yea or not, and was bound for Camelot, where I would become bard to King Arthur himself. I recited for them, unworthy though they were, some of the epic I had been composing.

"And they laughed," said my invisible knight.

They fidgeted in their seats, politely silent, for I was, after all, still their lord's son, every once in a while glancing in my direction, and then the laughter began with *Jeshute*, the beautiful *Jeshute*, whom I had loved from afar, a lady of high estate herself, who served my mother the Duchess, this *Jeshute* to whom I dedicated my many and exquisite verses—

"Before you got into the habit of burning them—"

"*She laughed*, and it broke my heart utterly, and all goodness was drained out of me, all faith in God, all *everything*—"

Then, to my amazement, he touched my hand tenderly, as if to comfort me, and he said, "That is truly a great tale of striving, of suffering, of heroic deeds, of temptations and a fall, as mighty as any recorded in the annals of chivalry—"

I drew away. "You ridicule me!"

"I swear to you Petrus, who would rather be called Theophanes, upon mine honor as a knight, that I do not ridicule your pain, which is to you as great as mine is to me, for losses great and small are as one before the eyes of God, if we allow ourselves, as the Enemy counseled Job, to *despair and die*. Therefore I command you, despair not, and live."

"Will you tell me your own story?"

"When it is time. Be patient."

We sat in the darkness. I felt my leather bag. It was empty.

"I've lost my books!" Doubtless they had fallen out in the struggle with the wolf-knights. I got up to search for them, but my knight hauled me back.

"You don't need any of them. Not even Isaac of Edessa."

Soon I was so cold, I barely managed to gasp, "Master! I'm freezing. I'll die."

He took me in his hard, metal arms, as a father might embrace his son, and said only, "Be comforted. You shall not die, for a knight must look after his squire even as a squire must look after his knight."

A strange warmth arose from him, like gentle fire, and I slept, and dreamed, or perhaps awoke from one lunatic dream into another.

* * *

I began to think of him as *my knight*, as if I truly were his squire, though I betrayed him again at the first opportunity.

It happened like this:

I awoke, as I said, from one dream, of darkness, into another, of light and warmth.

I was on a ship, in the bright day, surrounded by golden mist.

I stirred. The empty armor which still embraced me fell away into a heap. I looked up, but suddenly a maiden's voice spoke, commanding me to look *down*, to tend to my master's needs.

"But he's not here—" I started to protest.

"Petrus, would you deny him twice?"

And I was afraid again, for my name, my name was known here, too, though I had not told it. Twenty maidens in gowns of white samite danced in a circle around the mast of the ship to some impossible music I could *feel* but never quite hear, while the mast held up the slowly turning, golden sky as if it were the Axle of the World.

Seeing as much, of course, I had disobeyed. But I did not see any of the maidens' faces, because there was a light or glamour about them which my eyes could not penetrate.

Looking down at last, I found cloths and oils and such tools as I needed, and I cleansed and repaired my knight's armor, wiping away his own blood and that of his foes.

After a time, one of the maidens knelt down to offer me bread and wine, and I took them, and refreshed myself. She bade me gaze away from her, while she told me of my knight's adventure, how he had come to a castle of maidens, all of them dressed in white and wearing masks of white fire so he could not see their faces. They cried out to him, whether in fear or joy he knew not; and whether he was to rescue or ravish them remained uncertain to all concerned; and a giant strode out of the castle, to challenge him or make him welcome no one ever knew; and the two of them fought, bravely and fiercely and long; and the giant opened his huge mouth and bade the knight to leap in, and the knight leapt, devoured by the giant, but, led on in the darkness by the thunderous drumming of the giant's heart, he struck with his sword again and again until blood flowed around him like a burning sea—

And it was then that I realized that the maiden spoke with the voice of *Jeshute*, she whom I had loved, and she was not mocking me now, I was certain. *She* would rescue me from this slightly ridiculous predicament, and we would laugh about it while I formed the tale into a beautiful and somewhat satirical romance, feeding only the uninteresting parts into the fire, the parts I would have otherwise shared with the world. The core of the story, the pearl beyond price, I would write out for *Jeshute* alone, to treasure in secret.

And it was then that I caught her by the wrist, and pulled her toward me, and lifted the glowing veil from her face, and made to kiss her in the full expression of my love—only she was foul, and shrunken, her face filled with worms.

I cried out in disgust.

She wept black, muddy tears, and gasped in a coarse and broken voice, "Petrus, traitor, you've done it again."

* * *

I awoke then, to the sound of wind and of sleet rattling on the ruined roof of my hovel.

I sat up. I coughed long and hard, for the cold was settling into my lungs. Possibly I coughed up blood.

My knight stirred beside me.

Bewildered beyond all words, I groped about for my books. Even if I couldn't read them in the darkness, and my knight had forbidden me light, at least I could heft the familiar masses of useless verbiage, and take comfort from that.

"You're looking for Isaac of Edessa," my knight said. "But don't you remember? You lost him on your journey."

"But we haven't gone anywhere."

"Oh no, my dear and foolish Petrus. Already we have travelled very far."

I huddled beneath my only blanket, miserable and afraid, while my knight told me of his many adventures and sufferings. They assumed a certain sameness: the loneliness of the quest, terrible wounds acquired while battling black or red knights, monsters. My memories became uncertain, and I was somehow sure that I had been in his service all throughout his adventures; and on a thousand different occasions he had departed unseen from my abode upon his quest, then returned, that I might repair his armor and prepare his meals and cleanse his wounds.

"Chivalry is pain," he said to me. "Pain in the service of mankind."

"Who are you serving?"

"Myself, I suppose." He laughed bitterly, but not, out of despair. Like Job he refused to merely curse God and die, and, however grudgingly, I had to admire him for that. "And whom do you serve, Petrus, called Theophanes?"

"The . . . muses."

"You serve them by feeding your poetry into the flames?"

"That is perhaps my greatest service to them."

And my laughter was like his, tottering on the edge of despair without quite falling into the abyss. It echoed through the darkness in the Forest of Errors.

The episode in which I had been Dagnenac's brat, youngest son of the Duke of Nowhere You've Ever Heard of, *that* was the illusion. I was not the poet dreaming himself to be the squire, it seemed, but the squire dreaming, briefly, that he had been, in fact, a wretched poet, whose works deserved the flames.

I understood, too, that I had contributed to my knight's wounds by my treason. Each time I embraced falsehood, I drew him away from his goal.

Yet he held me in his arms as a father would, and he comforted me. I started to drift off into sleep once more.

"What are you questing for?" I asked him. "The Grail? Everybody seems to be looking for the Grail . . ."

He rocked me back and forth, and he wept softly, and I was both amazed and embarrassed as he bared his soul to me, as if to a confessor.

"Oh, I had the Grail at the very beginning," he said.

I shook myself fully awake.

"You *found* it?"

"No, no, good Petrus. I *saw* it, as we all did, on that terrible Pentecost, when the Grail floated through the room in a cloud of mystical light; and each man was satisfied with perfect wine and whatever meat he most desired, and a voice spoke to us in thunder, proclaiming, *Seek this, for the renewal of the land and the forgiveness of sins, that ye shall be made whole once again.* And Arthur wept, because he knew we were all sinful men, and most of us would perish on the quest. I think he even begged God take this cup away from us, but God did not. Meanwhile, I was perhaps a bit drunk from too much of that perfect wine we'd had—for our cups, miraculously, did not empty throughout the whole experience, no matter how many times we drank—and I thought, *I'll save us all a lot of trouble,* and I got up from the table and tried to seize the Grail right then and there. I actually *touched* it, and my hand was burned—if I were not invisible you could see the scar—and miraculously, too, I became invisible, not merely to the eye, but to the *mind.* I am forgotten, Theophanes, by all but God himself. No other knight would recognize my name now. To King Arthur I am perhaps a dream which leaves him uneasy upon awakening, though he has forgotten what he has dreamed. My name is not to be found in the chronicles, for *I have no name,* not even to myself. I too, have forgotten it, though God has not forgotten me, and he speaks to me often, in visions, and he directs me on the course of my penitential quest."

"But to what end?" I asked him at last. "How will you be redeemed?"

And then he said something more which pierced me to the very soul, and made me more afraid than ever, made me long for madness, that we two could be mad together and this might be no more than a lot of thunder and babbled nonsense.

"By the treason of another," he said.

* * *

The next morning it was still raining. I felt cold and sick and exhausted from a thousand adventures I couldn't remember, as if I had suffered wounds in every one of them. And I saw before me on the floor a disorderly heap of junk, which was my knight's armor, without him in it.

My hands knew what to do. I no longer sought Isaac of Edessa, whom I had lost in the forest. Instead I repaired and cleansed my master's armor, as a squire should.

During that day, I was tempted three times.

Jeshute came to the door, her face veiled in light.

"Fly away with me," she said. "Leave this."

"Begone," I said. And she was gone.

A giant came to the door, so huge that I could see only his eyes when he leaned to peer in.

"Follow and serve *me*," he said, "and I shall keep you in every comfort."

"My master is greater than you," I said, "and I care not for comfort."

"Indeed you do not," said Isaac of Edessa, who was my third temptation. The ancient philosopher stood before me, his filthy animal-skins soaked with rain, reeking. He handed me his book, saying, "You are swept along by that great river which is human striving. What you've got to do is climb up onto the bank and dry yourself out."

"It's raining," I said. "The roof leaks. Begone."

I cannot say when my soul changed, but it did, either then or earlier in the course of the many adventures I only remembered when my knight told me of them. Perhaps I, too, had been at Camelot and witnessed his fateful, fatal lunge for the Grail, and I too had become invisible with him. All I can say is that in the darkness of the returning night I heard his armor stir, as if filled by a wind, and then my knight was with me, and he put his hand beneath my arm and lifted me to my feet, saying, "Come, good squire, it is time for us to set out on our adventure."

And we mounted two steeds which awaited us beyond the door, he a huge, black charger, I a smaller mare. We rode, not in the darkness through the Forest of Error in the rain, but by pale moonlight, across the Waste Land, where ash stretched to the horizon in all directions.

We came to a plain of bare stone, beneath the moon and the pale white stars, and the hooves of our horses threw off sparks like fading meteors. I saw my master knight beside me, huge as any giant, or I saw his armor anyway, which was given to me to see. His visor was down. I could not—I did not attempt to—gaze within and see his eyes.

"Look, there," he said at last, pointing.

We reined our steeds and waited as one of the stars fell from the sky and touched the horizon, then drove toward us; and I saw that it was not a star all, but a champion in silver armor, wearing a mask of light; and somehow I knew, that however beautiful or striking his appearance might be, this was our foe, whom we must overcome if we were ever to complete our quest.

The silver knight circled. I saw that he had many faces, and none, the light of his mask shifting to form the face of a man, and a wolf, and a dragon, and even a maiden. He called to me in my father's voice, in Jeshute's, in Isaac of Edessa's, even in that of my master the invisible knight, but he spoke nothing and his voice was the wordless wind.

He circled, taunting. My master lowered his lance and the other lowered his. They crashed together. The lances broke. They smote one another with their swords. Sparks flew like stars. I drew my own weapon, the jeweled poniard I had once stolen, and tried to join in the combat.

But the silver knight unhorsed me with the backward sweep of his hand.

Then he and my master were far away, pursuing, turning, fighting.

I couldn't find my horse. I think I was blinded for a time, from blood where the enemy knight's hand had struck my forehead.

But I knew what I had to do. I followed, on foot, across the stone waste. Once I waded in red blood up to my knee. Once I walked upon the surface of a raging sea, but I did not sink. I came to a golden barge, and heard maidens singing, and the sea was calm. I saw my master and his foe lying in the barge as if they were both dead. I went to tend my master, but he raised himself on his elbow and pointed to the other and said, "Heal him first, for he is more hurt than I."

And I touched the other, and he was healed. We sailed together to an island, which rose like a black hump out of the sea. There was a white castle, in which the maidens dwelt. We feasted, though my master and his foe feasted behind a curtain, lest anyone see them. I heard them speaking together, not in anger or with taunts, but as if they were old friends.

I drank of heavenly wine, and ate of the perfect meat, and the room filled with light.

But when I got up from the table, there was only darkness, and I fell like a stone down a deep well, and found myself in the cold in the dark, inside my old hovel, in the forest.

Almost without thinking, I lit a candle.

I cried out at what I saw.

The silver knight sat astride my master. He had seized him by the throat, and shook him again and again, until I was certain he'd broken my master's neck.

"No!" I cried out, "You shall not slay him!"

I dropped the candle and drew my stolen poniard. I plunged it into the silver knight's back. I let out a great cry. *He* was silent. I twisted the blade, plunging it deeper. I didn't care if this was chivalrous or not.

And silently, he died, or merely ceased, for he collapsed into a pile of junk. There was no corpse, only old and crumbling scraps of metal.

I swept them away. I relit my candle. I leaned down to touch my master's visor.

He spoke. I drew my hand back. What he said didn't make any sense at first.

"You've still got my purse of coins."

I thought he was delirious.

"Of course I knew that all along," he continued, "but I thought as my treasurer, holding my wealth for safekeeping. Now, I think, as you go on, you will need it more than I. The poniard proved useful too, I see."

I wept then, and reached for his visor, to raise it.

"Petrus, would you betray me three times?"

"Yes," I said, between my sobs, "I would. I can't help it." I said this because I knew somehow that he was already dead.

So, did I betray him?

I raised his visor. The face there was fully visible. It was that of an ordinary man, with gray in his beard, his features lined by privation and pain.

I just wanted to see.

This was holy treason, committed out of love.

* * *

And what then? Say only that I awoke. Say that the dream of the Endless Quest raced forward like a tide. Say that I bore my master into the forest, until I reached a clearing where once we had battled the wolf-knights around a stone, on which was carven the image of a knight in repose. Say that I carved that image myself, somewhere in the course of my adventures, and that it was Petrus called Theophanes whom I buried beneath it, for surely he ceased to exist that day, and I, who wore my master's hairshirt and armor, who impersonated him in all things, went forth upon his quest. He, of course, could only be redeemed by God, in Heaven, but here on Earth his purpose had been to save the world from any more bad verse, whether tossed into the fire or otherwise.

Say only that I rode forth and had many adventures, saw visions, suffered many wounds, all the while working my way back to Camelot like a woodsman chopping through a tangle of thorns, so that the Invisible Knight might once more sit at the Round Table and rediscover his name, and serve King Arthur in a manner and through such deeds as are worth writing down.

The Great World and the Small

I did not kill my brother. In time, I hope we'll be able to joke about it, and say that for all fratricide is the most venerable of Roman traditions aside from, possibly, rape, I couldn't bring myself to emulate Romulus. My Remus survives yet. I never carried off any Sabine women either.

I remember telling him stories, more than anything else. That was how our childhood passed. Each summer the family would flee the heat of the City and seek refuge with grandfather, Serenus Falco, who had an estate in the north of Italy, in the foothills of the Julian Alps. Every night, all summer, Flavius and I slept in a broad, low room up under the tiled eaves. It was a spooky place, filled with ghosts, I was certain, but I was not afraid of them, and it was *there* that I could lie in the darkness listening to the wind among the mountain peaks, or to the secret conversations of the owls in nearby trees.

There I could well imagine that the world had never changed because everybody decided to worship a dead Jew, that the mysteries were still alive, that the gods still gazed down on us from Olympus, that the ancient heroes dwelt among the gods and looked down on us also, to inspire us to imitate mighty deeds.

There.

"It's time for a story," I would say, and sometimes my brother, when he was very young, would whimper, or when he was older protest, "No, that's wicked," or when he was older still dismiss it as "pagan rubbish."

But he always listened, silently, more fascinated than he dared to admit to himself, even when the telling turned to monsters and restless shades of the wronged dead, and the terrible Strix which comes out of the darkness to feast on the blood of children.

At the very worst, he would cry softly, hide under the blankets, and start mumbling Christian prayers. But he was still listening. I knew that.

Then I would stop and listen to the wind for a while, and imagine, and, beyond imagining, I was *certain* that the gods actually spoke to me then. They called out to me in the night. I heard their voices distinctly, but I could not make out their words. It was a kind of miracle, I decided. I wondered if Flavius could hear them too. Once, in the morning, I actually asked him, and he thought I was telling him another silly story.

But when I return to those nights again and again, in my memory, as if I were reading once more from an old and beloved book, I know why, for all he should have become my enemy, I could not kill my brother. He was my audience.

* * *

He should have been my enemy.

Though he was but five years my junior, my brother was the product of another time, another world. I was our father's son, he our mother's. I think that in the early years of their marriage, our parents called a truce in their constant bickerings, long enough to divide up the spoils. Mother got Flavius, raising him a Christian, naming him, as is increasingly fashionable, after the sainted emperor Flavius Constantinus, whom the Christians call the Great.

But Father taught me to revere the old gods and the old ways.

When my brother and I were boys, we fought like boys, made up, played, fought again, and the difference did not seem so great, but later, it became a chasm. We were torn apart even as the world is torn apart.

But first, we grew up. I put on the toga of manhood and tried to make a career as Father had, as our ancestors had all the way back to the days of the Republic: pleading cases, managing our estates, hunting, riding, hearing the complaints of tenants. I read old books and wrote poetry in the approved manner, which literary men said recalled the ancient masters. Soon I was to marry a girl of a lineage fully as venerable as my own. Father had arranged it.

Meanwhile, in the world beyond our immediate lives, Arbogastes, Master of Troops in the West, slew Valentinian Augustus and set up one Eugenius in his place. This Eugenius was the first emperor since Julian to worship the gods of Rome. He restored the altar of Victory in the Senate.

But he was also a usurper and the puppet of a murderer. His methods were those of his kind. He and his master swore they would turn the churches on the Vatican Hill into stables. Given time, they would have started heaving Christians to what few starving lions the circuses still possessed.

Yet Father went to serve the new regime.

I remember how it was when the word reached our house. Mother shrieked and wept. Flavius tried to comfort her. I had just come in from the law courts, and stood still as one of the numberless commemorative statues in the Forum, trying to look dignified in my toga.

Father dragged me into the library, shut the door, checked to make sure no one was listening, then said to me, "It is time to join the great world, my son. It is the end of being small."

"But—"

"Despite everything, it is Rome's last chance. I am certain of that. Truly the last."

I was to act as if nothing had happened, and to deny all knowledge of his actions and preserve the family wealth if fate went against us. He made me swear a solemn oath to obey him. I protested that this was unnecessary. But his look was hard and fierce, as if he were animated by the spirit of some ancient hero. I tried to believe he was. I swore.

Then he gave me certain, other instructions.

And so, in the summer of my eighteenth year, while the most Christian Theodosius Augustus marched from the East to do battle with Eugenius and the world awaited the outcome, I made my last trip to Grandfather Falco's. I rode on horseback, trailed by servants and a dozen pack mules laden with books and accounts and gifts. Behind them, Flavius lolled in a cart, prostrate with the heat.

When we got to Aquilea, the great city was filled with soldiers and with refugees from the coming battle. Smoke rose from sacrificial altars. Christian churches were closed. Flavius said the gods were devils and the stench of burning animals made him sick.

Ostensibly we were going to set our grandfather's affairs in order, since he was very old now, and his mind clouded. I tried to pretend it was nothing more than that. At night, I even told Flavius a few stories, for all he was in no mood to listen.

I hoped he would never find out that I bore letters for partisans of Eugenius. It was all we could do not to quarrel, since we'd both lived our lives weary of our parents quarreling. But he was old enough to have his own ideas, and for me not to trust him.

* * *

Somewhere north of Aquilea, the thing happened.

We had been on the road most of the day, hours beyond the last inn or posting station, when suddenly the woods around us exploded with screaming men waving swords and spears. One grabbed my horse's bridle. I kicked him in the face and sent him tumbling. Flavius awoke with a shout, then starting striking bravely on every side with a rake that happened to be in the cart with him. Once I saw him turn and stumble, and for a horrible second I thought he was transfixed with an arrow.

All was confusion, shouting. A servant screamed, his head cloven with an axe. The cart-horse reared up and the cart tipped over. Flavius went flying. Someone was on the horse behind me, but I shoved him off with a vicious jab of my elbow. A burly man in military armor went for my bridle again. I swerved away from him. He cursed in what sounded like German, drew his sword, slashed, missed.

I saw my brother struggling with three men who were trying to hold him down. One, my horse trampled. The other two rolled to either side. Flavius reached up with his hand. I caught him, hauled him up in front of me, and sped off.

I glanced back once to see the servants standing helplessly about while the robbers tore through the luggage, hurling papers into the air.

We galloped along a narrow path, up a rugged hillside, trailing dust. All the while Flavius was draped over the saddle like a blanket, his head one way, his feet the other. He struggled to sit up. I helped him. My hand brushed the arrow in his tunic.

"Are you hurt?"

He pulled the arrow out. It was merely through a fold in the tunic, not through him. "I don't think so."

"Jupiter be praised."

He didn't even upbraid my paganism then.

We rode for a while longer, along a ridge line, looking down over the vast countryside, the city of Aquilea below, and beyond it, the Adriatic. The world looked quiet, empty of armies and robbers.

The horse slowed to a walk.

"Who were they?" Flavius asked.

I shrugged. "Soldiers. Allies, deserters, brigands. It's hard to tell."

"But whose?"

He meant, of course, Christians or pagans, men of Theodosius or of Eugenius, friends or foes.

Toward evening, we looked down on Grandfather Falco's villa and farm, which seemed undisturbed, but was surrounded by hundreds of campfires.

"We can't go there," I said.

"They might be friends—"

"*Whose* friends?"

He saw the problem at once. For his age, I think he saw a great deal. But he didn't know what to say, and only managed a feeble, "I don't know."

"Besides, it wouldn't make any difference if they thought we had any money," I said.

So we turned away, walking downhill, Flavius leading the horse. There was nothing to do but find a secluded spot and camp for the night. In time we came to a little hollow, where water trickled among some boulders.

But we did not dare make a fire. Instead, we sat still beneath the trees, listening to the wind, gazing up at the darkening sky.

"Titus, what is going to happen to us?" my brother asked, and for a minute he sounded like a frightened child. It seemed as if the years were as nothing, and we were in the loft again, and it was time for a story.

But Flavius interrupted.

"We should be enemies," he said.

I stared at him, startled. "Why?"

"Because we're on different sides. Of everything. You know perfectly well."

Unconsciously, I fingered the letters, which I wore in a sealed packet around my neck.

"What do I know perfectly well?"

He was staring at me. As inconspicuously as I could, I withdrew my hand. But he lunged at me suddenly, and the two of us wrestled like small boys, rolling over the ground, startling our horse, while he shouted, "Give it, you bastard!" I dug my hand into his face and shoved him away with a mighty heave, but he had hold of the letters. The string broke. He tumbled backward, clutching his prize, then stood up, tore the packet open, and tried to read.

I tackled him. We rolled again. I got the letters back as he wriggled, tried to kick me in the face, and broke free.

We sat in the dust, panting, our clothing in ruins, glaring at one another. I'd scraped my knee painfully. But I held the letters. He had produced a dagger from somewhere.

"Now what are you going to do?" I said. "Kill me?"

"Or you me?"

"It would make a certain amount of sense."

"You're a traitor, Titus. You and Father both."

"Shut up. You don't know what you're talking about."

But he did. "Those men. They weren't robbers. They were looking for—" He pointed to the letters.

"Yes, they were. But they let us get away. Not very competent, were they?"

"They let *you* get away—"

"Do you think they would have treated you any differently?"

"It wasn't my fault—"

There was nothing to argue about. I felt a sinking, helpless feeling. I cursed Father for meddling in the affairs of the great world. I was losing my brother. Now it was all coming out, like a long-festering poison.

"Consider," I said after a while. "We are both Romans, and the soldiers on both sides are virtually all barbarians. Not one in a hundred speaks decent Latin."

"So?"

"That must count for something. Family must count for a lot more. Our lands, our ancestors, everything. So let us not be enemies, all right?" I held out my hand.

He clutched the dagger and drew back. "You're trying to trick me!"

* * *

I should have killed him right then and there. Logic dictated it.

A long, difficult silence followed. The sky became fully dark, moonless, filled with stars. Around us, the owls began to speak. Flavius sat very still, his face an inscrutable mask.

After a very long time he asked, in the tone of a child again, "What are we going to do?"

"I don't know. What do you think?"

"I think I should pray for you."

"That's a start."

But he did not. He sat still, listening to the sounds of the night.

"Do you hear them?" I said.

"What?"

"The voices of the gods. I heard them many times on nights like this. Sometimes when I went downstairs to piss, I'd look out a window, and see the gods up in the sky, huge as clouds, standing far away, with the stars like jewels in their cloaks."

"You were dreaming."

"No."

"It was clouds then."

"No. They spoke to me quite clearly, and said that because I still believed, I could call on them when I needed them the most, and they would answer—"

"What a crock of—"

"It wasn't the wind," I said. "I heard them." Again silence settled between us, and I listened for the voices of the gods in the night. Surely on this night, I told myself, surely now as the world hung in the balance, they would speak.

I was the one who began to pray, *"Mother Hecate, mistress of night, goddess of graves—"*

"Stop that!" Flavius hissed. "It's devilish!" He made the old sign to ward off evil, not the Christian one.

"I think it is time for a story," I said. "Will you listen?"

He said nothing at all, so I began my story, telling of two brothers who were lost in the woods, and how the spirits of the old gods gathered around them to hear one of them tell a story.

"I think I *know* this story," my brother said with ludicrously overstated irony.

"No you don't. Let it continue." All around us, the owls cried out.

In the story the brothers rose from where they sat and ran through the night, hand in hand, because one of them heard a voice calling out to him clearly, while the other, the younger, did not. The elder dragged the younger along, and the boy fought with him, and was afraid, but had lost his dagger somewhere.

In the story, he said I was bewitched, that the devil had me.

* * *

I did not kill him. I came to a cliff's edge and could have easily hurled him off.

Here a tree, there a stone. Again, the bending path. I knew the signs like something long remembered, like an old story, and the voices of the owls led me on, and shadows among the trees: a face like a man, a form not at all human.

In the story, in the story as I told it, the two of us crawled on all fours up steep hillsides, beneath thickets of thorns, until we came to a strange country where the very earth seemed transformed into crumbly ash, and the sky was black but there were no stars, and all the noises of the night were gone but for the voices of the thousand owls, which flew above us, invisible.

A single, black bird fluttered before my face; not an owl, and I saw its own face clearly: a woman's, with streaming black hair and snow-pale skin, eyes black and blind like a basalt statue.

It shrieked at me. Flavius cried out, stumbled. I caught hold of his wrist, yanked, dragged him on.

To this day I do not know if what followed was some kind of dream or an actuality, or if the distinction means anything.

Think of it as a vision.

We came to a ruined temple in a valley between two hills, beneath a starless sky that was utterly dark. The owls had deserted us, and we approached the fallen columns and roofless enclosure in absolute silence.

Flames burned noiselessly in a great, bronze bowl set on a tripod. In the firelight, amid flickering shadows, I saw shriveled corpses in heaps, and scattered bones, and great ravens rooting through the debris like robbers. My brother and I waded among them, but were not molested as they tore at the bones through fragments of fine garments, scattering jewels, scepters, diadems. Flavius babbled words in a whispering delirium.

At least one corpse had an animal's head, a dog, I think.

Then bones and tatters rose up before me, assembling themselves into the shape of a woman with wild black hair, her face streaked with blood, her eyes black as a statue and blind.

She groped for Flavius and caught him, quick as a striking serpent, hurling him to the ground, kneeling astride him, holding his arms down with her clawed hands. She rocked her head from side to side and hissed.

I saw that her teeth were like needles.

Strix. Devourer of children. Desperate, famished, mad.

My brother's eyes met mine. "Help me," he said. I think he wanted to say more, but couldn't find the words. I think he wanted to say that I had brought him here deliberately, to kill him.

But I turned suddenly, looking about for a weapon. I found a staff of some sort, picked it up, struck and the monster, then stumbled with the unspent force of the blow as the staff went right through the creature as if it were made of smoke.

Flavius let out a little cry.

I called on the gods then. I named them, great Jupiter, Apollo, Mercury, as many as I could think of.

Because in one of my stories there was a boy who spoke with the gods, and to whom the gods spoke. They promised to come if he called.

The temple filled with wind. Dust rose. The feasting ravens flapped their wings irritably.

In the far darkness, in the back of the temple, there was a light, like a candle before the face of a huge, seated statue. But the face turned toward me and opened its terrible eyes, and said, "She would have your brother's life. It will do her no good. We are all dying anyway."

"Stop her!"

Even then the black hag seemed to kiss Flavius on the side of the neck.

"Stop her!"

"I have no power left to stop her. Speak to her, Titus Serenus. Remind her who she once is."

"But—but—is she not the Strix?"

"No. Not always."

I thought I understood then, in my amazement, and if I can ever be called brave, if I ever can claim to have performed a heroic deed, it was this: I took the crone by the hand. She looked up at me, blood streaming over her chin. I spoke to her gently, my voice trembling, but I did not lose my words.

"Dread Mother of Darkness, I am honored to greet you at last."

She rose. I crouched down and helped Flavius to his feet. He leaned on my shoulder.

Together, he and I approached the seated one, and I saw a diademed figure clad in military garb like an emperor, larger than a man, mighty of limb, but the face was filled with pain and weariness. A spear had pierced the right side. Blood pooled before the throne.

I knelt and gathered the blood into my hands and poured it out again, as an offering to Death.

"Do you not know me?" The voice was like muted thunder.

"Yes, Lord, I do."

Flavius also knelt and dipped his fingers into the blood.

And all around us, the shadows shifted, and figures stepped out from behind the broken pillars. I saw them all, in their tattered clothing and tarnished crowns, in all their aspects and personas, those who were human in form and those who were not—the great ones, more perfect in shape than any mortal, and another, whose head was that of a startled bird, and another, green and clad in leaves—all of them feeble with age and neglect, truly as their king had said, dying.

I cried out then, and fell prostrate for I could no longer doubt that I was in the presence of the very gods who had made Rome a colossus, who granted immortality to heroes or smote them. The true gods, revealed to me, who was no one in particular, who was merely fond of telling stories in the dark.

I wept. The seated one leaned down and touched me on the shoulder. His touch burned, but very slightly.

"Get up," he said. "We are all waiting for you."

They were my audience. The ruined temple rustled with the wind of their voices. Dust stirred, rose, settled, rose again. I could not make out any words. At times they seemed to be laughing, at times weeping. At times it was like the soft chatter of pigeons under the eaves at Grandfather Falco's.

Then they all fell silent, and I was commanded to begin. I sat where I was, in the middle of the floor, and spoke haltingly, urged on whenever I could no longer find the words; all the while amazed that anyone would want to listen to a stuttering schoolboy who had forgotten his lessons and could only mangle Hesiod and Homer and Vergil. I felt like a boy again, like I was ten years old and had slipped down from the loft to relieve myself and looked out the window and saw, or imagined I saw, the gods in the night sky.

But it didn't seem to matter. After a while I came to understand that my listeners did not care at all about the quality of my delivery. They merely wanted to be reminded of old events. I think they merely wanted to hear the names.

Much to my surprise, my brother's voice joined my own. He crouched beside me, his face drawn, his expression bewildered, but he spoke gently, and together we told of Proserpine and of the passion of Demeter, or Orpheus and his descent into the nether world; only we left the ending off that particular story and made it seem as if the poet had found his beloved among the shades and been content to remain with her.

The lady who had been the Strix and before that a goddess sank down into sleep, into the darkness, bones rattling as they scattered across the floor.

"That was well done, for both of you."

I looked up.

"Come closer. I cannot rise."

And the dying god pulled the spear out of his side with a grunt, and his blood splashed over me, burning. It poured into my cupped hands, and for an instant it seemed I held a magic glass of some kind. Through it I gazed down as if from a great height on two armies in desperate combat. The place was the gorge where the river Frigidus cuts through the mountains above Aquilea. I saw a black-bearded, red-faced man riding furiously through a forest, up a steep hillside. His horse stumbled, broke a leg, threw him; but he continued on with three or four followers, all on foot, all of them at the absolute limit of endurance.

I knew this to be the murder-soiled traitor Arbogastes, who had promised to restore the old gods. Trapped at last in a cave, he clasped his friends to him one by one, then released them, muttered something, and fell on his sword.

The man who stood beside him, who steadied him as he fell, was my father.

I let the pooled blood drip out between my fingers. The image was gone.

"Why have you shown me this?" I said at last.

"I cannot tell. There must be a reason. I do not know it anymore."

When the god spoke no more, I knew he was dead. Even as I watched, the divine flesh sublimated away, rising like golden smoke. Bones poured out of the throne in a heap. Faint lightning flickered once or twice, and then there was absolute darkness in which Flavius groped his way to me and held me tight, his face against my chest.

He said something very strange: "What have I become?"

"You haven't changed at all. You're still my brother."

I think I had fathomed the final mystery then. I was to be a witness to the end of the great world. Only the small remained. We were to go on with our lives.

* * *

Flavius shook me awake that morning. We were still in the hollow, among mossy boulders. The horse grazed nearby.

"You've burned your hands," he said.

I looked at them dumbly. "They must have fallen into the fire."

"But we didn't make a fire." He turned his head to one side, wincing with pain. "Ow. I think a scorpion stung me."

"Do you know what happened, Flavius?"

"I had some kind of . . . dream. It was horrible at first. But in the end I was no longer afraid, and I dreamed of the angels."

"Really?"

He glared at me, but his fury faded into a kind of disoriented exhaustion. I didn't try to argue. I let him lead me to a stream. The cool water felt good on my hands.

* * *

I did not kill my brother. It wouldn't have mattered if I had. Not in the end.

In the end, the soldiers of Arbogastes went over to Theodosius and the Christians won the battle. Father vanished on the field or nearby. His body was never found.

But our family was spared, perhaps because as soon as Flavius and I reached Grandfather Falco's house I went straight to the kitchen and burned the letters in the oven.

My brother is not my enemy. That is all the consolation I have. If we had fought, if one of us had killed the other over the affairs of the great world, what difference would it have made, to Arbogastes and Eugenius, to Theodosius, or to the gods?

Father once told me that we are like barnacles on the hull of a ship, and the ship is the great world of caesars and empires and gods. We live in our own small world where what matters is more the hailstorm that flattened the crops and whether or not your belly is full. The events of the great world are as remote as the thoughts of the ship's captain to the barnacles.

"But what if the ship is wrecked?" I asked.

"Then we cling some fragment large enough that we won't notice the difference."

"Do you believe we can?"

"No," he said.

The ship was wrecked a few years later. Those same Goths who fought for Theodosius at Aquilea turned on the empire. On their way to Rome they ransacked Grandfather Falco's estate. He met them at the door, sword in hand, on his head the old helmet he hadn't worn in fifty years. A Goth laughed and ran him through with a spear.

The barbarians left the Queen of Cities a hollow shell. Now, though the Roman corpse may still be seated on the throne of the world, it is truly dead, its heart torn out, its limbs rotting in the sun.

I think of the old Stoic epitaph: *I did not exist. I existed. I do not exist. I care not.* So it is with all things, even the world, even the gods.

So it is in the great world, and in the small.

A Mildly Self-Deprecating Afterword, with a Progress Report on Collecting My Collected Works

I have been fortunate as many worthy writers have not been, that the great majority of my short fiction has been gathered into book form. With book form comes a shot at immortality, or at least recognition. The late Sam Moskowitz rightly observed (in the process of rescuing Robert Duncan Milne from oblivion) that nobody remembers old stories scattered in back-issue magazines, an observation made doubly true in this present age of small-press magazines, when much of the best fiction appears in often very humble magazines of extremely limited circulation. Believe me, it's going to be *hard* to find a copy of, say, *Lady Churchill's Rosebud Wristlet* (which publishes first-rate stuff by World Fantasy Award winner Kelly Link) in fifty years. Make that impossible unless you move in precisely the right circles, where ancient hoards of such periodicals end up on the tables at World Fantasy Conventions when the original recipients die or clean out their attics.

So, it's book form or oblivion.

Here I am, far more fortunate that Robert Abernathy or Arthur Porges or Robert F. Young or Jane Rice or Chad Oliver. None of them have had their Collected Stories published. My combination of good luck and sound strategy began back about 1973, when I established a firm relationship with W. Paul

Ganley's late, lamented *Weirdbook* magazine, after which I managed to appear in every issue until *Weirdbook* folded in 1997. This meant that a concentrated audience for my work had been built up in W. Paul Ganley's mailing list, which made feasible the first collection of my stories (none of them from *Weirdbook*, since the book was to be sold primarily to *Weirdbook* readers). This was *Tom O'Bedlam's Night Out* (1985) and it was followed in 1993 by *Transients*, which got me a World Fantasy Award nomination (only to be quite reasonably blown out of the water by Ramsey Campbell's 30-year retrospective collection, *Alone with the Horrors*).

I thought I was sitting pretty and would issue a collection every few years as good, new stories began to accumulate, also judiciously delving into my backlog as I went along. But then Paul Ganley decided to retire. It was only with a certain amount of whining and arm-twisting that I persuaded Paul (in collaboration with George Scithers of Owlswick Press, who is also not turning out books the way he used to) to let me have *just one more* collection. The result was *Refugees from an Imaginary Country* (1999), assembled after a very difficult process of selection: absolutely top-drawer, first-cut, a book which, if I were hit by a meteorite the next day, would be sufficient to preserve what I am about as a writer. I thought it very likely that there wouldn't be another Schweitzer collection for many years, if ever.

But then Fortune smiled, the gods showered me with blessings, and the miraculous John Betancourt came along, founder of Wildside Press and fruitful in many other projects, he who seems to issue two or three new volumes every time he exhales. In the course of the vast Wildside program, John found space for a volume of the equally-good stories that got left out of *Refugees*, published as *Nightscapes* (2000), and also for my collected collaborations with Jason Van Hollander, *Necromancies and Netherworlds* (1999), yet another World Fantasy Award finalist.

As if that were not enough, Sean Wallace suddenly asked to do a collection of my stories for his Cosmos Books (since made an imprint of Wildside Press, so everything comes home to roost).

Now what?

Looking through all these stories and assembling them into books has put me in a mood of retrospection. It also calls to mind some of that surprisingly self-effacing jacket copy August Derleth used to put on some of his own Arkham House collections, saying, in effect, "well this one isn't very good, a minor contribution to the minor domain of the macabre" or something like that, but suggesting that Arkham House readers might want it anyway for completeness' sake. Derleth was not, by most reports, a particularly humble man. It must have been a clever ploy to disarm his customers' sales resistance.

A Mildly Self-Deprecating Afterword

Fear not, Gentle Reader. You have not been ripped off. You have not been sold inferior goods. I will candidly admit that in assembling the book you hold in your hands I dipped into the barrel as far as I cared to go, but the reason that I offer you the result unashamedly and without apologies is that *I knew where to stop.*

This is important. Listen up, particularly if you are a writer or would-be writer. When I first started collecting old books and magazines, as a teenager, one of the first things I attempted to accumulate was all the uncollected stories of one of my favorite writers, Ray Bradbury. In the process, I learned an crucial lesson, which is that Ray is a sound judge of his own work, and if he decided to leave stories like "The Silence," "Doodad," or "The Ducker" out of his collected *oeuvre* there was very likely a really good reason for him doing so.

I have enough wordage leftover to fill two or three more volumes, but I'm not going to inflict such volumes on you. These, here, are the last uncollected stories that are *good.* I am not H. P. Lovecraft. You have no reason to want to read my equivalent of "The Beast in the Cave" or "The Transition of Juan Romero."

There are perhaps five uncollected Schweitzer tales published prior to 1990 which might someday find their way into a book. Otherwise, I have to stop. Any writer has to learn this. Some of your darlings are misshapen. They drool and gibber and they don't even shamble very well. Like a Victorian parent, you must keep them discreetly locked away in the attic.

This excepts the two story-cycles that grew out of my novels, *The Shattered Goddess* and *The Mask of the Sorcerer.* There will be a *Book of the Goddess* and *Sekenre: the Book of the Sorcerer* in 2001 or 2002. After that, as new stories refill the barrel, there will be more general collections. I have enough first-rate pieces now—"The Emperor of the Ancient Word," "Envy, the Gardens of Ynath, and the Sin of Cain," "The Fire Eggs," "Secret Murders of the Heart," etc.—but as I write this many of them are as yet unpublished or even unsold. Give me a couple more years.

Meanwhile, I look back on the contents of *The Great World and the Small.* Much of it is recent work. There are three Arthurian stories in my on-going cycle largely about doom-ridden chaps in iron pants, which I steadfastly refuse to entitle *Dark Knights of the Soul.* "The Invisible Knight's Squire" is one of my very best stories, only written last year.

"The Adventure of the Death Fetch" is my supernatural Sherlock Holmes story, something I'd contemplated doing for almost a decade before Marvin Kaye's book came along and sparked its creation. "I Told You So" is broad farce, something I tend to produce when confronted with the very narrow parameters of some modern anthologies. (Speculating that *Alternate Historical Vampire Cat Detective Stories* is only a matter of time, I have written such a story. It's presently in the Barnes & Noble anthology, *Crafty Cat Crimes, 100 Cat Tale Mysteries* and it'll be in that next general collection of mine in a few years.)

The really early stories here gave me pause, but as many other writers have observed, when you work on material like this it's like collaborating with another person. The kid who wrote "Wanderers and Travelers We Were," at half my present age, had probably learned more about romance from reading Roger Zelazny than from real life. There are definite echoes of "The Graveyard Heart" in this one, but I still look fondly on the result. It is my only interplanetary story, and it had a distinguished career outside of the United States, having been found worthy to appear alongside major works by Fritz Leiber and Larry Niven in its original (British) appearance, then reprinted several times in Germany. This is its first American publication.

"Silkie Son" was alleged to have a curse attached to it. I wrote it at Clarion in 1973, despite attempts to discourage me from doing that sort of thing. (Clarionites tended to be down on fantasy in those days; I was not so much a writer they wanted to encourage, but one they couldn't stop.) I sold it—are you ready for this?—*eight times* to various magazines (and one pamphlet publisher), all of which folded before the story came out. It was published, sort-of, in an issue of the Italian magazine *Kadath* in 1984, which never had any distribution, even to subscribers, as the publisher chose that moment to vanish from the face of the Earth. The story was touched up very lightly about 1990 when I typed it into a computer, but it didn't actually get published for real until the next-to-last issue of *Weirdbook* (that curse again!) a full *twenty-two years* after it was initially written. That it then garnered an honorable mention in Ellen Datlow and Terri Windling's *The Year's Best Fantasy and Horror* was some reward for such Job-like patience. I now find the brutality of the story disturbing. Christina's husband is the nastiest character I have ever created, though of course life (and police reports) is full of such people.

I touched up the three "Etelven Thios" stories for style, basically giving my former self (now a couple years out of Clarion, in his middle twenties) a heavy copy-editing. (Yes, despite my railings against such, I too have written a Fantasy Trilogy, but at least it's short.) The hapless hero of the final episode was originally described as committing his "penultimate mistake," as if "penultimate" somehow meant more-ultimate-than-ultimate because no further mistake followed. That's not what the word means, so I fixed it, even as I smoothed out the first story, which still seems the weakest of the three, yet necessary to maintain the structure of the other two.

But I knew when to stop meddling. The older writer should offer kindly advice to the younger, but not rewrite him. So this book a collaboration between the two of us, more me than him, but I let him out on the stage a few times between acts to do his bit.

So here we are. Enjoy the book. Now I will stop because it is time.

—Darrell Schweitzer,
Philadelphia PA
July 1, 2001

www.ingramcontent.com/pod-product-compliance
Lightning Source LLC
Chambersburg PA
CBHW020944310726
48980CB00001B/45

9781587152108